Newfound

Love

Also By Kay Brooks

Newfound Love

The Row Series, Book Three

by
Kay Brooks

KDB Manuscripts, LLC

Front Cover Design by SelfPubCovers.com/FrinaArt

Newfound Love

by Kay Brooks

eBook ISBN: 978-0-9996-0061-0
Print ISBN: 978-0-9996-0061-0

Printed in the United States of America

To my sister, Robin Scott,
my number one fan.

and

To Ann Wade,
who always has my back.

Prologue

December 2004

Miranda Cavanaugh, Randi for short, was buzzed from the Christmas party. Yes, she might have had two glasses of wine, but she was sober enough to drive home. Tim on the other hand had passed out in the passenger seat as soon as his head hit the back rest.

She looked over at her husband, wondered how she was going to get him inside. The last time she helped him she sprained her wrist when he stumbled and fell on her. Her father had never questioned it, but she knew he was worried. Even she was beginning to worry.

They had been married a little over a year now. The first six months had been wonderful but since winning the election to the Maryland General Assembly last fall, Tim had started drinking more than usual. The kind, considerate husband became arrogant and aggressive as alcohol became a regular part of his day. She had learned to read his moods and stay out of his way. Wondered how long he would be able to hide it from his constituents.

Randi pulled up to the curb outside their Baltimore home, turned to study her husband once more. Ought to leave him in the car, she thought. He can come in when he wakes up.

Then she frowned. It wouldn't look good for the neighbors in their gated community to see an up-and-coming Delegate passed out in his car.

She nudged him, but Tim was out cold.

She slammed the door when she got out, hoping the noise and motion would waken him. But he was still passed out when she opened the passenger door, leaned in to unbuckle his seatbelt.

"Everything okay, Ms. Cavanaugh?"

Randi jumped, knocked her head against the door frame. She stood straight, smiled up at the stout security guard that patrolled their gated community.

"Oh, Dave. You startled me. Yes. Yes, everything is fine. But Tim wasn't feeling so well when we left the party. He fell asleep on the way home and I was just trying to awaken him so I can get him inside."

Dave smiled. "Here," he opened the door wider, "let me help. I've been in the same situation a couple times myself."

Before Randi could object, Dave had Tim out of the car, leaning against him. Key in hand, she raced ahead to unlock the door while the men slowly made their way up the three steps into the house.

Tim grunted when Dave settled him to the sofa.

Randi smiled at the security guard. "Thank you, Dave. You're a lifesaver. I don't know how I would have gotten him inside. Can I offer you a cup of coffee?"

"Nah, but thanks. I'm about ready to go off duty. Wanted to make one last walk through the neighborhood. The wife is probably wondering where I am."

Randi followed him to the door. "Well, I certainly am glad you happened to be walking past our house. Stop by tomorrow and I'll have a bag of homemade chocolate chip cookies for you."

Dave chuckled. "Now that I will gladly accept."

Randi grinned as she closed and locked the door. She turned to find Tim glaring at her from the sofa.

"Making a date with the security guard now?" He snarled.

Her mouth dropped open. "No. I was simply thanking him for helping me get you inside."

"I didn't need him," he started to object.

"Tim, you were passed out!"

Cold eyes glared at her before he jumped up from the sofa, charged across the room. Before she realized his intentions, he slapped her across the cheek. Her head struck the door behind her, and she fell unconscious to the floor.

~~~~~

Seventy-five miles south of Baltimore, Deborah Gilman stood outside the Edmondsville Town Hall. She, Ginny, Brina, Marcie and Brad were having the time of their lives at the Annual Holly Ball Dance held the first Friday of each December.

She and Brina had stepped outside to cool off while the band took a break. When Brina turned to go back inside, Deborah said she wanted to stay a moment longer. She leaned against the railing on the concrete stoop, smiled up at the clear sky.

She had never been so happy. The limo ride, the music, the fun with her friends. More importantly, she was sure Brad planned to propose to her. Just didn't know when.

Ginny, Brina and Marcie certainly thought so. In fact, everyone in their small town seemed to expect it and Deborah wondered if it would be tonight. In the sparkling wonderland of the Holly Ball.

She and Brad had known each other all their lives. Their brother and sister relationship had blossomed into love six months ago when he cornered her in the library and kissed her. Since then, he had become so important to her. He loved her, listened to her, offered a shoulder to cry on. Gave her a reason to want to make something better for herself.

Her parents had died in a plane crash when she was three and she had been taken in by her mother's sister and her husband. Claire and Tom saw to her needs but cared more for their own daughter. Myra had always been a handful and they never noticed she had her own confusion and abuse. There was so much she needed to share with Brad.

Now that she was twenty-one, Deborah looked forward to moving out on her own. She worked at the library and squirrelled away as much of her paychecks as she could. Another few months, and she'd have enough for a deposit on the Turner's loft apartment on Elm Street.

Brad would be starting law school in the spring and was encouraging her to go back to the community college. She wouldn't have a scholarship this time.

Maybe, she shrugged her shoulder. But right now, she just wanted to get out on her own. Prove to Claire and Tom that she could do it. Make something more of her life than their spoiled daughter.

Deborah smiled. When Brad finished law school, they would get married, have a house full of children. Two boys and two girls. She would give them so much more than she had received from her aunt and uncle. She and Brad would take them places. Love them unconditionally.

Deborah hugged herself, glanced up in time to see a star shoot across the night sky. She sighed, hoped that was a good sign.

She stepped towards the door to return to the dance but was startled to see a shadow.

"Think you're going to hit it big with the Beckman kid?" Deborah cringed when she recognized the voice. "I don't think so."

Before she could grab the door, the shadow lunged, slapped her across the face. Deborah fell unconscious as her head struck the concrete platform and she collapsed down the steps.

Deborah Gilman never made it back into the Holly Ball.

CHAPTER ONE

*A**pril 2015*

"Mom, we forgot Ironman!" Scott and Sandy Cavanaugh hollered at the top of their lungs from the back seat of the car.

Randi Cavanaugh cast a frustrated look at her red-headed twins in the rear-view mirror. She had been up since five this morning trying to get ready for the long weekend in the mountains. Her father was anxious to get on the road and had already called twice.

"Didn't I ask if you had packed all your Power Rangers?" She spoke sternly. "I don't have time to turn around. We were supposed to be at GranPop's ten minutes ago."

Randi jumped, swallowed hard when both boys leaned over the console. "But MOM, GranPop says Ironman is the bestest. We can't save the world without him."

"Oh my gosh," she shrieked. "You two had better get your butts back in your seats. And buckle up before Deputy Peterson pulls me over for child endangerment! Then I'd have to go to jail and there would be NO vacation."

"Aww, Mom!" They hustled back to their seats. "We NEED Iron-man!"

Randi pulled to the side of the street, turned to make sure they had buckled themselves in. Shifting back around, she rested her head on the steering wheel and sighed. It was only eight o'clock and she was already exhausted. She had packed and repacked everything she was sure they would need for a week's stay in the mountains. Now Ironman had gone missing.

Really? She felt like screaming at the top of her lungs.

She lifted her head, locked eyes with her sons in the rearview mirror; made a quick U-turn. Racing back to the house, she kept her eyes alert for the deputies who liked to run radar along Main Street. She spotted Duane Peterson, waved and breathed a sigh of relief when he waved back.

Minutes later she pulled her maroon Escalade to a screeching halt outside their house and the three of them dashed inside. Searched all the likely places Ironman might have gone into hiding.

An interior decorator, Randi never had this problem in her office currently housed at the back of the house. Efficient, competent, totally organized, she was a perfectionist through and through. Never misplaced files, samples or catalogs. Things might get in disarray during a work session, but by the end of a long day, everything was as it should be. She looked forward to moving the office to *The Row*, a Fire House she, Brina, Ginny and Marcie were renovating in town.

Her home life was a different story. With twin six-year-old boys, there was constant clutter and disarray. No sooner would she clean the house, she would turn and find that her boys had found other toys to play with. For the most part though, they were good at putting their toys away, just not when she wanted and needed a straightened house.

Ironman could be anywhere, she worried as she searched between the cushions on the sofa. "When was the last time you saw Ironman?"

Scott was looking under the ottoman, Sandy behind the chair. They stopped, looked at one another.

Randi snapped her fingers, pointed to them. "This morning, in the bathtub." All three made a mad dash for the bathroom.

"There he is," Scott shouted.

"In the trash can," Sandy finished for his brother. They both reached for the missing Avenger.

"How in the world did he get in the trash?" Randi wondered.

Moments later, they were back in the car, making a fast get-away. "GranPop is going to be a little upset when we get there," Randi advised the boys. "He wanted to leave an hour ago so we're going to have to be super excited when we get there and maybe he won't say anything. Okay?"

"'Kay."

Since her first graders were on their spring break from school, her father thought it would be a great idea to go to Snowridge. They hadn't been to the mountain resort since her mother died five years ago. The main reason he was interested in going this year was because he had heard the developer was expanding the resort. She didn't know who this developer was, just that her father was set on showing his plans to the guy.

Retired, Sebastian Armstrong still dabbled in his passion for architecture and design. More so since reading about the planned expansion in the resort newsletter.

She still couldn't believe she had let her father talk her into accompanying him. "You need some down time. Time to relax," he'd explained.

She didn't disagree with him but would have been happy to relax at home. Sleep late. Do nothing for a change.

Six bridal showers and two weddings in four months had drained her.

Then there had been the never-ending problems with *The Row*. The public hearing. The fire. Brina's accident. They still didn't know how her brake lines had been cut.

She, Brina, Ginny and Marcie had been working non-stop on *The Row*, a side street they wanted to cultivate into a business complex in their small town, Edmondsville. She and Brina were converting the original firehouse into an office space for her interior decoration business and Brina's personal shopping service.

They planned to convert the sleeping quarters upstairs into a loft apartment. Originally, Brina was going to live there until she met Rafe last Thanksgiving. They got married two weeks ago. Now, Stacy Adamson, assistant to local lawyer, Brad Beckman would be living there. Stacy had just relocated from Richmond after her former boss – Brad's father – retired.

Once the firehouse was remodeled, they planned to renovate adjacent buildings for businesses. Ginny wanted to develop a Children's Museum; Marcie was looking to expand her wine shop. Their friend Scooter was interested in opening a second restaurant that would offer breakfasts and lunches during the day.

Randi's biggest challenge had been meeting Trevor, the contractor overseeing the project. Something always seemed to come up whenever she and Brina were scheduled to meet with him. It had become a joke between her and Brina that she usually got there in time to admire his cute backside. He had a lazy strut that just melted her bones.

"Mom, what's Snowridge like?" Sandy interrupted her daydream.

"Oh, it's a nice resort up in the mountains. They have horseback riding, hiking, golf, tennis, an indoor pool. I think they added a water park last year."

"Can we drive the golf cart?" Sandy asked.

"No."

"Can we race the horses?" Scott asked.

Randi laughed. "No."

"Can we hike up the mountain and hunt for bears?" They both whooped excitedly.

"Of course not!"

"Aw, Mom! We can't do 'nuthin."

Randi laughed as she pulled into her father's driveway. "I'm sure we'll find something to do while we're there."

Sebastian Armstrong immediately bounded out the front door.

"Bout time you got here." His gray hair glistened in the morning sun as he made it a point to look at his watch as he headed for his car.

"Aw, Dad!" Randi mimicked her sons. "It's only eight thirty," she called from her opened window. "We have plenty of time. Besides," she glanced at her grinning redheaded twins, "we had to go back for Ironman."

"What, you almost forgot Ironman," Sebastian pretended to be shocked. "In that case," he winked at his grandsons, "You're forgiven." He jingled his keys. "My car's all packed. You lead the way."

Randi frowned. This was the first she'd heard about driving separate cars.

"Why are we taking two cars? Surely, we can all go together. There's plenty of room in my Escalade."

"No. No. You never know what might come up. I may have to come back early for a golf tournament. Or we might want to go in opposite directions one day."

Randi felt like beating her head on the steering wheel. "Then why didn't you just go ahead? If I had known we were going in separate cars, the boys and I could've slept a little later, met you up there. Besides, you know how I like to take my time, visit a couple of the antique shops along the way."

Her father smiled, leaned in to kiss her cheek. "C'mon. I'll keep the boys one day and you can visit all the antique shops you want. But right now, we need to get going. Sandy, you ride with your mother. Scott, you can ride with me."

An hour later, Randi was ready to pull off the road but told her cell phone to dial Ginny instead. Her new Escalade had been a reward to herself after an article about her business. The unexpected advertisement had netted her some well-paying jobs.

She was still learning all the bells and whistles that were loaded on the car and the hands-free cell phone just amazed her.

"How's the trip going?" Ginny asked as soon as she answered.

"Crazy. I thought this was going to be a relaxing trip but before we could even get out of town, the boys realized they'd forgotten Ironman, so we had to go back to the house. My father got it in his head to drive separate cars and has been on my bumper the entire way. We can't get there soon enough."

"Why is your father driving separate? I figured you'd go together."

"My sentiments exactly. But he said something about maybe having to come back early. I thought he'd want to ride in my fancy new car."

Randi glanced in her rear-view mirror and was sure she could see her father's eyelashes. She deliberately slowed the car.

"Where are you?" Ginny asked.

"Approaching Brownsville."

Ginny laughed. "Your favorite town. I remember you telling us how you almost settled there."

"Yeah," Randi blew out heavily, watched an elderly couple holding hands as they strolled on the sidewalk.

Time apparently stopped in Brownsville fifty years ago. Businesses operated out of original framed buildings. Huge store windows in the grocery store and shops were decorated attractively, inviting anyone to come inside for their groceries, dresses, even snow shovels that were on sale. Brick houses, hundred-year-old churches, maple trees lined the streets. The only modernization had been the wing added to the small hospital and rehab center. She remembered stopping at the library where she observed a group of children enjoying storytelling in the small courtyard outside the facility.

The town would have been the perfect place for a new beginning.

"I would love to have settled here but with two small boys and a new business, I needed to be nearer the city. Besides, if I'd settled here, I would never have met you and Brina and Marcie."

"And you wouldn't have been me and Scott's teacher," Sandy yelled from the back seat.

"Scott's and my teacher," Randi and Ginny corrected him at the same time. In addition to being one of Randi's good friends, Ginny was also the twins' first grade teacher.

"Didn't you say you were looking for some new outfits for your storytelling?" Randi asked. "There's this neat antique shop in Brownsville and if my father wasn't breathing down my neck I'd stop, check out one of the booths. I remember she had vintage clothing."

"That would be nice. But I doubt I'll be doing much storytelling in the coming months."

"Why?" Sandy whined. "Me and Scott love your stories."

"Scott and I." Randi laughed as she reminded her son.

"Well, because Cliff and I are going to have a little baby."

"A baby!" Randi and Scott exclaimed at once.

"When did you find out?" Randi asked.

Ginny laughed. "Yesterday afternoon. I had been suspicions and the doctor confirmed it. You're the first person I've told."

"Aww." Randi gushed. "Now, instead of bridal showers we'll be having baby showers."

Ginny chuckled. "We've got plenty of time. Cliff is already tossing around baby names. He's decided if it's a boy, he doesn't want to name it Clifton Gerald the fifth. Thinks we need to be a little more creative."

"I must agree with him on that. Hey, I need to get off now. I'm coming up on the infamous roundabout and it looks like they've made a few changes since I was last here."

The only drawback Randi found with Brownsville was the round-about at the far end of town. She groaned as she approached the intersection. Three major highways met at this circle in the road, and you didn't just simply drive around. There were yield signs for one highway, stop signs for another coupled with highway markers. On a good day, it took some major concentration to stay on the proper path and the extra spring vacation traffic didn't make it any easier.

Normally the roundabout wouldn't bother her, but it had been a while since she'd been this way and with Sandy talking nonstop from the back seat, she failed to bear to the right, missing her turn. When she realized her mistake, she simply continued around the circle planning to catch the exit on the next go-round.

Her father immediately began honking from behind, broke her concentration the second time around. By the third loop, Sandy decided to join in the fun, hollered and waved at his brother while her father continued to honk at her.

Flustered, self-conscious and downright embarrassed by all the noise, on the fourth time around Randi gunned the Escalade as soon as she saw the Route Three sign.

From the gas station at one corner of the intersection, Trevor Graystone observed the chase around the circle and grinned. He watched the two boys, their red hair blazing in the sun's rays, wave and holler at one another, obviously enjoying the excitement of the adult confusion.

When the noisy convoy of two travelled through the intersection, he turned back to the gas tank. Glanced at his watch, reminded himself he still had several errands to run before heading back to the resort. Then he could relax for the weekend, not have to worry about any major problems or projects for the next couple days. The construction of the mini-mart was going as scheduled and the mini-movie theatre should be done in time for the ski season.

With everything going smoothly here, it would free him up to concentrate on the Edmondsville project. He appreciated the fact that Brina Hollingsworth, now McGuire, and some friends were restoring a section of their town instead of trying to build a new complex. Renovating was more appealing than demolishing. The old fire house offered a unique setting for offices.

Apparently, the project didn't stop with the offices. He recalled overhearing Brina and her blonde friend talking about some sort of children's museum. There was also another friend who was interested in moving her wine shop there. Then there was the interior decorator who was going to share the firehouse with Brina. He'd decided she must be scatterbrained as she never made it in time for any of his meetings with Brina and he had yet to meet her. He was sure they would butt heads before this project was over. He hadn't met a decorator yet that was easy to work with. Always dreaming up all sorts of crazy ideas with even crazier color schemes.

For now, he looked forward to a long weekend doing nothing. With the change in weather, his coming days would be busy completing projects with his crews, his evenings planning new projects. He might be boss and could delegate work, but it went against his nature to sit back or idle for long. He enjoyed the fresh air, doing some of the hard labor. His crews seemed to respect him more because of it.

Hammering a nail also helped him to ignore some of his problems. Like the Greenwillow Corporation in Atlanta. They'd been after him for almost a year now to develop a resort like Snowridge. He still had big plans for Snowridge and wasn't interested in taking on such a large project. Certainly not so far away from home.

And he wasn't getting any younger. At thirty-seven, he had everything a man could want. Thriving business, beautiful chalet home on the side of a mountain, three vehicles, an active social life. Thanks to his early morning workouts and jogs, his six-foot two body was healthy, trim, and pleasing to many of his lady friends.

Lately though he caught himself observing those lady friends a little more closely. He should be happy, but something was missing. What good was money and success if he had no one to share it with?

Trevor returned the nozzle to the tank, nodded to the guy at the next car. He'd tackle his loneliness another time. When there weren't more pressing matters to attend too.

~~~~~

Two hours later, Trevor headed back to the resort. Johnny Cash walked the line on the radio, the cool mountain air whipped through the windows. It might be spring, but Mother Nature hadn't warmed up to the idea yet.

He caught a whiff of fried chicken as he approached the convenience store at the intersection to the resort and smiled. This convenience store wouldn't be so convenient once he got his own mini mart completed. He'd noticed how people always stopped here before heading up to the resort. The new mini mart should be finished next month. The pizzeria was next and before long, vacationers wouldn't have to leave the resort for anything.

With chicken on his mind, Trevor pulled up outside the store. He paused briefly to admire the maroon Escalade parked next to his dirty truck, then proceeded inside the store.

CHAPTER TWO

R andi pushed a cart and tossed packages of hot dogs, hamburger, chips, crackers, cereal, milk, eggs inside the basket. She couldn't believe as organized as she was, she had left the cooler of food next to the back door.

"Should smell wonderful when we get home," she muttered to herself. "Have to remember to give Marcie a call. Ask her to stop by to put everything away." She closed her mouth when she noticed the couple standing in line at the register, cast worried looks her way.

If Snowridge had a mini grocery store on the resort, she grumbled silently, she wouldn't have had to drive five miles to the nearest convenience store. It seemed everyone else had forgotten something as baskets bumped baskets in the small supermarket. Any other time she would have appreciated the quaintness of the narrow aisles and wooden shelves.

Thank goodness, she had remembered the DVD's. She'd left the boys and her father settled on the sofa watching one of the Avenger movies. When they realized she had left the cooler, her father simply shook his head, then waved her on. "The boys and I will be okay."

"What would I do without him?" She once again muttered to herself. He might dote on her and the boys a little too much, but he never interfered with her decisions, was always there when she needed him.

Just like when she'd decided to divorce Tim.

Tim's drinking escalated to the point that he received several DUI's. Then she found out she was pregnant with the boys and refused to go with him to the socials. She knew he saw other women at the parties but by then she didn't care. Political success and inflated ego had taken the spark out of their new marriage.

For the most part, he left her alone. Until one night when one of his lady friends had rebuffed his advances and he came home in a rage. The fact that she was six months pregnant with the boys didn't stop him from taking it out on her. She'd become immune to his insults and whenever he came home drunk, she stayed in her bedroom. Waited for him to pass out on the sofa.

But this time, his anger escalated, and he came looking for her. When she tried escape downstairs to call her father, he slapped her.

She flinched as she remembered screaming as she fell down the stairs then lost consciousness. Sharp pains had awakened her, and she called out to Tim. When he didn't answer, she crawled to her cell phone, dialed her parents who took her to the emergency room.

She spent four long weeks in that hospital bed, flat on her back, trying to prevent a premature delivery brought on by Tim's attack. It was her parents, not Tim, who stayed at her bedside, held her hand, offered support while she wrestled with her conflicting emotions. Her mother had cried, encouraged her to come stay with them.

Her father didn't say much but Randi worried about the anger in his eyes. At one point, she didn't see her father for two days and when he returned, there was a calmness about him. She often wondered if he had confronted Tim. Especially when she made her decision to divorce Tim and he never objected. Her father had quietly arranged to have her things moved back home where both parents remained by her side until the boys were born.

Her mother died from cancer the next year, but her father remained her rock. Even moved to Edmondsville with her when she decided to relocate.

Today had been no different. After her meltdown, he apologized for being so insistent about getting to the resort. "Maybe if I hadn't rushed you, you wouldn't have forgotten the cooler."

He'd handed her a hundred-dollar bill, told her to go get what she needed. Promised when she got back, he would prepare dinner and she could relax a bit.

The brief meltdown helped to relieve some of the stress. Randi smiled as she bent down to grab a can of beans from the bottom shelf. The boys always liked beans with their hot dogs. That should be easy enough for her father to heat up tonight.

She straightened, backed into a solid human wall.

"Oh, I'm sorry." She turned and stared up into chocolate brown eyes. Why was it that men always had the long lashes? She thought to herself.

"No problem," Trevor answered. A smile tugged at his lips as he reached above her head for a can of peas.

Pinned between his chest and the hard shelf, Randi felt the heat of his body, caught a whiff of sawdust. Rough and tough ran through her mind while her heart skipped a beat. It had been a long, long time since she had been this close to a man. And judging from the twinkle in his eyes, he enjoyed her predicament, wasn't in a hurry to move on. She inched her way around him and grabbed for her cart.

Trevor watched her move down the aisle, appreciated the worn jeans that hugged her shapely hips. His gaze travelled up her slim back to the silky blonde hair that peeked from the baseball cap. Smooth as silk sprinted through his head. She'd looked up at him in surprise, but he'd seen tiredness in her eyes; watched it in her walk. Her day had apparently been as long as his.

Randi checked the basket to be sure she had everything. Decided she needed to get out of this store. Away from the man who had such a potent effect on her. Her body temperature had spiked a few notches and she knew her cheeks were flushed.

She grabbed a bottle of Pinot Grigio off the wine shelf, headed for the checkout counter. A glass of wine would complement her long bubble bath while her father cooked dinner.

Fifteen minutes later, Randi walked along the mountain road.

"This should have been a pleasant evening," she yelled to the dark skies as she headed back to the convenience store. It would have been a pleasant evening if she'd looked at her gas gauge before leaving the store. Hadn't left her cell phone on the table at the unit.

"What else can go wrong today?"

Maybe it was a good thing that her father had driven separately. At least when she called him from the store, he could come get her.

She inhaled the pine scent as the cool spring breeze whipped through the trees. At least the traffic was light, she didn't have to worry about dodging a convoy of vehicles. Instead, she appreciated the much-needed peace and quiet as she made her way along the winding road back to the convenience store.

She kicked a rock. Hopefully this wasn't an omen of their long weekend. Obviously, these past few months had affected her more than she thought. She wasn't usually this scatterbrained. Or maybe it was the new car. She never thought to check the gas gauge. Or question what the ringing noise meant when she pulled out of the parking lot.

She approached the rock, gave it a harder kick.

What happened to the woman who had picked herself up after the birth of her sons, struggled to give them a good healthy home? Built her successful interior decoration business?

The same woman who had moved to a new town three years ago. Made new friends? Met Ginny, Brina and Marcie.

She reached for her cell phone to call one of the girls, groaned when she remembered she didn't have it. Now would be a good time to hear one of their voices. Brina and Marcie would laugh. Ginny would be concerned, keep her on the phone while she walked.

Randi shook her head. Despite being stranded on a dark, narrow road, life was good. Ginny and Cliff were going to have a baby; Brina and Rafe were newlyweds and Marcie was busy learning about making wine.

Their vacation might have gotten off on a rocky start, but she was determined it would be a wonderful time away. She and the boys were going to go to the pool every day. Her father was going to talk to this developer guy. They would go to the water park. Yes, life would be good.

Much as she could use the exercise, Randi didn't like walking alone along the winding narrow road. Especially now that dusk was settling in and the treetops were starting to resemble those strange creatures Scott and Sandy's Power Rangers were always battling.

There were no lines on the road and with the approaching darkness, it appeared to be a wide path with the side of the mountain on the other side of the road, cliff overhang on her side. Walking against the traffic, she worried about missing a step and falling into what appeared to be a black hole.

She heard an engine, then saw the headlights of an approaching vehicle. Slowed her pace and focused on walking as close to the shoulder as possible. It wasn't completely dark, but she worried that the driver wouldn't see her. As it came closer, she could tell it was a big pick-up. A big, muddy pick-up.

Even though the vehicle was headed in the opposite direction it stopped beside her.

Randi breathed a sigh of relief when she saw the Snowridge Resort logo emblazoned on the side of the truck but still felt uneasy being by herself. She moved a little closer to the edge of the road, watched as the window came down. Then her heart almost stopped for a second time as she recognized the man from the store.

"Need a lift?" he asked.

"No." She waved a hand. "I'm, I'm fine." She stepped forward, breathed a sigh of relief when she heard the engine then groaned when the truck reversed instead of going forward.

"You know, you really shouldn't be out here all by yourself. On this dark road."

"I'm fine. Really. Just going back to the store for something." She picked up her pace, hoped he would get her message.

"Suit yourself," she heard him call out.

Minutes later, another car came towards her, swerved sharply to the left when the lights reflected off her jacket.

"Maybe this wasn't such a good idea," Randi fumed to herself when she heard another vehicle coming up behind her. It stopped beside her and when she looked over, she saw that it was the same Snowridge truck. Same man. He had obviously turned around when he saw her car.

"Is that your Escalade back there?"

Randi stopped and sighed. "Yes. I ran out of gas."

"Get in," he leaned away from her, opened the passenger door of the truck.

"Excuse me?" Randi's mouth fell open. "I most certainly will not. I don't know you. Why would I get in your truck?"

"Look lady, I have a tank of gas in the back and the sooner we get you off the road, the sooner I can go home."

"Why should you be so bothered?" Randi retorted angrily as she stood her ground, her hands on her hips. She glared at the logo on his truck. "If your boss had had the good sense to put a convenience store on the resort, I wouldn't have had to drive so far. I wouldn't have run out of gas. Nor would I have ice cream melting all over the back seat of my brand-new car."

"I'll tell him." He nodded his head at the truck's passenger door. "Now get in."

Trevor waited for her to make up her mind. He couldn't really blame her not trusting him. After all, there was no way she could know for sure he worked for Snowridge. Forget the fact that he owned it. He wasn't certain he'd approve of his own sister having to make the same decision.

Randi's tightening calves decided for her. She stomped around the front of the truck, stepped onto the running board. He leaned over to offer a hand and she felt an instant jolt at his touch. Sparks travelled through her body. Her cheeks felt warm, her heart raced. Expecting a gentle tug, she was unprepared for his hard pull and had to brace herself before she fell across the seat into his lap.

He must have felt something too, Randi concluded. There was a puzzled look on his face. A frown creased his forehead and his eyes squinted slightly. Before she could consider jumping out of the truck, he managed a quick U-turn in the road and headed back towards her car.

"I take it you just arrived today?"

"Yes." She answered breathlessly. She scanned the interior for any stray tool she might be able to use in case she needed to defend herself. He had smelled of sawdust in the store, but she had to wonder if he really was one of the construction crew. He didn't seem to carry many of the tools of the trade with him. Then she spotted a hammer between her seat and the console, closed her hand over the handle.

Trevor had watched from the corner of his eye and couldn't help but smile.

"My father stayed at the unit with my sons while I went to stock up on groceries. I was on my way back to the store to call him when you so kindly stopped to help." There, she thought, she would be pleasant and as soon as he got her car going, she would offer to pay him for the gas then make a quick exit. "I hope this doesn't put you out too much."

"No problem. That's what we're here for."

He pulled up behind her Escalade and Trevor left her to get out by herself. He lifted the tank of gas out of the bed of the truck, walked over to her car and began pouring the fuel into her car.

While he poured, Randi moved to get her purse out of the car. She pulled on the handle, but the door refused to open. Her forehead puckered, she tried again. When it still wouldn't budge, she looked inside and could barely make out the key fob resting in the cup holder of the console.

Why? She groaned to herself, rested her head against the top of the car. What next? She heard his chuckle and with her head still resting against the door, she turned to glare at him.

Her Good Samaritan was obviously enjoying her run of bad luck.

"Let me guess," he started to comment, stopped when she straightened and faced him. There was anger in her stance, fire in her eyes. Trevor was beginning to like the way she put her hands on her hips when she was flustered.

"Don't. Say. One. Word." She inched her way towards him then threw her hands up in frustration and paced back and forth. "I can't believe this is happening. It's been one thing after another all day." She kicked the front tire. "First the boys forgot Ironman." She gave the tire a second harder kick, groaned when her foot jolted.

"Then there was the fiasco in Brownsville." She swung around, stomped toward him. "My father was behind me. Honking that stupid horn all through the town. Can you believe it? Then when I got to the unit and started unpacking, I realized I'd left the cooler of food at home. Damnation!" She threw her hands in the air once again.

She ventured a step closer, glared up at him. "If your boss had thought to put a convenience store on the resort I wouldn't have had to drive so far. Or run out of gas," she exclaimed.

Yes, Trevor decided he liked her fiery temper and tried not to laugh. He simply emptied the gas into her tank, stepped around her to put the can in the back of his truck.

Randi watched him, furious that he could be so calm, nonchalant about everything. She started to follow him, continue her tirade but backed up when he turned and advanced towards her.

Oh Lord, she thought to herself. Now she'd done it. With her luck, he was one of those psycho employees who would probably knock her senseless then toss her off the mountain. She'd never see her boys again. Never watch them grow up, get married, father her grandchildren.

Trevor picked up on her attack of nerves when she backed away from him. And much as he wanted to laugh at her, he understood her ranting. He simply stopped in front of her, stared into wide, nervous moss green eyes. When he was sure she was in control once more, he reached for her hand.

"C'mon," his firm grip pulled her towards the truck.

There was strength in those coarse hands that scared and excited her at the same time. "What? Wait a minute," she tried to pull away, "I'm not going anywhere with you. With the day I've had, how do I know you're not going to have your way with me? Then throw me off this mountain and steal my car? My groceries? My ice cream," she exclaimed as she looked back at the car.

Trevor yanked the truck door open. "Do you smell that chicken? Much as I would probably enjoy having my way with you, as you put it, I haven't eaten all day and am more interested in enjoying the chicken than your delectable body."

His eyes narrowed, dared her to interrupt. "What I tried to say was that I will take you to your unit, you can borrow your father's keys," he paused a moment, "he does have a spare key to your car doesn't he?" When Randi quietly nodded her head, he grabbed her around the waist and lifted her up into the truck. "Good," he barked, before slamming the door and marching around to get in his side of the truck.

"We'll get you straight; I'll give my boss your message. Tomorrow."

Ten minutes later, Trevor chuckled as he drove towards his home. She had three things going for her – shapely hips, a temper and meekness. As soon as he pulled up to her unit, she had jumped out, thanked him, said good night before he could even shift into park. When he got out to follow her, she'd stated her father would be able to help her. She didn't want to take any more of his time. He had simply bowed silently, returned to his truck.

Then he laughed out loud. These next few days might be interesting.

First thing tomorrow, he planned to stop by the office, find out the identity of the little lady in unit thirty-eight.

~~~~~

Randi sat on the deck outside unit thirty-eight enjoying a second glass of wine. She had just put the boys to bed and her father was watching a golf tournament on the sports channel.

True to his word, Sebastian had cooked dinner after driving her to retrieve her car. She hadn't mentioned her companion. Simply said a Good Samaritan had stopped by, gave her some gas, then brought her to the unit when she realized the car was locked.

She settled her feet on the railing, stared up at the clear skies. The stars sparkled like diamonds, the full moon glowed, and the weather forecast promised exceptional spring temperatures for the weekend. She looked forward to just taking it easy. After the day she had had, it couldn't get any worse.

She reached for her cell phone to check the time. Nine-thirty. Marcie should be closing the wine shop about now. She was sure Ginny and Cliff, Brina and Rafe were otherwise occupied, but Marcie would probably appreciate talking to her while she locked up.

She answered on the second ring. "Hey, what's up? I thought you were on vacation. What're you doing calling me on your first night away?"

Randi laughed. "Sorry to say you're not the first to talk to me. I chatted with Ginny on the way."

"Well then, what's wrong? That was a nervous laugh. I know when something is bothering you."

Randi reached for the wine. "Today has been so discombobulated."

"You're on vacation. You're supposed to be relaxing."

"I wish," she groaned. "You won't believe what has happened," she took a sip of wine.

"You met the man of your dreams?"

"Hardly," Randi said thinking about her Good Samaritan. Yeah, he might clean up good but after her reaction to his touch, she wasn't sure she wanted to tempt herself. "Well, I did meet someone today but not under the best of circumstances."

"What happened?"

"For starters, Dad had us leaving almost at the crack of dawn. Then I got turned around in Brownsville and it took forever to get here."

"You mean the round-about?"

"Yeah. When I missed the turn the first time, Dad started honking at me. That got Scott and Sandy all excited. You should have seen us. Dad honking his horn, the boys hollering at one another as we went around four times. Four times," she exclaimed. "Can you believe it? It was so embarrassing."

Randi heard the metallic sound of Marcie's key locking the door to the shop.

"So? You made it there okay, right?"

"Well yeah, but then when we unpacked, I realized I had left the cooler of food next to the back door. That reminds me, can you go over, take care of it for me?"

"Sure," Marcie laughed as she unlocked her car. "What else?"

"Well, I went to the store," Randi paused for another sip of wine, "and on the way back, I ran out of gas."

Marcie snickered. "You ran out of gas?"

"And locked my keys in the car."

For once Marcie stayed quiet. "Wow. You really have had a bad day. Surely someone stopped to help you."

"Well," Randi stretched the word while her heart skipped a beat, "this guy did stop."

"Guy?" Marcie interrupted. "Did you say guy? As in a member of the male species? Was he old? Young and cute? Fat and bald?"

"Definitely young. And I guess he cleans up good."

"He what?"

"He works for Snowridge. And had apparently been working most of the day. The truck was muddy, and he smelled of sawdust."

"You got close enough to catch his manly cologne? Randi, you're going to have to check him out. Or look up his boss one. Doesn't Trevor Graystone have some connection with Snowridge? You know, the one with the cute butt you're always talking about?"

"Yeah, now that you mention it, I think Brina mentioned something about him when I told her we were going to Snowridge." She chuckled. "I guess I'm just going to have to check all the butts around here. That could be interesting but I'm not sure my father would understand."

Randi heard Marcie's car chime. "I'm at your house. You keep the key under the flowerpot, right? I'll go put the food away. Go get 'em girl!"

CHAPTER THREE

The following morning Randi was boisterously awakened at six-fifteen when Scott and Sandy bounced on the king-size bed. "We're on vacation, guys," she moaned. "You're supposed to sleep late. Ump." Sandy plopped on her stomach, stared down at her.

"Do they have cartoons here at Snowridge?"

"Yeah," Scott snuggled at her side, "can we watch Tom and Jerry?"

"Why didn't you go bounce on your grandfather?" she groaned as she reached for her robe, stumbled down the steps toward the living room. She shouldn't have drunk all that wine last night.

Randi reached for the remote, surfed the channels. Sure enough, there was Tom and Jerry. Just like in Edmondsville. She chuckled, amazed that they always asked about the old cartoons.

She settled the boys on the sofa with their favorite blankets, thought about going back to sleep for a while but didn't dare. Not after last night. She'd forgotten to tell Marcie about the fiasco with the Jacuzzi.

While her father cleaned the dinner dishes, she had let the boys bob around in the Jacuzzi. As soon as the timer stopped, she left them to play with their Avengers while she went in search of their PJ's. She was only gone a few minutes, but in that short time, one of the boys had managed to jam an action figure in a Jacuzzi jet.

"We thought he could hide in the cave," Sandy had explained.

Her father had simply laughed, suggested she call housekeeping this morning. "With the luck you've had today, one of us will do more damage if we try to fix it."

Randi glanced at the clock on the stove while she poured water into the coffee maker. Surely no one would be there at this hour but maybe she could leave a message. Hopefully, the earlier they got the message, the earlier they could be here to fix it. And she wouldn't have to waste the whole day waiting. She hated wasting time and was sure the boys would be raring to go somewhere after breakfast.

She dialed the number, expecting it to ring endlessly before going to voice mail and was surprised to hear a breathless male voice on the sixth ring.

"Yeah." The voice was brusque and husky.

Randi stared at the phone, wondered if she might have dialed the wrong number. "Is this the Snowridge business office?"

Trevor recognized her voice. "Last time I checked."

He had been out for his early morning jog and detoured by the office to leave a message for Sandra, his office manager. Technically, they weren't open yet, but he decided to answer. Was glad he did.

"Oh- ah- this is unit thirty-eight. I have a slight problem with the Jacuzzi and was wondering if you could send someone to fix it."

Trevor frowned. The Jacuzzi systems were top of the line.

"What's the problem?"

"Ah- one of the jets is jammed with an Avenger action figure. I would have tried to get it out myself, but I thought it might be best to leave that job to maintenance."

Trevor shook his head and chuckled to himself. This lady was a regular calamity.

"Hello?" Randi asked when she heard no response on the other end.

Trevor cleared his throat. "Yeah, we'll send someone to look at it as soon as we can."

He studied the clock on the opposite wall, calculated he should be finished with his jog, shower and breakfast by eight-thirty. Then he had a nine o'clock appointment with one of his foremen. "It might be ten o'clock."

"Ten o'clock," Randi tried not to groan too loudly. "Does someone need to be here? I mean, you should have a master key to the unit. Right?"

"Somebody's got to show him which Jacuzzi." Trevor knew it would only be a matter of checking the different bathrooms but this way he could guarantee she would be there.

"Oh, yeah, I guess you're right. Okay. I'll stick around then. And, ah, thank you for taking care of this so quickly. I really hate to be a nuisance."

"No problem. That's what we're here for."

Trevor broke the connection, laughed out loud. She could be a nuisance anytime she wanted. He smiled as he left the office to resume his jog.

Randi hung the receiver on the wall and frowned. That last phrase jogged her memory. It was the second time she had heard it and decided it must be the Snowridge motto.

While the boys watched cartoons, she fixed a big breakfast of cereal, fruit, eggs, bacon and biscuits. Knowing she didn't have to rush around or get the boys ready for school, she suddenly felt alive and full of energy.

The coffee aroma lured Sebastian into the kitchen just as she was putting the food on the table. "Well, well, what have we here?" He smiled, rubbed his hands together as he sat at the table. The boys were already munching their cereal, their eyes glued to the TV visible from the den.

"Okay kiddos," he asked reaching for some bacon. "What do you want to do today?"

"Go swimmin'" they answered together, never once looking away from the TV.

Randi reached for some melon.

"I wonder if the Club has any special activities planned. Maybe we should check their schedule of events." She winked at her father. "And I think I saw the Water Park on the way into the resort."

"Water Park?" Scott dropped his spoon, stared at his mother.

"Can we go? Pleeez?" Sandy pleaded.

"It'll depend on how well you two behave. We'll also have to wait for the maintenance guy to look at the Jacuzzi." She frowned at her sons. "To get Ironman out of the jets, remember."

"You've already called?" Sebastian asked.

"Yeah. I took a chance, figured I'd leave a message at the office. Some man answered. Said he would send someone by this morning. Let's just hope the boys don't do anything else in the meantime."

"How about if I take them over to the Club and let them swim? Then you can join us after the Jacuzzi is fixed."

Randi smiled. "Okay with me. Okay with you guys?" she asked her sons.

"Yeah!" The twins started to jump up from the table.

"Not till you finish your breakfast," Randi laughed. "Besides, the pool isn't even open yet!"

After breakfast, Randi took the boys on a short hike while her father researched the resort online. When it was time to go to the pool, she helped the boys change into their suits, stuffed their towels and some toys into the bag. She was reaching for a change of clothes when her father hollered from the bottom of the stairs. "Are we ready yet?"

She laughed to herself. Her father seemed almost as excited as his grandsons.

She made it a point to leave the front door ajar when she followed everyone out to the car. Sandy said his goggles were missing so Randi dashed back inside to find them. She raced back to the car, failed to hear the door close behind her.

Minutes later, she waved good-bye and promised to join them as soon as possible. As she made her way back to the unit she shivered. Spring might be here, but the mornings were still cool. Maybe she'd have time for another cup of coffee before the handyman came.

She approached the door, turned the knob but it wouldn't open. She nudged the door, hoping it wasn't completely closed but it wouldn't budge. She pushed and rattled the door harder, but it remained steadfast.

She threw her hands up in defeat when she realized she was locked out of the unit.

"This just can't be happening," she cried out in frustration. Friday the thirteenth was yesterday. Today was Saturday, the first day of her vacation. She should be enjoying herself. Wanted to enjoy that second cup of coffee.

She searched her jeans pockets, hoped that the key card might still be there from last night. No such luck. She looked in the window beside the door and there it was. Next to her cell phone. Not only was she locked out of the unit, but she had no way of calling anyone.

"What is the matter with me?" she thought out loud. She hadn't been this forgetful in a long, long time. Not since she came home from the hospital with two small babies and a mountain of bills to pay. She huffed out a deep breath. She'd survived then, she'd survive now.

She leaned against the door, tapped her head against the entryway. Feeling sorry for herself wouldn't solve anything; she needed to do something. She squared her shoulders, headed toward the parking lot. Maybe another vacationer was out. Would give her a ride to the office that was two miles away, at the top of a steep hill.

She found no one and after last night, she didn't feel like another hike. She also didn't want to have to explain her klutziness to a stranger when he arrived to fix the Jacuzzi. Even though he might have a master key, she just didn't want to have a reputation of being an absent-minded mother. Especially if he talked to the other guy that gave her the ride to the unit.

She recalled the decks outside different rooms on the other side of the unit. Maybe one of the doors would be unlocked. She was pretty sure the upper deck off the boys' room was locked because she remembered checking it when she put them to bed last night.

Her father had the downstairs bedroom. Maybe he had stepped outside to enjoy the sunrise and prayed that he might have left the screen door ajar or unlocked. She jogged around, jumped over the railing, pulled on the sliding doors but they wouldn't budge.

Randi glanced at her watch. Almost ten. Guessed she'd have to wait for the handyman after all. But what if he didn't believe her? She could be anybody, as far as he was concerned.

She remembered having coffee with her dad on the deck off the den and stepped away from the unit to see if the door was open. Breathed a sigh of relief when she saw that it was.

Unfortunately, this deck was higher. She stepped away from the building, studied the arrangement of decks. Decided if she stood on the railing of the lower deck outside her dad's room, she might be able to reach the floor of the deck to the den and pull herself up. At this point she was willing to do anything. Might even be lucky enough to get inside before the handyman arrived. She rolled up her sleeves, advanced towards the railing.

~~~~~

At the Club, Trevor shook hands with his foreman then sprinted across the parking lot toward his truck. Steve Green was dependable, competent and organized but he talked too much. He looked over, saw two red-headed boys entering the front of the building. Both boys talked at the same time to an older man that walked between them. Trevor could understand their excitement. That early morning phone call kept replaying over and over in his mind.

Finally, he was on his way to unit thirty-eight, anxious to get reacquainted with the lady of the house. She had not only detained him from his dinner last night but haunted his dreams. His heart hummed as he recalled some of the wild fantasies.

Five minutes later Trevor parked the truck outside the unit and sprinted up the steps to the front door. He knocked, waited, frowned when no one came to the door. He distinctly remembered telling her someone would have to be there to show him which of the three Jacuzzi's was jammed.

He started to knock again but thought he heard some noises coming from the other side of the unit. He vaulted the railing and dashed down the slight decline. Someone could be trying to break in from the wooded side.

He rounded the corner and stopped in his tracks. His heart skipped a beat when he saw the woman of his dreams trying to balance herself on the lower railing while reaching for the wood beam in the floor of the upper deck.

"What the hell are you doing," he roared. His heart skipped another beat as he watched her lose her balance. He bolted quickly, caught her in his arms just as she fell backwards.

Reeling from shock, Randi wrapped her arms around his neck, hugged him tightly. Where had he come from? And why had he hollered at her? Caused her to lose her balance?

She leaned back and stared into familiar chocolate brown eyes.

"What do you mean, what am I doing?" She wiggled, trying to get out of his arms but he held her tighter. "C'mon! If you hadn't hollered at me, scared me, I would be on the upper deck by now."

"There is no way you would have been able to pull yourself onto that deck."

"Well, we'll never know now, will we?" She wiggled again but he simply smiled.

"You seem to be a regular damsel in distress. What happened this time?"

Since he wasn't going to put her down, Randi slid her arms from around his neck, crossed them beneath her breasts. She planned to wait him out but quickly realized that the top button of her shirt had come unbuttoned and he was enjoying the exposed cleavage.

"This is so ridiculous," Randi groaned. "Would you just put me down?"

"Please," he answered. When she stared up at him in disbelief he laughed. "After I just saved your life, the least you could do is say please and thank you."

Randi squinted her eyes up at him. "Please and thank you."

Trevor released her legs but hugged her close as her feet settled in front of him. He rather enjoyed the feel of her breasts against his chest and took his time letting her go.

"That's better. Now," he put his hands on his hips and stared down at her. "Why were you trying to climb to that deck?"

"I locked myself out of the unit." Her nose went up another inch as she stood her ground, stared up at him. "I was trying to get back inside before you got here."

She turned, headed along the path to the front door. "I hope you have a master key card or whatever you call those things because I can't get inside."

Trevor watched her stomp away, appreciated the long legs and sway of her hips. "It just so happens that I do," he spoke softly to himself as he followed her.

She was waiting for him at the door and had obviously forgotten the unbuttoned shirt as she once again crossed her arms beneath her breasts. His mouth twitched as he leaned forward to unlock the door. Giving her exposed cleavage one last look, he pushed the door open, stepped aside for her to enter ahead of him.

Just as Randi stomped past him, something scurried across the carpet from under the table and ran into the wood box on the fireplace. She stopped, then backed into him.

Trevor had also seen the mouse and wasn't surprised when she backed into him. Hadn't met a woman yet that had a fondness for mice. He felt the shiver and saw that her face was chalky white. "You okay?" He whispered into her ear.

"I. Hate. Mice." She stated flatly.

Trevor chuckled as he nudged her aside. "Wait here."

He quietly made his way into the den, grabbed the newspaper from the table, placed it over the top of the box. In one brisk movement, he whisked it out the door next to the fireplace, stepped across the deck and turned the contents onto the ground below. The timber scattered and the mouse ran for the woods.

When he returned to the room Randi was leaning against the door. "I just don't understand how something so small can rattle me so."

"We all have our phobias. I'm not crazy about snakes." He stepped towards the stairs. "Now that I've done my two good deeds for the day, why don't you show me which Jacuzzi I need to fix."

Randi started to answer him but stopped. There was something about that swagger that was awful familiar. She shook her head in confusion. Probably because of last night she thought as she followed him.

He waited for her at the top of the stairs, then shadowed her to the master bathroom. Squat down to check the tub and smiled up at her. "Surely a woman your age should know better than to get your action figure stuck in the jet." She narrowed her eyes at him, opened her mouth to speak but turned and left instead.

Trevor watched her sashay out of the room, imagined those long legs wrapped around him. Flashbacks of seeing and feeling her breasts pressed against him gave his body a jolt and he doubted that he'd get any sleep again tonight. This lady most definitely affected him, and he decided he just might enjoy making sure her stay at Snowridge was a memorable one.

He reached for the action figure stuck inside the opening, gently twisted and tugged until it came loose. Chuckled when he recognized Sgt. Slaughter. He didn't know G.I. Joes were still around.

He returned downstairs and wasn't surprised to find her gone. With her run of bad luck, he couldn't blame her for not wanting to stick around. She obviously seemed to have a problem with keys and now action figures.

Trevor reached for a paper towel, scribbled a note about Sgt. Slaughter being the culprit and left the note and figure on the table. He added a postscript, *"I'll also pass your message along to the boss."*

He smiled. Decided he might keep his identity a secret a little while longer.

CHAPTER FOUR

Trevor returned to the Club, recognized Ken the golf pro working on the ninth green with an older gentleman. Both men were thoroughly engrossed in sinking the older man's putt. Trevor remembered seeing the man earlier with two young boys. He heard some noise and looked over to find the two red-headed boys pretending to drive the golf cart.

Just as the ball fell into the hole, the golf cart seemed to come alive. Trevor stopped in his tracks, watched the boys excitedly call out as the cart moved slowly towards the pond on the other side of the fairway.

He raced across the green, running at full speed to catch the cart. By now the boys realized they couldn't stop the cart and were anxiously looking in every direction for an escape. They spied Trevor just as he was almost alongside them.

"Jump," he hollered, opening his arms to catch them. They scrambled over the seat, bailed out the back, one landing in each arm.

Trevor managed to stop himself as the cart rolled down the bank into the pond. All three stared at the slowly sinking vehicle. Then both boys shivered in his arms and clung to his neck. He had to admire them though, scared as they were, they never cried. He heard footsteps running behind him.

"Are they okay?" The older man asked, concern all over his face.

"I think so. Just a little shaken up." The boys refused to let go, their heads resting on his wide shoulders.

Trevor winked at the older man. "Nothing some ice cream won't cure."

As expected, both boys raised their heads and stared at him. Even though their eyes were big as saucers and their little bodies still trembled, they managed a smile.

"I'm not sure they deserve ice cream," Sebastian scolded sternly.

"Accidents happen," Trevor defended the boys. "It's a lot easier to replace the golf cart than these two."

"Well, I agree with you there. I want you to be sure and send me the bill though. The name is Armstrong. Sebastian Armstrong. And these two munchkins are Scott and Sandy, my grandsons."

The boys started to wiggle. "Can we get our ice cream now?" They chorused.

Trevor laughed as he put them down. "Sure. I was on my way for a snack." He winked once more at Sebastian. "If it's okay with your grandfather, you can join me."

"Please, GranPop, can we?"

Sebastian frowned down at them. "Don't you think you have something to say first?"

The boys' smiles disappeared as they stared down at the ground.

"We're sorry we crashed your cart," Scott said as he peeked up at Trevor.

"We won't do it again." Sandy added for good measure.

"NOW can we have our ice cream?" They turned their pleading eyes back to their grandfather.

Trevor laughed out loud. "Can't argue with that." He held out his hand, introduced himself. "Trevor Graystone."

Sebastian jerked his head. "Graystone. I've heard that name before."

"Maybe you've seen the name on the different sites. I own the resort and my company is doing all the construction."

"Construction is a tough business. But you've done a great job here at Snowridge. Up until a few years ago, I used to come on a regular basis. I'm impressed with the changes. Understand more changes are in the works."

"You in construction too?"

Sebastian nodded. "Design. I retired from Keymaster Architects last year."

"Keymaster." Trevor recognized the name. "They're a big firm."

"Yes. We worked with a lot of corporations."

By now they were seated at a table on the patio outside the small Clubhouse café. One of the waitresses joked with the boys while taking their orders for 'nilla ice cream and promised to be back as soon as possible.

"By the looks of things, you seem to be about finished with most of the construction around here."

"Yes. Most of the newer units are completed. Just need the finishing touches in some, odd jobs in others. We have another phase to go, but I don't plan to start that for a couple months. Also trying to decide whether I want to work with a developer who wants me to build a resort outside Atlanta."

"Do they plan to use your design here? Or do they want something different?"

"They like this project but are leaving everything up to me. Anxious for me to agree to do the project."

Sebastian hesitated. "I've done a few designs if you think you might be interested. My family and I will be here for a few days, if you want to look at them sometime."

Trevor tilted his head. "I might be interested." He watched the boys enjoying their ice cream. "Just you and your grandsons here?"

"Oh no!" Sebastian laughed. "I can only handle these two for a short time. My daughter is with me. She had an appointment this morning but plans to take them for their second swim this afternoon."

"I have some free time this afternoon. Maybe we can get together. My office is upstairs."

"Sure." By now Scott and Sandy had finished their ice cream. "We really should be going. My daughter was supposed to have been here by now. Can't imagine where she might be."

Both men shook hands, agreed to meet at two that afternoon in Trevor's office.

~~~~~

At two o'clock, Randi relaxed in the hot tub while she watched the boys play in the children's pool nearby. She rested her head against the side, let the motion of the water sooth her weary body. "Ah," she moaned as her sore muscles relaxed.

The hot tub and children's pool were located at one end of the Olympic size pool. The entire area was surrounded by glass. One long side displayed a magnificent view of the lush green mountains, the other a glimpse of the game rooms and basketball court.

Two levels of windows looked down from each end. One end housed the restaurant and sports bar, the other the executive offices. The drapes in some of the office windows were drawn but in most, they were open, overlooking the activities in the pool.

During lunch, her father had relayed the events of the morning. The runaway golf cart and the daring rescue by none other than the owner of Snowridge Resort. It was obvious to Randi that all three of the males in her family were smitten with this big-time developer. She herself had to appreciate that he had saved her son's lives and hoped that she would be able to thank him.

"I hope you told him he needed to build a mini market," she had grumbled, still upset by her morning adventure with the handyman. Not even the second trek along the nature trail had helped. She hadn't planned to tell her father what happened, but they had found the note the handyman left for her.

"No, but we plan to meet this afternoon at two while you and the boys are swimming. I'll try and remember to mention it."

She jumped then laughed when Sandy squirt her with his water gun from the children's pool. She splashed him back then rested her head on the edge once more.

Her heart skipped when flashbacks of her brief moments in the handyman's arms crowded her thoughts. It had been a long time since she'd been in a man's arms. The boys consumed much of her attention and then there was the struggle to build up her business. Most of her clients and closest friends were women and her evenings revolved around the boys. Men and a social life were non-existent, and she was obviously rusty. Had forgotten how men could ruffle the emotions and was more than a little exasperated at her clumsiness this morning.

She turned her head to check on the boys, noticed they were waving at someone behind her. Already self-conscious that the people in the offices could gawk at anyone swimming, she turned and looked up. High above, her father grinned and saluted.

She stood, waved then turned to follow the boys who wanted to swim in the big pool. She didn't see Trevor join Sebastian at the window.

Trevor's brows shot up; he couldn't help but appreciate the view. He braced a hand against the window when his stomach suddenly lodged in his throat. All he could do was stare down at the woman stepping out of the hot tub. Normally immune to the near-naked beauties, he couldn't take his eyes off the magnificent view of the scantily clad lavender bikini. He watched as she rounded the corner of the pool and instantly recognized her as the little lady in unit thirty-eight. Then experienced a sense of loss when she dove into the water.

When she came up, he watched her help Sebastian's two red-headed grandsons into the water. Her smile was very much like theirs.

He frowned. Suddenly things began to fall into place. It occurred to him that Scott and Sandy resembled the red-headed boys at the Circle in Brownsville, and he now understood why her car had seemed familiar when he helped her last night. She'd even mentioned that she was vacationing with her boys and her father. Then there was their escapade this morning with Sgt. Slaughter that just happened to coincide with Sebastian's comment about the daughter who had an appointment.

Trevor turned to Sebastian. "Is that your daughter?"

"Why, yes." The older man beamed. "Beautiful, isn't she?" Having watched Trevor's reaction, he asked, "Have you met her before?"

Trevor laughed. "You might say that. First, I watched the two of you chase one another in Brownsville yesterday."

Sebastian grinned. "It wasn't really a chase. She kept making a wrong turn."

"So, she said." Trevor chuckled, continued when Sebastian eyed him suspiciously. "I was the one who gave her the ride back to the unit last night."

"And judging from the note on the table, I don't suppose you were by any chance the handyman who came by this morning?"

"The one and only." Trevor sauntered over to the mahogany desk covered with Sebastian's plans. "Don't take this the wrong way but she certainly seems a little overwhelmed at times."

Sebastian chuckled. "I will admit she's had a rough time of it lately. The holidays, Ginny and Cliff's wedding, then Brina and Rafe getting engaged on Valentines and their wedding last month. She was looking forward to some down time before she and the girls started working on their project again."

Trevor collapsed in his chair, realized there were suddenly too many coincidences.

"Wait a minute. Are you talking about Brina Hollingsworth? From Edmondsville?" The two men stared at one another. "What's your daughter's name?" Trevor wondered if this little lady was also one of Brina's partners.

"Miranda Cavanaugh."

"That's Miranda Cavanaugh?" Trevor pointed a finger toward the window. Now, he had heard of that name. From his sister. Who was always telling him he needed to collaborate with her when he put the finishing touches on the new units.

Trevor stood, walked back to the window, watched her frolic in the water with the boys. She was laughing just like the picture in a recent magazine.

He turned back to Sebastian. "That's the Miranda Cavanaugh that has been in the magazines?"

Sebastian nodded.

"And the same Randi Cavanaugh who's working on a project with Brina Hollingsworth?"

Sebastian frowned, nodded again.

"I'm the contractor that's working on the Edmondsville project. With Brina."

Sebastian laughed out loud. "How strange is that? Randi has never mentioned you."

"We haven't officially met. Now that I think about it, we always seem to miss one another. She's usually coming in one door as I'm leaving another. And if I recall, Brina was always talking about how Randi had all these plans for the project."

"They all do," Sebastian agreed. "Brina her personal shopping office. Ginny a children's museum and adult center. Marcie a wine shop. And Randi an office for her interior decorating business."

"Yeah. Now that we seem to have gotten past all the public hearings and the weather is warming up, I'm sure they're looking forward to getting the project done."

Sebastian laughed. "Yup. And you certainly have a full plate. Here, Edmondsville and that project in Georgia?"

Trevor smiled. "Haven't decided on the Georgia project. And I have a good foreman and crew to handle the Edmondsville project." Although now that he had met Randi, he might be spending a little more time on *The Row* project himself.

"Randi has a full plate as well. Because of that article in *Decorating Today*, her career has suddenly taken off. She says the phone never stops ringing. Fortunately, the boys are in school so that frees up her days. It's also the main reason she wants to move everything to an office at the fire house. Separate the business from her home life. These past six months have been a little overwhelming which is why I talked her into bringing the boys here for their spring break. I'm trying to get her to slow down a little. Enjoy life again."

"Yeah. She seemed strung-out last night. I almost felt a little sorry for her."

"Hah! She might have a few bumps in the road from time to time but overall, my Randi is very focused and independent. Takes after her mother."

Trevor chuckled. "I said almost. She let me have it when I teased her about walking after dark by herself and then a few minutes later she was hesitant when I offered to carry her back to her car. Her bark is louder than her actions?"

"That's my Randi. Fiercely independent. Not one to let things get to her. And don't ever tell her she can't do anything; she'll prove you wrong. Only people she depends on are me and the girls. Lately though, she's been so stressed out with the business and weddings. Hopefully some R and R this weekend will get her back to her normal self."

"Don't know what her normal self is like, but she has definitely made my last twenty-four hours interesting."

"She can be hard-headed but deep down, she's sweet and easy-going."

"I don't doubt that. No, I'm very familiar with her reputation as an interior decorator and as a businessman myself, I know how we sometimes push ourselves too far." He winked at the older man. "We'll just have to make sure these next few days help her loosen up."

It occurred to Sebastian that Trevor Graystone had more than a passing interest in his daughter. Trevor just might be the answer to some of his plans for his daughter.

"Are you by any chance doing anything tonight?"

Trevor leaned back in his chair. "Well, no, not really."

"Would you be interested in a home-cooked meal?"

"What sensible man wouldn't be interested in a home cooked meal?"

"Would you like to join us tonight?"

"Sure. But don't you think you ought to ask your daughter first?"

"Oh," Sebastian waved a hand, "she'll be okay with it. And I'm sure there will be more than enough food. Once I tell her that I invited the developer of Snowridge to dinner, I'm sure she will be anxious to tell you all about the improvements you need to do."

Both men laughed.

"If you're sure she won't mind," Trevor worried. He remembered how his mother had felt whenever he invited his friends without asking her permission.

Sebastian stood, crossed his fingers behind his back.

"Of course, I'm sure. I tell you what, why don't I leave these plans with you, and you can look them over. We have plenty of time to discuss them."

"Sure thing," Trevor said as he walked Sebastian to the door. "Seven?"

Trevor closed the door, returned to his desk but was no longer interested in the plans. Especially now that he knew the identity of the lady in thirty-eight.

The door opened and Sebastian poked his head around it. "I won't tell her who you really are. Let's let her find that out when you get there."

Both men laughed, each anticipating a different reaction.

~~~~~

Sebastian sprinted down the stairs to join Randi, prepare her for the plans he'd made. Apparently, she and Trevor had had a rocky beginning and he was more than a little interested in seeing how they would adjust to one another.

"How'd your meeting go?" Randi asked as they drove back to the unit. Scott and Sandy were already half asleep in the back seat, their heads nodding from side to side.

"Interesting," Sebastian said.

"Interesting as in he's interested in your ideas? Or because he's an interesting man?"

"Both, actually." He wasn't ready to spring the news about their surprise dinner guest. "He's come a long way in six years."

"Six years? Wow. That is impressive. Not too many people could have accomplished all he has done with Snowridge in such a short time."

"Yes. And he has other projects in the works as well. But you know, you haven't done so bad yourself, young lady."

Randi smiled as she parked the car. She appreciated his confidence in her. "Well, I don't have the capital he seems to have."

"Your time will come."

Each carried a twin inside, settled them on their beds for a short nap.

"What's for dinner?" Sebastian followed her into the kitchen.

"Pot roast. I'm on vacation, remember?"

"Yeah, okay. But could you fix some of those farmer's potatoes? And didn't you pick up the ingredients for that bean casserole I like?"

Randi leaned against the counter, crossed her arms and feet. "What have you done? Who've you invited to dinner?"

Her father was famous for inviting someone for dinner. Usually, he took them out. But tonight, she would be doing the cooking. And he always had an ulterior motive for his invitations.

Sebastian opened the refrigerator, reached for a beer. "What makes you think I invited someone over?"

"Why else would you ask for your favorite dishes when it would be so much easier for me to fix plain potatoes, carrots and green beans?"

"Well... I did mention that you were a good cook." He wasn't ready to spring Trevor's identity yet.

Randi gaped at her father. "You invited the owner of Snowridge to our unit? The owner? For dinner? Dad," she groaned, "I thought I was on vacation. Not a personal chef."

"Aw, honey," Sebastian rested his hands on her arms. "I know, but it just happened. Besides, it might convince him to consider my plans."

Randi narrowed her eyes at her father, then accepted the inevitable. She stepped towards the fridge.

"Lucky for you I happened to pick up most of the ingredients last night. Just hadn't planned on cooking them so soon." She reached for the roast. "What time is he coming?"

"Seven," Sebastian answered sheepishly.

Randi shook her head. "I don't know why I let you do these things to me."

"Because you know I love you."

"Mom?" Sandy stood at the door. "I'm hungry. Can me and Scott have some popcorn?"

"Scott and I," Randi corrected him. "That was a short nap," she noted as she put the package of popcorn in the microwave.

Sandy started to race to tell his brother but turned at the door. "Mom?" Big brown eyes stared into green ones. "I love you to."

~~~~~

Two hours later, Randi relaxed in a mountain of bubbles enjoying a glass of wine. The meat and potatoes were in the oven and her father had handed her the glass, suggested she take her time getting ready. He and the boys would set the table and fix the appetizers.

Now that she could relax, the evening ahead worried her. Why did she feel nervous? Because it involved a man, she scolded herself. Up until now, the only members of the opposite sex she ever had time for were her sons and her father.

Now, suddenly there was another man intruding on the scene. Make that two men – the handyman and the owner. They seemed to be coming out of the woodwork here.

And why did she feel there was one last trick to be played before her day was complete?

Her thoughts went back to the handyman this morning. Recalled how she had simply dropped into his strong arms. He had flustered her with one simple look. She felt her cheeks flush as she recalled how he had stared down at her unbuttoned shirt, then squirmed as she remembered how he seemed to enjoy holding her close. With a sparkle in his eyes and smile on his lips. He was very potent, and she wasn't sure she was up to handling him.

Randi rested her head against the tub, let the goose bumps thrill down her body. Felt a throbbing and an itch she hadn't felt in a long, long time.

"You are so horny," she scolded herself as she reached for a towel. The shivering wouldn't stop so she grabbed her cell phone, scrolled for Marcie's number, pressed send. Hopefully she wouldn't be too busy to talk.

"What's up?" Marcie asked.

"Nothing really," Randi leaned against the door, the towel wrapped around her. "Just getting ready for some company."

"I thought you were on vacation."

"I thought so too. Then my father decided to invite the owner of Snowridge to dinner."

"Hmm, this sounds interesting. Hold on a minute so I can put you on speaker phone. Brina and Ginny are here in the tasting room." A few seconds later Randi could hear the hum of the deli case in the front room of the wine shop. "Now," Marcie continued, "tell us about this dinner guest."

"Probably some stuffy old guy Dad wants to impress. He said he ran into him this morning, then pitched his business proposal to him this afternoon. Must have gone well as he invited the guy to dinner when he said he wasn't busy."

Randi heard Brina laugh. "Are you sure he's old? You know how your dad is always trying to match you up with someone."

"Yeah," Marcie added, "remember the dentist he tried to hook you up with last year?"

"And the realtor before that?" Ginny added.

"Very funny," Randi responded. "Judging from the improvements he needs to make I'm sure the owner is still living in the last century. I just might give him an ear full."

"So, what are you going to wear?" Ginny asked. "In case he happens to be a handsome devil."

Randi was silent a moment. "Considering that I packed only jeans and sweaters, I guess it will be jeans and a sweater. After all, I AM on vacation."

"Be sure and wear those dangling earrings I gave you for Christmas. They make your eyes sparkle."

"And add an extra dab of your Rapture perfume," Brina added. "Remember how Rafe and Scooter always tease you about smelling good? Who knows, this Snowridge guy just might be a handsome devil like Ginny said. Reel him in, girl."

Randi laughed. "I have enough men in my life. Besides, I'm saving myself for Trevor, remember?"

There was a loud knock at the door. Her father's warning that she had thirty minutes.

"That's my cue to get my ass moving. Wish me luck."

"We'll call you later," Marcie shouted before breaking the connection.

Randi hung the towel on the rack, studied her reflection in the mirror. Her breasts were small but firm, her waist still slim, and her hips as trim as when she had raced on the track team in high school. Not bad, she decided. At least her cheeks had a natural blush, and she had a full head of hair. Why was she worrying about whether her figure would appeal to some old goat? If she was going to doll herself up, she'd make sure he was young and good-looking first.

She decided to leave her hair down and put a little more effort into her makeup. "Just in case," she thought to herself. In case he happened to be the handsome devil Ginny suggested he might be.

She was dressed and ready for the evening ahead when she heard her father open the door downstairs. She added an extra dab of perfume, gave herself one final look over before heading downstairs. She smiled, pleased with what she saw.

She stopped at the top of the stairs when she heard a very familiar voice.

CHAPTER FIVE

"What are you doing here?"

Trevor was seated on the sofa between the boys and had just reached for a chunk of cheese when he heard her voice. It occurred to him that he would never tire of seeing her. She might be wearing worn jeans and a faded sweater, but he decided she'd probably look just as good in a potato sack.

In the short time he had known her, he had probably witnessed every emotion possible. Frustration with her vehicle and then being locked out of the unit. Nervousness about accepting his help. Shyness, then anger when he knew he might have been a little arrogant. And now confusion at his appearance for dinner. That left passion, desire and ecstasy. All of which were worth pursuing.

He decided he enjoyed her anger the most and waited for the explosion as she put two and two together. Her shoulders had stiffened, her hands were fisted at her waist. Emerald green eyes glared at him, and he was sure he could feel the pricks of daggers she sent his way.

No one had spoken since she entered the room. The boys gaped; their mouths open in surprise. She obviously had never raised her voice like that to a stranger. Sebastian appeared to be beside himself. Trevor was sure her father had expected confusion, certainly not the anger that was brewing.

Since her eyes bored into him, Trevor decided to give her an answer. "Your father invited me. Didn't he tell you?"

"Oh, he told me all right." She crossed her arms in front of her, "he said he had invited the owner and developer of Snowridge. Not,"

Randi paused, felt her stomach knot in tension. It suddenly occurred to her that this man had never really identified himself. She had just assumed since he had so conveniently appeared to offer her a ride last night, then fixed the Jacuzzi this morning that he was the handyman. And now to realize that he was the actual owner. She turned to stare at her father.

"Mom," Scott asked, "why are you fussing at Mr. Trevor? He's the bestest."

"Yeah," Sandy chimed in. "He's almost as good as Sgt. Slaughter!"

"Honey, I thought you knew Trevor was the owner of Snowridge."

"How would I know that? I've never met the man. Wait a minute," she paused, backed away. "Did you say Trevor?" She pointed a finger at Trevor. "You," she ordered. "Stand up and turn around."

Trevor lifted his eyebrows in surprised but obliged her.

"Walk over to the fireplace," Randi commanded then groaned when she recognized his strut.

"Honey, are you okay?" Sebastian asked.

"I'm, I'm fine," Randi turned to the kitchen. What else could happen this weekend? She called over her shoulder, "Boys, go wash up while I put dinner on the table."

"Does that mean all of us?" Trevor asked from the door.

She pivoted, squinted her eyes at him. "Cute," she muttered.

Trevor stuffed his hands in his pockets, leaned against the door jam and smiled. "I need to ask though. Why have me stand, walk to the fireplace?"

"Because that's all I've ever seen of you," she threw her hands in the air. "Your butt. Walking away whenever I came to the Firehouse." She wasn't about to tell him how much she admired his butt. "And if you knew who I was, why didn't you tell me?"

"Because I only found out this afternoon. Considering our past two meetings, I was curious about how you would react."

"Well, I hope you had a good laugh. I'm sure you've been chuckling all afternoon. Now put this roast on the table."

She handed him the plate, reached for the potatoes. Tried to ignore his smirk but paused to appreciate his strut as he sauntered to the table.

"So," she filled the boys' plates minutes later, "besides taking our hard-earned money to renovate the fire house, what do you really think about the project?"

"I think it has a lot of potential." Trevor poured the cabernet he had brought into their wine glasses. "I like the fact that you're renovating and not tearing down. Not that a couple of the buildings don't need to be demolished but for the most part, the project will be an asset for the town."

"Wish everyone felt that way," Randi mumbled, thinking about the three public hearings they had had to endure. At the first one, the Town Council discussed the project; the second, several on Council tried to vote against it; but the third time was the charm when just about everyone in Edmondsville came out and supported them. They were still trying to find out why Myra White and her father Councilman Tom Marshall were so against it.

"Yeah. It's not unusual but you girls seem to have had more than your fair share of opposition." Trevor hadn't attended the public hearings but had provided Brina with the ammunition to use. She had also given him a blow-by-blow account after the hearings. He recalled the fire that had happened weeks after the public hearing.

"Did they ever determine who started that fire? I asked the guy at the garage behind the firehouse to keep an eye on the place but never heard anything."

"They think it was a homeless guy," Sebastian announced as he spooned another serving of potatoes on his plate. "Homeless Hal hung around the town for a while, then he disappeared shortly after the fire."

Trevor looked at Randi. "You girls need to be careful whenever you are there. At least until the construction is finished."

Randi knew he meant well but bristled anyway. Tim had always said she was careless and pointed it out every chance he could. She had learned to tune out his hurtful barbs.

"We try to meet as a group whenever we visit the site."

"Still, I've caught Brina there by herself a couple times," Trevor countered.

Randi quietly set her fork on her plate, stared across at him. "Not since her car was tampered with, you haven't." She dared him to say anything else about the project.

"Scared the crap out of me that day." Sebastian said. "When you called about keeping the boys, I thought you had been in the accident. Not Brina. And then hearing about that boy dying the next day. Did they ever find out who hit him?"

"No." Randi stiffened, frowned at her father. She didn't want to remind the boys about their first conversation about death. It had been difficult having to explain why Mark Smith wouldn't be doing any more chores around the house. "Who's ready for dessert?"

"Me," the boys said together as Randi reached for their clean plates.

She carried the dishes into the kitchen, stared at the wall behind the sink. Mark's death had been difficult for her, Brina, Ginny and Marcie. With the public hearings, the fire, Brina's accident and then Mark's death, they wondered if *The Row* was jinxed. Or if someone was deliberately trying to sabotage the project.

"You okay?" Trevor set the left-over meat and potatoes on the counter beside her.

Randi jumped. She hadn't heard him follow her into the kitchen.

Trevor stood directly behind her, tilted his head closer to her ear. His nostrils filled not with the flavors of the meal but with her perfume. She smelled good. He was tempted to wrap his arms around her and hold her close, but he knew he shouldn't.

Randi cleared her throat. "Yes. Yes," she repeated as she started the water into the sink. "Mark Smith's death was a difficult time for all of us. We began to wonder if someone might be sabotaging the project."

Trevor whispered in her ear. "It never hurts to be careful."

Randi gave a half-chuckle, tried to ignore the tingle that shot down her spine.

"Oh, we've definitely become more careful." She turned to get the dessert out of the refrigerator, realized too late how closely he stood behind her. She was trapped between him, and the counter and he didn't seem to be interested in moving anywhere soon. She stared up into chocolate brown eyes that had shifted to her lips.

"Did anyone ever tell you you have very attractive lips?" His head inched closer.

"Mom," Sandy hollered from the dining room. "Where's our pudding?"

Randi jumped at the sound of her son's voice, tried to nudge him away but Trevor remained steadfast, smiled down at her.

"You know, we might have just met but I feel like I've known you for months." He took one last glimpse at her lips then turned and headed back to the dining room. He paused at the door and gave her a saucy smile and wink. "Hold your horses," he called out to the boys.

Randi leaned back against the counter, breathed a sigh of relief. No man had rattled her like that in a long time. She grabbed the pudding and bowls, made a beeline for the table. The sooner they finished dinner, the sooner he would be on his way.

After dinner, Trevor started a fire in the fireplace then settled on the floor for some battle planning with her sons. Randi relaxed on the sofa, watched Scott and Sandy bombard him with questions while they set up the scene. He seemed to enjoy answering them.

It suddenly occurred to her that her boys probably needed more male companionship. Not that her father, Cliff and Rafe ignored them, but Trevor was new. Somebody different. They asked about learning to play golf like GranPop, but Trevor had to explain that the Club didn't have golf clubs small enough.

"How about soccer?" He looked at Randi for her opinion. "Some of the staff are trying to include it in the activity schedule. I think they're having a clinic tomorrow."

The boys cast excited brown eyes at their mother. "Can we, Mom?"

Randi smiled. "I guess we can try it out. I was going to check with the Recreation Department when we get home, but we can certainly give it a try here too. I'm not sure I understand all the rules, though. Not like I do baseball."

Suddenly there was a loud thud outside the front door.

The boys immediately jumped up. "What's that? A bear?" They asked at the same time.

Trevor chuckled. "If I'm not mistaken, I believe Max has trailed me here."

"Who's Max?" Scott asked.

"My St. Bernard."

"A dog!" Both boys made a beeline for the front door.

Randi quickly tried to intercept them. "Wait a minute, you two. St. Bernard's are very big, and you don't want to surprise him. Wait for us."

But Scott and Sandy were already out the door. Just as she moved to follow them, a tremendous dog raced through with the boys in hot pursuit. The adults jumped to action. Randi grabbed for the lamp near the door, Sebastian gathered the scattering dishes as Max raced under the table and Trevor snatched the ceramic figurine in the corner when the dog continued down the hall.

"Max," he hollered, then whistled. The dog quickly returned to the den, sat in front of his master. In a matter of minutes, Max had made a running tour of the entire unit. Scattered the area rugs, overturned the bookcase filled with paperback books, left the boys' toys strewn from one corner of their bedroom to the other.

Trevor immediately grabbed for the dog's collar while Randi and Sebastian each held a twin like a bag of potatoes. Everyone – adults and children – were breathless from the wild chase.

"You two are going straight to bed if you don't watch it." Their mother scolded them.

"Aw Mom. It wasn't our fault! Besides, we was having fun."

"It will be more fun tomorrow when you can romp outside." Trevor stated as he returned from putting Max on a leash outside the door. "There will definitely be more room."

"Can we, Mom?"

"Can we play with Max tomorrow?"

"Let's see how fast you can get your teeth brushed and ready for bed. You two have had a busy day today."

The boys raced up the stairs while the adults collapsed in the den.

"Do you normally allow your dog to just roam the resort whenever he wants?" Randi reprimanded Trevor in her motherly tone.

"No. But occasionally, he gets out of his pen. Never gets very far but has a way of finding me wherever I am."

"Reminds me why I've refused to let them have a dog."

Trevor chuckled. "Aw Mom, every boy should have a dog."

"That's debatable," Randi said as she rose to check on her sons.

She and the boys had a bedtime routine that included stories, secrets and prayers. Usually this was the only time she could relax with them, and she tried to make it her quality time with them.

Tonight, Scott and Sandy asked if they could share a secret with Trevor.

She was surprised that they had taken to him so quickly. With her lack of a social life that didn't include many men in her life, she'd expected them to have been shy and reserved, but instead, they had taken right to him.

The boys waited until Randi was in the hall before they hunkered down to whisper their secret to Trevor.

Trevor laughed to himself as he made his way down the steps. Those two might be innocents but they had plans for their mother.

"What deep dark secret did they tell you?" Randi met him at the bottom of the steps.

"No real secrets. Just some man-talk."

Having loaded the dishwasher and cleaned the kitchen, Randi turned to look for her father and immediately noticed some changes in the den. The lights were dimmed, music played softly. Her father was up to his old tricks, and she turned to see if Trevor noticed.

Sebastian called to them from the deck where he enjoyed a cigar and port.

"I envy you your solitude," he commented to Trevor as they joined him. "Considering the size of the resort and the number of people who stay here, it's quiet. If I had a place like this, I doubt that I'd ever leave it."

Trevor leaned against the railing – the same railing she had been reaching for that morning, Randi thought. Wondered if Trevor remembered.

"Well, it's been a good investment and I stay here as much as I can. I'm originally from outside of Richmond though. Still have the home that's been in the family for over a hundred years. Caretakers oversee it, I visit from time to time, but this is really my home now. I've made friends here and there's still a lot of work to be done. Also gives me plenty of room for exercise since I jog and swim to keep in shape."

And have a cute butt, Randi thought as she sat across the deck from him. No wonder he had felt so solid when he caught her this morning.

She suddenly realized that her father must have said something to her because both men were looking at her.

"I was saying," Sebastian repeated, "it's such a clear brisk night. Why don't you and Trevor take a stroll? I'll stay here with the boys."

Randi opened her mouth to refuse when Trevor interrupted.

"I usually take a late stroll with Max in the evenings. You're welcome to join me."

Randi squirmed in her seat, uncomfortable with the thought of being alone with him. Not that she hadn't been alone with him before but now that she knew who he was, it seemed different.

"Go ahead, Randi." Her father encouraged her. "Do you some good to get out."

Randi was sure her father was doing some matchmaking and didn't want to encourage him with too many objections or excuses.

It had been a long time since she had been alone with a man. A man who seemed larger than life. Too good to be true. What would they talk about? How would Trevor act? Especially after two near-kiss episodes. Or did she want to see how far he would go?

Trevor watched Randi from across the deck. He was pretty sure he knew what was going through her head and if he didn't somehow maneuver her along, she might never give them a chance. Even though she was experienced, there was an innocence about her which intrigued him. He was pretty sure she questioned his intentions, and, in a way, he could rightfully understand.

"I tell you what," he spoke out loud. "We'll take the short trail to the Club and back."

Did he just quirk his eyebrow and challenge me, Randi thought? The nerve of the man.

"I agree with you Dad. A walk will probably do us both some good. Why not?" Before she could chicken out, Randi headed inside. "Let me get my jacket."

Trevor unleashed the dog when they stepped outside the unit. "This is Max's favorite time of day."

"I hate to admit it, but my father was right," Randi tucked her hands in the pockets of her jacket as she followed him down the shortcut to the Club. "A stroll under the full moon is already relaxing." She inhaled deeply, caught the scent of the pine trees, brisk cool air. Pine needles softened their steps, the full moon lit their path as they walked side by side. "It's certainly a clear night. Almost as light as daytime. And it's so quiet."

"Yeah, that's why I like it here. No smog, no streetlights, no noises. Just plenty of fresh air, lots of peace and quiet." He bumped shoulders with her. "I really had to think long and hard about whether I wanted to develop this area." He looked down at her. "Allow people to intrude on my paradise."

Randi smiled up at him. "I'm glad you did. Although there's still a lot more that needs to be done," she teased.

"Like what?"

"Well, a small convenience store for starters. I wouldn't have been stranded on the road last night."

"And we wouldn't have met."

Randi laughed. "Between my father and my sons, I'm sure our paths would've eventually crossed."

"I guess you're right," Trevor recalled Sebastian seeking him out to pitch his plans, the boys' mishap in the golf cart. Fate apparently had a plan, and he was more than a little curious about what the future held. "Like I said earlier, we may have just met but I feel like I've known you longer."

The corner of her mouth quirked up. "Yeah. We heard a lot about each other even though I kept missing you whenever you met with Brina."

A raccoon dashed across the path ahead of them with Max in hot pursuit. Trevor grinned when Randi jumped, moved closer to his side. He rested an arm across her shoulders. "I thought you were only scared of mice."

"That and any dark movements I can't distinguish at night." She smiled up at him. Found his lips inches from hers and she couldn't help but wonder if he was talking about the raccoon or himself.

"It's okay." He turned them towards the Club. "We don't normally have any wild animals roaming around here. They're further up the mountain." He paused. "And I just plan to take a walk, that's all."

Randi stopped, slipped him a curious glance. "Do you normally read people's minds?"

"No. Your eyes tell it all."

"Well, just to let you know, despite my father's intentions, I don't have time for men in my life. As a single parent, all my energy is focused on the boys. If I don't work to support them, who will?"

Trevor studied her with narrowed eyes. "Don't you get child support?"

Randi stepped ahead. How do you explain that not having the father in her boys' lives was the best child support? Tim had never wanted the boys and she certainly didn't want to expose them to his abusive ways. When he finally agreed to the divorce, she and her father had examined the divorce papers, demanded some changes. In exchange for child support and visitation rights, Tim would establish a trust fund for the boys' college education.

The first few years she had lived with her father while he adjusted to life without her mother. Then she started the business and this past year had been a good one due to the newspaper article. She was determined to give her boys a normal home life and the trust fund would take care of their college education.

"Randi?" Trevor grabbed her elbow, interrupted her thoughts. "You do get child support, don't you?"

"Now, no. But when the boys are older, yes."

Trevor frowned, stared down at her in disbelief. "What does that mean?"

Randi tugged her elbow free, turned to take another step. "I really don't want to talk about my ex-husband. He hasn't been in my boys' life since before they were born."

Trevor stopped her once more; his hands grabbed her upper arms to hold her still.

"Let me get this straight. You're saying that your ex-husband has never, ever, been in Scott and Sandy's lives? And paid no child support? What kind of father is that?"

"A father that didn't want the children in the first place." She pulled away, continued down the path. "Trevor, you don't know my ex-husband."

"Maybe it's a good thing I don't," Trevor growled. It angered him that any man would refuse to support his children.

"Look," Randi turned to face him, "you don't have to worry. I'm doing fine. Now. And when it comes time for the boys to go to college, the money will be there."

"And how do you know that?"

"I just know. Okay?" Suddenly, her cellphone chimed but she ignored it. "Look, we're better off without him in our lives" her cellphone chimed a second time. In exasperation, she reached for it, worried it might be her father. She breathed a sigh of relief when she recognized Brina's number.

"Hey," she answered.

"Hey, hope I'm not interrupting anything."

"No, just out on a moonlight stroll."

"By yourself?"

Randi chuckled. "No. As a matter of fact, you know him," Randi put the phone on speaker.

"Hey Brina." Trevor spoke, "you never told me about your partner."

"Trevor? Is that you?" Brina laughed. "What are you doing there?"

"Snowridge is Trevor's resort," Randi responded. "He owns it. I've been giving him an earful of changes he needs to make."

"Well just make sure the firehouse is done before you tackle some other projects."

"Everything going okay?" Trevor asked. "The crew's supposed to be working on those changes we discussed with your offices."

"Oh, yeah. Can't help wondering where the next obstacle will come though. I sure will be glad when we get this project done."

"Shouldn't be more than a month, six weeks at the most." Trevor assured her.

While talking, Randi had turned, steered them back towards the unit. She was happy to see the parking lot, her front door within sight.

"Well, you two have a good time." Brina laughed. "Glad you two finally hooked up."

"See you in a couple days," Randi ended the call. She continued towards the unit, but Trevor stopped her.

"Randi," his hands on her upper arms turned her towards him. "Look, I'm sorry about the temper earlier. I guess you have your reasons for keeping your ex out of your life. I just know if Chuck did that to my sister, I'd beat the crap out of him. So..." he leaned down to look directly into her eyes, "I'm sorry. No hard feelings?"

Randi felt her eyes water, her heart warmed when he'd said he was sorry. Other than her father, there had been no other man in her life to be concerned for her.

"Thank you. I really hate talking about my ex-husband. The boys and I have created a life without him and we're better off that way. I appreciate your concern and am sorry I never had a brother to talk to."

She leaned up and kissed him on the cheek.

Trevor held her in place as he stared at her lips, her eyes then her lips.

"We need to get something straight," he murmured. "I certainly care about you and your boys but not in a brotherly way." He paused to be sure his words sank in. "I want to see you tomorrow. You, me, the boys, even your father if he wants to come along. We'll spend the day together, then you and I will have dinner tomorrow night."

Randi's hand rested against his chest. His heart beat steady while hers raced. It had been a long time since a man had shown any interest in her.

"Ah... that will be nice, but I should warn you, I don't have time to start a relationship with you or any man."

"That so?" His eyes twinkled; his mouth curved into a smile. "Seriously, I'm kind of on vacation myself and I'd like to show you and the boys around. As for a relationship," he leaned down his mouth inches from hers, "count on it. A hot and heavy one."

~~~~~

Is anyone still up? Randi texted her friends praying that one of the girls would call.

"Oh my God! The man is incredible!" She declared when Brina rang her moments later.

Brina laughed. "Is his butt as cute in the flesh as you say it is in jeans?"

"I wouldn't know, we went for a stroll after dinner. Brina, Trevor said he wants to show us a good time while we are here. We've only just met officially. I told him I didn't have time for a relationship, and he has all but promised we will be lovers. Brina, I've never felt like this," she gushed.

"Wow. That'll put a different spin on our project. We need him to get the job finished. Not spend all his time in your bed."

Randi laughed. "You forget I have two boys. And I haven't been with a man in a very long time. Somehow, I doubt that we will progress that quickly."

"He moved pretty fast tonight," Brina reminded her.

CHAPTER SIX

Trevor whistled softly as he meandered down the path towards unit thirty-eight. He hadn't felt this good on a Sunday morning in a long time. Slept like a baby, got up with the birds, was ready for some more time with Randi. He'd include the boys during the day but planned on more alone time with their mother tonight. He was sure Sebastian would help him.

His smile slipped as he recalled her comment about her ex-husband not supporting them; decided he needed to have a conversation with Sebastian about that.

Now that he'd met Brina's elusive partner, he just might be spending more time on the Edmondsville project. He recalled Randi's comment about not having time for a man in her life. We'll see about that, he thought. They might have just met but Randi had grabbed his attention and he intended to pursue a relationship with her. He could be persistent but would be patient and understanding too.

Maybe Sebastian could shed some light on why she didn't think she could have it all. Love, a relationship, kids and a business of her own.

He started up the steps towards the door of the unit then heard Scott and Sandy playing in the shade under the deck. He peeked over the railing saw that they were setting up their action figures.

"Who's winning?" He studied the soldiers lined up along a mound of dirt. All the soldiers faced a few Cobra enemies and Darth Vader's storm troopers.

"Rey is going to lead a team against Darth Vader and needs to get over there to Sgt. Slaughter," Sandy announced.

"And Captain America will fly down from here." Scott added. "Hulk will be moving in too."

"Wanna play?" They asked together.

Trevor vaulted the railing, sat and crossed his legs. "That depends. Do I get to choose my side?" When both boys nodded their heads, he rubbed his hands together. "I'll take Sgt. Slaughter. He's more my style."

"But he can't stop Darth Vader." Sandy argued.

"Wanna bet?" Trevor lined his men along a fresh mound of dirt. "What's this?"

The boys looked at one another before Scott finally spoke. "We found a bird."

"A bird?"

"Yeah. A dead bird." Sandy stammered with a sad face.

"Well, gee, I'm sorry to hear that." Trevor apologized.

"But we buried it there."

"You did? You buried the bird here?"

"Yeah." Scott nodded "We said a prayer."

"And sang *Silent Night*," Sandy said.

"Why *Silent Night*?" Trevor asked, puzzled that they would choose a Christmas Carol for a bird's funeral.

"'Cause it says sleep in heavenly peace."

Trevor pressed his lips together to prevent the chuckle. "Well, that was mighty thoughtful of you guys. Did you tell your mother?"

"Tell me what?" Randi asked as she smiled down on them from above.

"We buried a bird!"

Trevor watched her eyes grow big as saucers. "We need to get you inside to wash your hands." She exclaimed. "Right now."

"Aw Mom. We was just getting started with our battle."

"And Trevor's going to play too."

"Yeah, Mom." Trevor mimicked the boys. "I'm sure another ten minutes won't harm them. Besides, I need to prove Sgt. Slaughter is man enough to fight Darth Vader." He picked up the action figure, knocked down several of the First Order Stormtroopers. "You boys better hustle."

Scott and Sandy immediately positioned themselves, did battle with Trevor while Randi cheered from above. Ten minutes later Darth Vader's forces lay in a mound in the center of the battlefield.

"Okay guys. Let's pick up your soldiers while I go back inside, look for the car keys. I know I set them on the table this morning."

"Did you go to the Soccer Clinic this morning?" Trevor asked as he helped gather the figures.

"Yeah!" They exclaimed excitedly. "And Mom said we could go back this afternoon."

"Glad you enjoyed it." Trevor tossed some soldiers into the box, noticed something shining at the bottom of the box. He lifted the fob, looked at the boys. "Do you suppose these might be the keys your mother is looking for?"

The twins exchanged guilty looks, nodded their heads.

"Any reason why you're hiding the keys from her?"

"We... we figured if we hid the keys then...then she wouldn't be able to find them, and we could play longer."

Trevor looked from one twin to the other. "Suppose she really needed her keys? What if something happened to one of you or your GranPop and she had to leave in a hurry?"

The boys looked at one another, lowered their heads.

He wondered if this might be the first time they had tried to pull a fast one on their mother. Trevor stood and put the keys in his pocket. "We better get inside before she comes out and finds them."

"The boys told me they went to the Soccer Clinic this morning," Trevor commented as he followed the boys inside. "Does this mean you're going to let them play?"

"Yes, in fact they have another practice this afternoon. I had planned to take them to the park for a picnic lunch before the practice but since I can't find the keys, we might not have the time."

"The park! Aw, Mom, can't we go? Pleeease?"

"I can't find the keys, remember."

Trevor raised his eyebrows, looked down at the boys as if to say, *I told you so*. Then he winked. "Why don't we help you look. Who knows, maybe you missed, them. Right boys?"

He wandered over to the table that held the ceramic figurine Max had almost overturned last night. While Randi stood with her back to him, he quietly set the missing key fob on the floor beside the table. Both boys stared at him wide-eyed.

Noting their expressions, Randi turned, saw Trevor walk towards the fireplace. When she began to turn back around, she glanced down, noticed the keys on the carpet behind the leg of the table.

"Now how did they get over there?" She wondered out loud, cast a suspicious look at Trevor as she bent to retrieve them.

"Must have fallen in the excitement of Max's visit last night. You reckon?"

"But I used them this morning."

"Yeah, Mom," Sandy interrupted his mother. "That's what happened. Now can we go to the park?"

"I don't know..." she was skeptical now.

"I tell you what." Trevor interrupted. "I don't have any plans for this afternoon, so what do you say I tag along. To help, that is. I've been meaning to check out the water park we built last fall. We can go there after their practice."

"I'm not sure we have time, now." Randi studied her watch.

"Time for what?" Sebastian asked from the bottom of the steps.

~~~~~

Randi fed everyone a quick lunch of PB&J sandwiches before they headed for another round of soccer practice, then the water park. The boys were too short for many of the rides but still enjoyed working their way up the Snowridge Alps, then sliding down to the bottom.

The Pine Hollow innertube ride was the most challenging for Randi. She and Trevor each had a child between them, but she kept sliding against him. At one point, Trevor had one arm around a twin and the other around Randi holding the other twin as they bumped each other down the path.

She finally relaxed at the Wave Pool as she, her father and Trevor watched the boys ride the surf. It was late afternoon when they carried two exhausted boys into the unit.

Randi was surprised to find a big box leaning against the door. "What's this?"

She looked at Trevor, but he shrugged, shook his head.

"Well, open it up and see," Sebastian suggested.

Randi opened the box, found a card on top of the tissue. *"Happy birthday. Thought we'd get Cinderella something special for her evening out. ~ the girls."*

Randi nudged the tissue paper aside, lifted out a halter scarf hem midi dress, three-quarter sleeve wrap, heeled sandals, earrings, even a small purse.

Trevor smiled. "Have to say it's good timing."

"I called Brina last night but certainly didn't expect her to do this. That'll teach me not to share problems with her."

"What kind of problems?"

"I told her I didn't have anything to wear for dinner tonight."

"You mean our date?"

Randi cringed when her father chuckled.

"What's a date?" the boys asked, instantly awake.

"I'll explain it to you later," Sebastian said as he led the twins upstairs. "Let's get our PJ's on and I'll watch *Captain America* with you."

Trevor watched Randi brush a hand across the material.

"Looks like 'the girls' have high expectations for this evening. Guess I'll have to dress for the part, not disappoint them." He leaned down, whispered in her ear. "That dress looks kinda sexy."

Randi nudged him out the door, then turned to fix the boys and her father an early dinner. Once they'd eaten and were nestled on either side of their grandfather, with *Captain America*, she sprinted upstairs to get ready.

She dialed Brina on her cell phone as she headed up the stairs.

"You shouldn't have," she scolded Brina.

"We wanted you to look hot tonight. Do you like it?"

"I love it. And I certainly appreciate it. How did you do it so quickly?"

"Called in a favor from a colleague that lives near there. Sandra's also a personal shopper and once we checked online and put the outfit together, I asked her to pick everything up and deliver it to your doorstep."

"I love it."

"Did Trevor see it?"

"Of course. We'd just gotten back from the Water Park, and he was here when I opened it."

"Good thing I didn't order the sexy underwear." Brina laughed. "Have a good time."

~~~~~

Randi smiled when Trevor knocked at her door an hour later. The sapphire blue shirt complemented his scruffy auburn whiskers, the coal black slacks boasted his long legs and the tight butt she always appreciated.

She stopped in her tracks when she saw the shiny black convertible parked next to her Escalade.

"Thought we could enjoy the fresh air," he whispered near her ear as he opened the door for her.

She stroked the soft grey leather seat. "It's very beautiful."

Trevor smiled. "I kinda like it myself. Don't drive it as much as I'd like though."

Owning the resort obviously had its advantages, Randi thought. Special parking space, special seating. She was impressed that although he was the owner, his staff didn't single him out. Simply escorted them past the other diners to his special nook in the far corner of the room. She couldn't help but admire him. Not only for his self-confidence but for the respect everyone seemed to feel towards him.

She appreciated the romantic ambiance with the soft lighting, linen tablecloths, hushed conversation and splendid view of the mountainside. Easy-listening music piped throughout the room.

"VIP treatment," Randi smiled. "I like your idea of having fine dining in addition to a sports bar."

"When I'm with a beautiful lady, I want to enjoy the moment. Not have to talk over the crowd. The dining room has become so popular we've started recommending reservations."

She glanced out the window. The mountainside reminded her of Christmas as the lights from the villas and streets twinkled across the way. She was surprised to see the moon sparkled on the water of a pool.

"Trevor," she exclaimed, "I had no idea there was an outdoor pool."

"Don't really advertise it much. It's more for staff use although we've sometimes allowed private parties."

Randi reached for her glass of sauvignon Blanc wine, offered a toast. "Job well done. I'm impressed more each day. You should be proud."

Trevor watched her gaze travel around the room, waited until her eyes rested on him and smiled.

"Now that I have you to myself," he murmured huskily, reached across the table for her hand, "we might as well enjoy the evening to the fullest. Come dance with me." He led her to a small corner in their secluded nook.

He took her in his arms, moved to the slow beat of Neil Diamond's *September Morn*. Her perfume surrounded him as he gathered her close and they danced cheek to cheek.

"Who would have thought two nights ago that I'd have you in my arms tonight?" He whispered in her ear.

Randi leaned back to look up at him, her arms around his neck, surprise in her eyes.

"You sound as if you have big plans."

Much as she enjoyed being in his company, she hoped he wasn't planning an evening of seduction. She wasn't sure she was ready to take that giant step.

They silently sized each other up. He saw a woman who wanted to be loved but never had the time. She saw a man capable of giving so much love, no questions asked. Neither was certain how to take the first step, handle the other. So, they simply smiled, decided to take whatever the evening had to offer.

"I hope you don't mind that I took the liberty of ordering our meal," he spoke when they returned to the table. Saw the salads had already been set.

"Of course not. This evening is turning out to be a novel adventure." She took another sip of wine then turned to observe the other people in the room. Many were couples huddled together in private conversations. A large group was apparently celebrating a special event in the small room off one side.

Suddenly her gaze fell on a couple seated midway across the room. She didn't recognize the woman but something about the man's profile was familiar. Her stomach knotted when she realized it was the way he held his head, drank his wine. Talked to his companion. When he turned, stared directly at her she froze, caught her breath.

"Randi?" Trevor touched her hand. "Are you okay? You look like you've seen a ghost."

Randi quickly turned to Trevor.

"You could say that," she whispered. "My ex-husband. He's here. Across the room."

Trevor looked across the way, immediately locked eyes with the guy. Salt and pepper hair, slight build, dressed in a suit, stern expression. They stared at one another. Trevor didn't normally let things bother him, but he didn't want Randi upset either.

"Do you want to leave? I can have everything boxed. We can take it to my house."

"No. No." She tried to smile. "He doesn't scare me. I'm just shocked, that's all. I haven't seen him in over six years. And Snowridge is the last place I expected to run into him."

Randi breathed a sigh of relief when the couple stood to leave, then fretted briefly when Tim walked towards their table. She squared her shoulders, refused to let him intimidate her, simply looked him in the eye when he stopped by their table.

"Randi," he glared down at her, expressionless. "It's been a long time."

"Yes," she answered. Trevor squeezed her hand then stood. He knew he towered over the man by a good six inches and smiled when the ex-husband hesitated then looked back at Randi.

"I'd like to introduce you to my wife, Miriam. Miriam," Tim never looked at his wife, kept his eyes on Randi, "this is Randi, my first wife."

Miriam extended her hand, offered a nervous smile. "It's so nice to finally meet you. Tim has told me about you and the boys."

Randi tried to smile. "It's nice to meet you. This is Trevor Graystone. Trevor, my ex-husband, Tim Cavanaugh."

Both men nodded to one another before Trevor rested a hand on Randi's shoulder.

"I hope you're enjoying your stay at Snowridge," Trevor said.

Miriam smiled. She was a small woman and Randi was sure Tim used his slight height to dominate her. He certainly couldn't do that with other men.

"Oh yes. It's so quiet here. Just what we needed."

"Trevor owns Snowridge," Randi announced proudly.

Miriam's smile broadened. "Well, you should be proud. All I've heard is compliments. We just got here this afternoon but plan to check out all the amenities." She looked at Randi. "Are you and the boys staying here as well?"

"Just for a long weekend," Randi said.

Tim placed his arm around Miriam's shoulder, nudged her along.

"Randi, good to see you. Mr. Graystone," he nodded to Trevor, "maybe we'll run into each other these next few days." They walked away.

"Not if I have anything to do with it," Randi mumbled.

Trevor sat, watched her shaking hand reach for her wine. "Are you sure you are okay? You're white as a sheet."

"Nothing a little wine can't take care of." Randi shivered, tried to smile. "Give me a couple minutes. He just surprised me, that's all."

So much for their romantic evening, she thought. She was determined not to let Tim spoil things.

"So, you haven't seen him since the boys were born?"

Randi nodded.

"And he hasn't paid you any child support?"

Randi looked at him, then nodded again.

Trevor was baffled. "How does he get away with it?"

"Hey, it beats the alternative. It's worth not having him in our lives. You have no idea what my life was like back then."

"But Randi," Trevor reached for her hand again, "there are laws. A father is obligated to support his children."

"Trevor, I know that. Believe me, I know that. Now," she took another sip of her wine, "if you don't mind, I'd like to just forget all about Tim Cavanaugh and see if we can recapture some of the romance my ex-husband chased away." She looked at him and sighed. "Trevor, I appreciate that you want to take me out. I'd like to just enjoy the evening."

Trevor stared at her. Randi Cavanaugh and her two boys had suddenly made his life more interesting. He'd already decided he wanted
to spend more time with them. Even offer a shoulder for her to lean on
if necessary. If it meant shutting up now, so be it, but he and Sebastian
would be having a conversation real soon.

For now, he'd do as she'd asked. Recapture the romance, enjoy
a quiet evening with a beautiful woman. Much as he desired this
woman, planned for a more intimate relationship, he also realized he
was going to have to give her more time. Court her.

When their meal was served, Randi stared into Trevor's eyes and
smiled.

"Trevor, I want you to know that I thoroughly enjoyed today. I
don't think I've seen my boys so excited to be with another man as they
are with you. And this evening, it's been a long time since I've dressed
up for dinner; been treated like royalty. You have apparently put a lot
of thought into all this, and I don't want a chance meeting with my
ex-husband to spoil things."

After dinner, they took advantage of the warm evening and enjoyed
a slow drive around the resort. He showed her his chalet home, but
they didn't go inside. They drove along the golf course, stopped to
walk around a green.

It suddenly occurred to her that Trevor's quiet, calm, patient demeanor relaxed her. Unlike Tim who wanted to be in control, Randi
realized Trevor's confidence, sense of humor, strong belief in himself,
and her, was like a breath of fresh air. He soothed her.

She reached for his hand as they strolled along the fairway.

The moon was bright just like last night, but tonight she felt a sense
of peace. They walked in silence, paused ever so often to watch the
deer that wandered out of the woods to graze. Once, Trevor tugged

her hand, stopped her as a skunk scurried ahead of them, intent on finding food.

"Good thing Max isn't with us, huh?" He whispered. "I'd much rather smell you."

Randi snickered, covered her mouth. "Where is Max anyway? I haven't seen him all day."

"At home. In the kennel. I didn't want a repeat of last night."

Trevor parked outside the unit, walked her to the door where he gave her a tender look. "Tomorrow?"

When she nodded, beamed up at him, he leaned forward to softly brush her lips.

"Tomorrow it is," he whispered, then turned to leave.

He couldn't help but smile. One step at a time, he thought to himself.

CHAPTER SEVEN

R andi decided not to tell her father about seeing Tim. It would only upset him. He had been her rock throughout the divorce proceedings and would not appreciate having her ex-husband back in their lives. Besides, the likelihood that they would run into each other at such a large resort was minimal so why say anything. He'd play his round of golf and she and the boys would go to the soccer camp, then swim.

She had fifteen minutes to find the boys shin guards for their soccer practice but was having difficulty concentrating on the task. Her heart fluttered for the umpteenth time as she recalled her evening with Trevor. He had been so gentle and caring the entire evening. She sat on the side of the bed, pressed her fingers to her lips, reliving the brush of his good-night kiss.

When she heard voices, she jumped up, dashed down the steps. Her father had already left, and the boys were supposed to be watching TV. Who could it be? She stopped abruptly at the bottom of the stairs.

"Boys, what have I told you about opening the door to strangers?"

"But it was Mr. Trevor," Scott answered.

"We saw him in the window," Sandy added.

"I don't care. You should have called me."

"We did. Then we let Mr. Trevor in."

Randi saw the twinkle in Trevor's eyes. "Well, lucky for you it was a friend. Next time might be different," she scolded her sons.

"I came to see if you guys were going to the soccer clinic. Thought I'd ride along. See if you two are learning anything."

"Yay," both boys exclaimed. "Mom? Can we?"

"Of course. Why do you think I've spent the last fifteen minutes looking for your shin guards?"

Randi looked at Trevor and sighed. "I wasn't expecting you so early."

"Couldn't keep me away. What else can a guy do with a good-lookin' Mama and two handsome dudes in the neighborhood."

The boys giggled.

Twenty minutes later, the boys were playing at soccer on the long narrow field, trying to remember which of the two nets was their goal. Trees lined one side of the field; bleachers interspersed with open spaces for those who preferred to bring their own chairs on the other. Parents mingled along the sidelines, some sitting in the sun, others seeking the shade. Randi and Trevor settled in their chairs under a row of pines to watch.

They had split the twenty boys into two teams and the two coaches practiced with their team at opposite ends of the field. The last ten minutes of the session would be a mock game. Thankfully Scott and Sandy were on the same team and Randi could focus her attention on one end of the field.

"I wish they'd chosen baseball," she sighed as she leaned back. "I understand the game. Soccer? Too many rules."

Trevor smiled. "There's still time. I remember being in little league, but it wasn't till I was about seven that I understood the game and took it seriously. Who knows, maybe they'll like both sports."

Randi laughed. "They're busy enough as it is. My mother always said busy bodies stay out of trouble. I'm not sure I agree. No matter how busy I keep them, they're always into something."

"Watch, Mom," Scott called out.

Randi cheered when he scored a practice goal. "They look so small on such a big field."

When the game finally started, she, Trevor and most of the other parents laughed as the boys raced up and down the field, some running in the wrong direction, others missing the ball or tripping each other up. The coaches tried to steer them in the right direction, reminding them that they had to kick the ball with their feet. Everyone roared when one of the boys subconsciously picked the ball up with his hands and threw it towards the net.

Randi was still laughing when she happened to look across the field and locked eyes with her ex-husband. Tim and Miriam sat on the other side, watching the boys. She froze, caught her breath while her heart sank to her stomach. She was so sure their paths wouldn't cross in such a large resort.

Unless Tim was deliberately shadowing them.

Trevor knew the instant she saw Tim. He'd scanned the area when they arrived, spotted the couple right away. He was sure she would be upset so he had tried to keep her preoccupied rather than tell her. He squeezed her hand. "It's okay."

"No. No, it's not," Randi mumbled. "He has no business spying on my boys. Why is he here?"

"Maybe he's trying to get a rise out of you. Don't let it bother you."

"Trevor, he has never been in their lives. Why now?"

"Just wait. Ignore him. See what he does."

"Trevor, all I wanted to do this weekend was to relax. Spend some quality time with my father and two sons. If we hadn't come here, I wouldn't be having this problem."

Trevor leaned forward, looked directly into her eyes. "If you hadn't come here, we wouldn't have hooked up. Gotten to know each other. Besides, if he wanted to see the boys, he would have found a way. For all we know, the boys may be why he's here now."

"That's what worries me. And if so, how could he have known we were here?"

Trevor shrugged. "Anything's possible. He could have someone watching you."

Randi shivered. "Now you're making me paranoid," she nervously looked around then back across the field where she saw Tim staring at her. She started to get up. "I can't do this. We need to go."

Trevor tightened his grip. "Randi, they're almost finished. Give it a few more minutes. You don't want to let him know he's upsetting you. Do you?"

Randi stood, reached for the boys' water bottles. "How can I not worry? He has always rattled me. Even when we were married."

Trevor stood. "Another reason to stay calm."

When she ignored him, he reached for her, swept her into a dip. "If he's going to unnerve you by watching you, maybe we should give him something to stew about." He smiled at her shocked expression, then took hungry possession of her mouth.

Surprised by his sudden move, Randi grabbed his shoulders for support. Her head was dizzy, her spine tingled with heat. When he hugged her closer, deepened the kiss, her hands moved around his neck. She murmured softly and returned his kiss.

The sound of giggles ended the kiss but not the dip. Trevor looked over at the boys who were laughing and jumping in place at the same time. "You like that?" He teased them.

"Yeah," they both exclaimed.

"Then watch this." He turned back to Randi and kissed her again.

"Umm, Trevor," Randi hissed against his lips, tried to push him away. He lifted his head, waggled his eyebrows before he brought her upright.

"That'll give him something to think about."

Randi tried to hide her smile. "Okay boys, time for some lunch. Then we'll stop by the Club House to see what GranPop is doing."

She handed them their waters, stuffed their shin guards into the bag and turned to head for the car. Her heart tripped when she spied Tim and Miriam walking towards them.

"Randi," Tim said as they approached.

She wondered if he suspected she would bolt. "Tim," she answered firmly.

"You boys did a great job," Miriam praised the boys.

Scott and Sandy stared up at the strangers, then looked at their mother.

"Boys, this is Mr. Tim and Mrs. Miriam." She refused to use Tim's last name. Or mention that Tim was their father. "They're staying at Snowridge too."

"Yes," Tim studied his sons, "maybe we can get together sometime while you're here."

Trevor decided it was time he stepped in. "Boys, why don't we go put your stuff in the car. Let your mom talk to Mr. Tim. Miriam," he turned to the other woman, "would you like to walk with us?"

Miriam was shocked, then smiled. "Why, yes. I'd love that."

Randi watched them walk away. She appreciated that Trevor had taken control and was determined to continue it. Tim liked nothing more than being in charge and she resolved to not let him intimidate her. Their marriage ended five years ago; he no longer influenced her life. She took a deep breath, stared directly into his eyes.

"What do you want, Tim?"

Tim scowled. "To see my sons, of course."

"You gave up that right when you signed the divorce papers. In fact," she crossed her arms under her breasts and glared up at him, "I seem to recall you saying you were glad to be rid of us. And while we're talking about the divorce, I went online, checked the boys' trust fund. See that you're behind by almost eighteen months. If you want to make trouble for me, I can certainly reciprocate."

"Look, I'm not trying to make trouble. I just want to see my sons, that's all."

"Why now? Why are you suddenly so interested in your sons' welfare?"

"Look, I've remarried, okay. Miriam knows about the boys, wants to get to know them."

"Then have your own children. Leave mine alone." She turned to walk away.

Tim grabbed her arm to stop her, dropped it when she stared at his hand. He threw his hands up. "I'm sorry. We've been trying to have children. For two years. First there were the fertility tests, then the IVF attempts. Nothing took. That's why I fell behind on the payments. IVF procedures are expensive. After several attempts, the doctors finally determined she can't have children. That's why I brought her here. To relax. Get away from everything for a while."

"I'm sorry. I am. But that's not my problem. You signed away your rights five years ago. Scott and Sandy have adjusted to not having a father in their lives and I don't want to upset them. They wouldn't understand."

Tim squinted his eyes, glared down at her. Randi was immediately reminded of his mood swings, prepared herself for the backlash. "Looks like you're working on a substitute dad."

"Trevor and I are friends, that's all."

"Looked pretty chummy to me," he growled.

Randi stared icily at him. "Tim, you don't scare me anymore. Your days of control and abuse are in the past. And I'm not going to stand here and argue with you."

She turned to leave and once again Tim grabbed her arm.

"Okay, okay. I'm sorry. I had a brief relapse."

"Brief relapse?"

"Yeah. I've changed. Miriam is helping me to be a better person. That's why I've been trying to be patient and understanding. But now it looks like there will be no children in our future. That's why we came here."

"Wait," Randi interrupted him, "did you know we would be here? Have you been watching me? Spying on me?"

"I had a private investigator track you. That's all. He found you at Edmondsville, just happened to overhear you telling your friend you were coming here."

"He was that close to me?" Randi exclaimed. "That close to my boys? You had no right," she fumed.

"All I want is for Miriam and me to be a part of the boys' lives. Now."

Randi shook her head, threw her hands in the air.

"Not going to happen," Randi stated vehemently, then turned to walk away. She was shaking inside from fury. And fear. Much as she wanted to run away from him, she paced herself and was thankful Tim didn't try to stop her a third time. She needed to get as far away from him as she could.

She walked up to Trevor, Miriam and her sons. "Okay boys, time to load up." She turned to Miriam, tried to smile. "Miriam, it was nice seeing you. I hope you and Tim have a pleasant visit here at Snowridge."

She looked at Trevor. "Didn't you say something about going to a movie?"

"Sure." Trevor played along. "What'll it be boys? Action movie or chick flick?"

"What's a chick flick?" Sandy asked as he followed his brother into the back of the Escalade.

~~~~~

Randi paced the small deck off the den. They had gone to a matinee and the boys were resting in front of the TV before their next adventure. "I cannot believe Tim wants to see the boys," she moaned.

Trevor let her walk off her frustration while he sat in the chair nursing a beer. "Is that what he said he wants?"

"Pretty much. It seems Miriam can't have children so he's looking to the boys as a replacement."

"Maybe you need to get some legal advice. Don't you and Brina have a friend who's a lawyer? Brad Beckman? Maybe Brad can help you."

"I'll certainly be giving Brad a call when we get back." She stopped, stared down at him. "Can you believe Tim hired a private investigator? he investigator not only found out where I live but was close enough to overhear me talking to Ginny about coming here. If he was that close to me, what about the boys? Chills went down my spine when Tim told me."

Trevor balanced his chair on the back legs. "I'm surprised he admitted to doing it. Yes, you need to talk to Brad. Make him-" Trevor stopped when his cellphone chimed. "I've got to take this. It's one of my foremen."

Randi leaned against the railing, sipped her wine. Her own cell phone rang, and she recognized Brina's number.

"Hey, what's up?"

"Just wanted to let you know that someone must have had a party in the firehouse this weekend."

"What? I thought it was locked. Secure."

"They broke a window in back. There's graffiti all over the walls, trash and bottles everywhere. Duane Peterson is investigating, trying to see if anyone saw anything. But it's going to be another hiccup to get through."

"Wait. Are you there?" Randi asked. "At the Firehouse? Not by yourself, I hope."

"No, Rafe is here. He's talking to Duane. I just wanted to let you know. Ginny, Cliff and Marcie are on their way."

"Should I be concerned? Maybe the boys and I need to come home."

"No. We've got it under control. Besides, you only have one more day, right?"

"Yeah," Randi answered softly.

"What's wrong? Is everything okay? Is Trevor behaving himself?"

"Trevor couldn't be better. Just some hiccups here as well. I'll tell you about it when I get back." She heard the concern in Brina's voice but didn't want to get into things over the phone. "Tell everybody hey for me. And you might see us sooner than you think." Randi had a sudden thought. Maybe she could use this as an excuse to leave early, not have to see Tim again.

"I've got to go to Edmondsville," Trevor said moments later.

"I know. Brina just called."

"They think it's kids. Foreman says it's under control but I'm going just to be sure it's only graffiti. Might even stay there tonight to be sure they don't come back."

"Where will you sleep?"

"In the loft."

Randi forgot about the apartment they were putting in the firemen's sleeping quarters on the second level.

"But there's no electricity. These spring days might be nice, but the nights still get cool."

Trevor grabbed her upper arms to stop her pacing. He forced her to look up at him. "Randi, I've got a cot I can take with me. I've done this before. I've slept on the job in November, the month of April should be a piece of cake."

"Then I'm coming too."

"To stay with me in the loft?" Trevor teased.

Randi laughed. "Of course not. But I will cook you some breakfast in the morning."

Trevor stared down at her. "Nice to see you smiling again."

"I need to get away from here. I hate to cut their time short, but I need to get the boys away from Tim."

~~~~~

He watched the activity from his office window. People came and went. First the woman in charge, then the deputy, then the rest of the group. He noticed that one of the group was missing.

He sneered when the deputy walked away, got in his car. They'd never find who did it.

Then he smiled. It hadn't taken much to convince Josh that the firehouse would be a good place to party. Stupid teenagers. Always looking for a good time. Never paid any attention to the news around them so they'd never questioned it when he told them the firehouse was due to be demolished. Another reason to party there.

Fortunately, they'd been smart enough to wait till after dark.

And the graffiti added a sinister touch. The mess would have been fine, but the beer probably had something to do with the signage.

Everyone in town was talking about it. He was annoyed that they didn't heed his other warnings. The public hearings. The fire.

Maybe this would finally end the project.

The longer they worked on it, the greater the risk they would find out.

CHAPTER EIGHT

"Should I be worried?" Randi asked Brad. She'd had a constant headache since returning home late yesterday and couldn't focus on anything. It was all she could do to fix breakfast for Trevor. The boys had a play date with some friends and as soon as she dropped them off, she'd delivered Trevor his breakfast. She still hadn't told her father about Tim and thankfully he hadn't stopped by to join them for breakfast.

As soon as she'd returned home, she'd called Brad. When he'd said he could see her in an hour, she changed into the first decent pair of jeans and shirt she could find.

"I mean, technically, he signed over his rights when he signed the divorce papers. Right?" She'd never told anyone about Tim's abusive ways. Not Ginny, Brina, Marcie and certainly not Brad. Maybe now it would be necessary.

Brad gave her a concerned look. Dressed in his plaid shirt and khaki pants, he looked more like an old friend than a lawyer. She understood he only wore suits on court days.

"If you don't mind my asking, I'm curious why he'd even sign away his rights." Brad leaned forward, stared at her from across his heavy desk. "And why you let him. Legally, a father is responsible to support his children."

"Oh, he does," Randi answered quickly. "He does. We set up their college trust and he agreed to contribute to it on a regular basis. Only - "

"Only what?" Brad asked.

"Well," she hesitated, "I checked the account, and he hasn't made any contributions for the past eighteen months." She paused when Brad leaned back in his chair, a look of disbelief on his face. "I guess it's my fault," she continued. "I should have checked it before now."

Brad put up a hand to stop her. "Wait a minute. It's not your responsibility to monitor the account. Surely your lawyer assigned someone to check it, at least on an annual basis."

"Then why wasn't I informed?"

Brad reached for his phone. "What's the Law Firm?"

"Burnside and Associates."

"Peter Burnside? In Maryland?"

Randi nodded.

"I know him. We've handled a couple cases together." Brad asked Stacy, his assistant to put the call through. When the phone rang minutes later, he put it on speaker. "Peter, Brad Beckman here. How's it going?"

"Great," Peter answered. "These past few months have been hectic but I'll be in the Caribbean next week so I guess I can hang in there a little longer."

"Let's hope so. Hey, I have Randi Cavanaugh in my office. She says you handled her divorce."

"Yes. I worked with her dad on it. Why?"

"I understand the husband is supposed to be contributing to a college fund in lieu of child support. Do you have anyone monitoring the account?"

"Yeah, my secretary assigned one of our clerks to do it. She was supposed to check it quarterly."

Brad frowned. "Was?" He asked. "Not anymore?"

"No. Not after Cavanaugh called her to say Randi had agreed to switch to annual contributions. Sent a letter which we have on file. Not sure when Pam last checked. Hold on," Peter put them on hold.

Brad looked at Randi. "Did you agree to switch to yearly contributions?"

"Of course not. Why would I do that? I haven't had any contact with Tim since the divorce."

"Brad," Peter interrupted, "Pam said he called June of last year. She has a letter Randi signed in the file. She just checked the account, says nothing has been contributed since then. Do I need to put some pressure on him?"

Randi couldn't stay quiet. "Peter, it's Randi. Until the other day, I have had no contact with Tim since the divorce. I certainly would not have agreed to that change and have not signed any letter."

"Hmm," Peter responded. "I will put Pam onto it; have her scan you a copy of the letter. Funny you should call, Randi. I had an email from Tim's lawyer this morning stating that Tim wants to pursue joint custody of the boys."

Randi gasped. "But he can't," she exclaimed. "Can he? I mean, he signed away those rights. Didn't he?"

"Doesn't mean he can't change his mind. Frankly, I'm surprised he hasn't done so before now. I seem to recall telling your father the same thing when we worked on the conditions. Your father said you wouldn't have to worry about that happening. Has something happened?"

"I ran into him the other day. He says he's changed. Remarried and since his wife can't have children, he wants to spend more time with the boys. Peter, I thought all that was taken care of."

"Like I said, despite the original divorce agreement, he has always had the option to petition for joint custody."

"I can't go through this again." Randi sobbed. "Peter, you know the hell I went through. The boys don't even know their father." She looked at Brad. "This can't be happening."

"I understand," Peter stated. "Let me talk to Tim's lawyer. See where they're going with this. I'll call you when I know something."

When Randi remained quiet, Brad answered, "That'd be great Peter. Maybe you can let me know what you find." When Brad cast a questioning look towards Randi, she nodded. "Good talking to you buddy. And enjoy the cruise."

Brad disconnected, then looked across the desk at Randi. "Now, if I'm going to help you with this, you need to tell me exactly what happened. What is this 'hell' you mentioned? Did he abuse you?"

Randi stood, crossed her arms across her nauseated stomach, paced to the window. "My ex-husband was an alcoholic. The more he drank, the meaner he got. I tried to stay out of his way but when I was six months pregnant with the boys, he came home in a rage. We argued and I ran upstairs. He followed me and when he slapped me, I tried to get away from him. He ended up pushing me down the stairs in anger. I spent a month in the hospital trying to prevent a miscarriage. My dad had always suspected Tim was abusive and when this happened, he threatened to report Tim to the authorities unless he agreed to a divorce. Dad and Peter drafted the terms. Tim agreed."

"Are you talking about Delegate Tim Cavanaugh? In Maryland?" Brad asked.

Randi nodded.

"And Peter knew all this?"

Randi nodded again, paced back to the chair. "Tim has been groomed since youth for politics. His father was a local politician. Tim was supposedly on the road to governor, and it wouldn't look good for a delegate, much less the governor, to have abuse charges brought against him. So, Tim agreed.

"Then he showed up out of nowhere the other day. Said he'd straightened up. Told me he had remarried, and they were having fertility issues. They'd just found out his wife can't have children. But he never said a word about joint custody."

She leaned forward, rested an arm on the edge of his desk.

"Brad, what am I going to do? Until the other day, my boys had never met their father. They don't know that the man they met at Snowridge is their father. What am I going to do?"

Brad rose, came around the desk to pull her into his arms. Randi had been his friend for almost five years, and he never knew the horror she must have endured. "I'm sorry. Sorry you went through what you did. Sorry he is upsetting you now. All we can do is wait to hear back from Peter. See what Tim's intentions are."

Randi rested her head against Brad's shoulder. "But can he do this? Can he just barge back into our lives? Demand joint custody?"

"Unfortunately, it's his right. Happens all the time. If this is the case, more than likely some guardian *ad litem* will be assigned to the boys."

Randi leaned back, stared up at him. "A what? I thought they were for abusive situations."

Brad steered Randi towards the soft brown leather sofa. "In many cases they are. But their main purpose is to make recommendations to the court in the best interest of the child. They interview the child, parents, teachers- "

"You mean Ginny might have to be involved."

"As their teacher, yes. The GAL does home visits, observations, anything that involves the boys. Then he or she makes a recommendation which the judge considers before making his decision."

"But Scott and Sandy hardly know their father. And Tim has never made any effort to contact me before now."

"Well, that's something in your favor but he might also try using his political position. You say he has remarried? Just found out his wife can't have children?" Randi nodded. "Maybe it's the wife that is behind this."

"I don't know," Randi collapsed against the sofa, "this is all so upsetting. Just when things were going so smoothly. Brina and Rafe are married. Ginny and Cliff are going to have a baby."

She thought about the fun she and the boys had had with Trevor.

"We had such a great weekend with Trevor. Scott and Sandy are crazy about him. They're near the end of their school year, I hate to have something like this upsetting them."

Brad squeezed her hand. "Let's wait and see what Peter says. If you want me to help, I will."

Randi gave him a watery smile. "I appreciate it. I was so sure when he signed the divorce agreement Tim would be out of our lives. For good."

Brad stood, offered her a hand. "It still might work out, but if not, we'll face it. I know several GAL's in the area. They're all honest and caring people. Some are counselors. Some, retired lawyers. All will recommend what's best for the boys. I don't think you have anything to worry about. You've certainly proven yourself to be a responsible parent. Your ex-husband has been the negligent one."

~~~~~

Randi left Brad's office and headed home. She felt drained. She hadn't slept good last night, and her energy was nil.

She drove by the firehouse and saw Trevor's truck. That's odd, she thought. It was her understanding he only planned to stay the one night. Planned to head back home this afternoon. Had something else happened?

She parked next to his truck and noticed the county vehicle on the other side. She stepped inside to find Trevor talking with the building inspector.

"Come to see how soon you can move in?" the inspector asked.

Randi smiled. "I'm sure there's still a lot more to be done but it will be nice when everything is finished."

"Yeah, you girls have had more than your fair share of problems. But" he nodded toward Trevor, "this guy knows what he's doing. Probably another two months and you and Brina will be hosting your Grand Opening."

Randi smiled. "Let's hope so. I saw Trevor's truck; thought I'd stop by for a progress report. I'll let you two finish your business first." She smiled again and headed toward the back of the building.

"Progress report, huh. Not because you missed me?"

Trevor reached for her hand, pulled her into what would be her office.

"Well, I admit it was a nice surprise to see your truck. Maybe you can join us for dinner? Before you head back? I'm sure the boys will enjoy seeing you."

Trevor stepped closer, stared down at her. "What about their mother?"

"Me too," she sighed.

"Well, a little more enthusiasm might be appreciated. What's wrong?"

"I just left Brad. We had a long talk. It seems Tim is filing for joint custody."

"Hmm," he rested his forehead against hers.

"And he hasn't contributed to their college trust fund in over a year," she added.

"What?" Trevor raised his head and frowned down at her. "I thought you said he was obligated to do that in lieu of child support."

"He is." Randi stepped away, wandered across the room. "It seems he called my lawyer last year; said I had agreed to allow him to do yearly contributions. Even forged my signature on a letter. Nobody questioned it and then he just neglected to follow through."

"Another reason to make him accountable."

"Trevor, there's a reason why my father drafted the divorce conditions as he did." Her eyes pleaded with his from across the room.

Finally, Trevor thought, we're getting to the bottom of this. Now he worried he might not want to hear what she had to say. He sat on the make-do bench, leaned against the wall, rested a foot on a knee. "I've got time."

Randi stared at the two-by-four board across the cinderblocks, determined it was sturdy enough for the two of them. She sat beside him, leaned against the concrete wall.

"When I first married Tim, things were wonderful. I knew he planned to enter politics and for a while, our life was one social event after another. Then he won the delegate seat and there were more meetings, more parties. Most of the parties involved liquor. One drink led to another and before long, he convinced himself he needed the drinks to get through the evenings. He was able to hide the addiction from the public but behind closed doors, his personality changed. I tried to be the good wife, but nothing seemed to please him. He was always impatient. Irritated. Constantly going to this function or that meeting and expecting me to go with him. To cover for him. I got pregnant with the boys and used that as an excuse to stay home. Then," she paused, caught her breath, "then, one night he slapped me. I was shocked and he was instantly apologetic. But when it happened again, and a third time I made it a point to stay out of his way."

Trevor felt the anger building. "Did your dad know?"

"Not at first. Then I think he started to be suspicious. And I was so embarrassed I tried to cover it up."

Trevor reached for her hand. "It wasn't your fault."

"I know that, but I was so angry at myself for letting it continue. He could be so kind one minute, cruel the next. He wasn't happy when I got pregnant, and I tried to just stay out of his way as much as possible. Then when he pushed me down the stairs,"

"He what," Trevor growled. He jumped up, walked across the room to rest his forehead against the wall. Then he walked back to stand in front of her, his hands clenched at his side. "He what," he asked again, softly.

Randi looked up at him. "We argued and I went upstairs to our bedroom to get away from him. He followed me and when I refused to talk to him, he started getting physical. He slapped me. And when I tried to run, he just shoved me down the stairs. I don't know what happened after that. I must have blacked out," she sobbed. "All I know is when I awoke, he was gone."

Trevor sat beside her, put his arm around her.

Randi rested her head on his shoulder. "I must have been in shock at first. When I had some pains, I crawled over to the phone, called my parents. Dad had the foresight to call nine-one-one, got there about the same time the rescue squad did. The pains increased and the doctor worried that I might miscarry, so he ordered me on complete bed rest. I was in the hospital almost a month. My parents moved me back home and I think that's when Dad hired Peter to start the divorce process. He must have said something to Tim because Tim stayed away and after the boys were born, he quietly signed the papers. Until the other day, I haven't seen Tim in over five years."

"I'm glad I didn't know this when I met him the other night. Things would have been a whole lot different."

"Trevor, I don't know what to do. He says he has straightened up but to be honest, I don't believe him. I don't want to allow a man like that around my boys. Even if he is their father."

"I would hope that if it comes to that, all visitations will be supervised. Considering the boys don't even know he is their father; I would demand it."

Randi stared up at Trevor and smiled. "You know, Scott and Sandy just met you, but I would have no problems allowing you to take them somewhere. Tim? I just can't."

"What did Brad say?"

"To wait and see what Peter finds out. Peter said Tim's lawyer had emailed him just this morning inquiring about joint custody." Randy trembled. "It just spooks me to even think about it. Brad said some guardian ad litem would probably be called in. All I can hope for is that this person will see Tim for what he really is."

"Then we'll wait and see. If he files for joint custody, we'll face it." He stood, pulled Randi into his arms. "You look beat. Why don't I pick up a pizza when I finish here? You go home. Relax. Have a glass of wine. Let's not worry about it until we have too."

~~~~~

Twenty minutes after Randi left, Trevor locked the firehouse doors, walked the two blocks to Brad's office. He'd driven by it enough times and considering that there was no other lawyer's office that he knew of, he was certain this was the Brad Randi was talking about.

He opened the door, smiled at the blonde seated behind the desk.

"Can I help you?"

"Yes. I understand Randi Cavanaugh was here earlier. Can I speak to the man in charge?"

"I'll check. Can I say who's asking?"

"Trevor Graystone."

"Trevor." The blonde smiled, extended her hand. "You're working on the firehouse. I'm Stacy Adamson, Brad's assistant. Friends with Brina, Ginny, Randi and Marcie." She reached for the phone, dialed Brad's office. "Trevor Graystone is here to see you."

Seconds later, she smiled at Trevor. "He said he'll be right out."

"I guess in a small town, everybody knows everybody."

Stacy laughed. "That's for sure. I used to work for Brad's father and moved here from Richmond a couple months ago. I've learned to keep my mouth shut. You never know who might be related to whom."

The door opened and Brad stepped out, offered his hand. "Trevor, it's good to meet you. How's the project coming along?"

"Hopefully another month, six weeks at the most." Trevor stuffed his hands in his jeans. "Do you have a couple minutes?"

"Sure. Come on in. Stacy, it's almost quitting time, why don't you go ahead and call it a day?"

Brad closed the door behind him. "What can I do for you? We don't have another problem with the firehouse, do we?"

"No. Things are going good now. I understand you met with Randi this afternoon."

"Yes. Yes, I did." Brad settled in his chair. "Why? Is she okay?"

"She stopped by the job after she left here. Told me about her ex-husband. I know you're probably bound by this attorney-client thing but is he really planning to file for joint custody?"

Brad stared at Trevor. He'd heard a lot about the contractor from Brina and the girls, knew Trevor was a friend. "Yes, it appears he is. I just got off the phone with her divorce attorney. Peter says we should be getting the paperwork within twenty-four hours."

Trevor shook his head. "That's what I was afraid of. Have you met this guy? Do you know what he did to her?"

"I haven't met him, no, but Randi told me about her marriage this afternoon."

"Then you'll understand why I say there is no way in hell that piece of scum is going to be alone with her or those boys. And if Randi needs money, you let me know."

"I will. I had no idea that you and Randi were that close. She's always complained that she keeps missing you."

"Well, we connected at Snowridge this weekend and I'm sorry we didn't do so sooner. Listen, she's pretty upset about this. I'll be seeing her this evening but I'm not going to say anything. Can you wait until tomorrow to tell her?"

"I will. And Trevor, I'm glad she has you in her corner."

"Just make sure that asshole doesn't get in the same corner."

CHAPTER NINE

T revor followed the GPS directions although in the small town of Edmondsville, Idyllwild Lane wasn't that hard to find. He recognized some of the four cars parked in front of her house and understood the five pizzas. Randi had company.

"Hope you didn't mind the extra food," Randi nervously greeted him at the door. "Brina called and since you were in town, we thought it might be good to have a group meeting. About the firehouse." She reached for her purse. "I'll be glad to pay you for it."

Trevor set the pizzas on the table, reached for her. He saw the worry in her eyes and felt the tension in her body.

"No problem." A smile tugged at his lips as he brushed his hands up and down her upper arms. "I think I can afford a few pizzas. And I agree, it might be good to discuss the project."

Sandy raced into the dining room. "You gonna kiss mom again," he shouted.

"Want me to?" Trevor gave the youngster a cheeky grin.

"No," Randi exclaimed. "I'm nervous enough about Tim, now the whole world knows you've kissed me." She grabbed one of the pizzas, handed it to Sandy. "Here take this in the other room. I'll bring the rest. Trevor, you can grab the beer in the fridge."

Thirty minutes later everyone sat in the den while the boys played in their room.

"You know, Trevor, if you're going to stay in town, you don't have to stay in the loft at the firehouse." Ginny sat beside Cliff on the sofa. "You're more than welcome to stay in the cottage at Spicer Meadow. I lived there for a few years and Brina stayed there when we started the project. Now that she and Rafe are married, it happens to be vacant."

Trevor knew Cliff and Ginny had served as executors to Claudette Spicer's estate, which led to the rekindling of their feelings for one another. Newlyweds, they were married two days after Christmas. He thought he'd heard some whispers about Cliff being Claudette Spicer's grandson, not nephew, but figured it was none of his business.

"Thank you, I might take you up on the offer," Trevor considered. One night on the cot had been enough for him. It'd be good to sleep in a real bed. Give him a reason to stay in Edmondsville. "Hopefully it won't be for too long."

"I'm glad this recent incident can be rectified with a can of paint," Brina stated. "I don't understand why we've been plagued with so many problems at the firehouse. At least they've been minor ones. Even the fire was minor."

Renovating the firehouse had originally been Brina's idea. Then Randi, Ginny and Marcie had become partners in the project. Brina had moved back to Edmondsville then married Rafe six weeks ago after Rafe had hired her to do his Christmas shopping.

"I'm trying to catch up with this 'Homeless Hal' everyone seems to think might have started the fire," Travis leaned back in his chair, rested his ankle on his knee. "He's also a suspect with the graffiti but I'm not so sure. I can understand his starting the fire to keep warm, but not the graffiti."

"Yeah," Cliff agreed as his Paul Newman eyes stared into his beer. "Guess we'll all have to keep our eyes and ears open, if you know what I mean." Everyone smiled at Cliff's use of an old song in his conversation. A music fanatic, Cliff often inserted song titles whenever he could.

Trevor looked at Randi who mouthed, "I'll explain later."

"Tell us about your stay in Snowridge," Marcie crooned. "I'm glad you two finally met. Randi was always saying," Marcie paused, almost said 'you have a cute butt' but stopped herself.

"Saying what?" Trevor teased.

"Did she tell you? About your cute butt?"

"No but that would explain why she made make me walk across the room when she put two and two together."

Brina, Ginny and Marcie chuckled while Randi's cheeks turned pink.

"It was great getting away," Randi prattled. "Dad played golf, the boys played some soccer and I just relaxed. Trevor took us on a couple adventures, and we enjoyed that."

"You know," Brina said, "you didn't really have to come back a day early. We could have handled the graffiti situation. I just wanted to keep you in the loop."

"Yeah, I know. But I was ready to come back. I needed to come back."

Ginny frowned. "Needed? I don't think I've ever needed to come back from vacation a day early. Did something happen?"

Randi looked at Trevor. "We had a great time until the last two days. When I ran into my ex-husband and his new wife."

Everyone was silent until Marcie spoke up. "You've never talked about your ex-husband. Is everything okay?"

"Yes. No. I don't know." Randi shrugged her shoulders. "We've been divorced since the boys were born. Part of the divorce agreement was that he would fund an education account for the boys. Other than that, he has had no contact with them."

"Never?" Ginny looked at Cliff. "Their father has never seen those beautiful boys?" Randi knew Ginny was thinking about the child she and Cliff were going to have and how Cliff would never agree to not being a part of his son or daughter's life.

Randi sighed. "It was for the best, okay? And I thought things were going smoothly until I realized he hasn't contributed to their education fund for eighteen months. Now he's petitioning for joint custody of the boys."

"Why now?" Rafe asked. A financial advisor, he calculated the missed investment opportunities the absent child support would have benefited the boys' education fund.

"Apparently, Miriam, his wife, can't have children so he wants to share custody of mine."

Trevor reached for Randi's hand. "When we both got the phone calls about the firehouse, we figured it was a good reason to come back early."

"Especially after I found out that Tim had hired a private investigator."

"I certainly understand that feeling," Brina cast a look at her husband. Rafe had secretly hired Brad's father to investigate her past. In the long run, it had brought closure – the identity of her parents – but she remembered the shock and hurt she'd felt when she found out. Rafe squeezed her hand.

Randi looked at Ginny. "The guy got close enough to overhear a conversation you and I had about the trip." She shuddered. "It gives me the creeps to think that someone has been watching me. Taking pictures of me, and probably the boys, without my knowledge.

"I talked to Brad this afternoon about what to do and he's going to help me. Said if Tim followed through, some guardian ad litem would probably be assigned to the boys. He or she, whoever it is, will be talking to all of us. Ginny, you will probably be interviewed since you're their teacher. The rest of you because you're my friends."

"I don't think you have to worry about us," Brina stated. "We will all attest to how great a mother you've been and how happy the boys are. You've done so much on your own. I know I will certainly be making this guardian whatever aware of how your husband has shirked his contributions to their education fund."

Randi smiled. "Thank you. All of you. Let's just hope it doesn't come to that, though."

Trevor decided not to share that the process had already started. That was Brad's job and Randi didn't need to worry about it till tomorrow.

"Ginny, if your offer still stands, I think I'd like to check this cottage out and settle in tonight. It's been a long day and I'd like to get an early start tomorrow. I also need to make a quick trip home for more clothes."

"Of course," Ginny reached for Cliff's hand. "I've been more tired myself these past few weeks." She rested a hand on her stomach.

Cliff kissed her cheek. "Been eating a little more too."

Randi called the boys in to tell everyone good-bye. The adults exchanged smiles when Scott and Sandy rushed to Trevor's side and he squat down to talk to them, man to man.

"You take care of your mom, okay?"

"'Kay," they both responded.

"See you for breakfast?" He turned to Randi who nodded.

"Don't worry," Marcie hugged Randi after Trevor backed out of the drive, followed Cliff and Ginny to Spicer Meadows. "We're all here for you but it looks like you already have your knight in shining armor."

~~~~~

Trevor awoke early the next morning with no back ache and feeling refreshed. It wasn't quite six and he was sure it was too early for breakfast at Randi's. He'd missed his early morning jogs the past couple days, decided to check out the terrain of Spicer Meadows.

He took a deep breath, enjoyed the smell of dew on the hay as he headed up the long drive. The sun was just coming up when he reached the end of the drive and started back. He followed the path between the manor house and cottage to the back fields. Past the barns, cemetery and open fields. New territory made for an interesting run.

He was worried about Randi. Wondered how she would react to the bad news Brad would be delivering today. She didn't deserve any of this and it irritated him that her ex-husband would suddenly decide to pursue custody.

Before going to Randi's for breakfast, he drove by the job where Aaron, his foreman assured him nothing had happened in the night. On the way to Randi's, he kept an eye out for Homeless Hal. If he didn't see him today, he planned to talk with the deputy.

Randi poured him a second cup of coffee after breakfast.

"Brad called. Said he needed to see me today." She sat across the kitchen table. "Guess that means he's heard something."

Trevor leaned back in his chair. "If Tim decides he wants shared custody, we'll do what needs to be done."

"I haven't told my father anything and if Tim is going to pursue custody, that will upset him even more."

"Maybe, but I'm sure he'll do whatever is necessary to help you. I don't know Brad that well, but hopefully he'll look out for your best interest."

Randi stared at her cup. "What am I going to tell the twins? How do you tell six-year-old boys that the man they just met is their father? A man that had no desire to see them until now?"

She rubbed the back of her neck. The headache was gone but not the tension. She looked at Trevor, saw the concern and frustration in his eyes. Wanted to tell him he had been more of a father to them than Tim.

She kept her thoughts to herself. Didn't want to put Trevor on the spot. After all, they'd only just met.

"When are you supposed to see Brad?"

"Sometime this afternoon. He's going to call."

"Who's watching the boys? Do you want me to take them?"

Randi's eyes grew wide. "Oh my gosh, I hadn't thought that far. And they have their first soccer session with the recreation department." She rested her elbows on the table, her head in her hands. "Too much is happening all at once."

"Randi, you don't have to worry about the boys. What time is the practice? I'll come by, take them to lunch and then to practice."

"But you have your own work. Didn't you say you had to go back to Snowridge?"

"One more day won't matter," he shrugged a shoulder. "And if need be, I'll go late tonight. As for the job, that's why I have a foreman. He and the crew are finishing up the loft. I've also been trying to track down this Homeless Hal and the boys can ride along. I want to talk to him."

"I'd appreciate it. I'm sure the boys will enjoy an adventure in your truck."

~~~~~

Randi sat in the car outside Brad's office. Tried to calm her nerves. She'd been a wreck ever since Brad had called to say Tim had filed for joint custody. Asked if she could meet him and the guardian ad litem in his office.

She'd waited until after Trevor left with the boys to react. Her headache was back, her eyes hurt from crying. She took a deep breath; needed to get control. Too much was happening all at once. Less than a week ago, her life had been great. She and the boys were relaxing at the resort, and she'd just met Trevor.

Now, because of Tim, she'd have someone interfering in her life. Observing her, dictating what she could and couldn't do. All she knew was this GAL was a woman. A retired lawyer that took on special cases for Judge Reamy. Randi hoped having a woman in charge would be to her advantage.

Another car pulled up beside her. Randi watched a woman get out. That must be her, she thought. Short and grandmotherly came to mind when the woman smiled at her then headed towards Brad's office.

Randi pulled the visor down. checked her makeup. Her eyes weren't as puffy. She reached for her purse, added some lipstick, then opened her door. It was time, she squared her shoulder, tried to encourage herself. She could do this.

Stacy was coming out of Brad's office when Randi entered through the front door. She smiled, walked across the room to give Randi a hug.

"I'm so sorry you're having to go through this, but I want you to know Brad and I will do everything we can to help."

"Thank you." Randi tried to smile. "I guess they're waiting for me."
Brad appeared at his door.

"Randi, glad you're here. I want you to meet your GAL." When
Randi followed him into his office, the woman from the parking lot
chuckled.

"That's short for guardian ad litem. Not his girlfriend as it insinu-
ates." She extended her hand. "I'm Harriet Young. Your GAL. I retired
from my law practice a couple years ago; now serve as a GAL part time.
Judge Reamy asked me to take your case."

"This is all so new to me," Randi confided softly. "I feel like my
private life won't be so private anymore."

"Things will be a little different for a while," Brad agreed, "but once
the preliminaries are done, things should go back to normal. Let's
hope your ex-husband will be cooperative."

Harriet smiled. "And I will certainly make my part as painless as
possible. I'll be interviewing everyone involved, reporting to Judge
Reamy. The reports will be sealed. Shared with no one. I will attend
all court hearings and handle any mediation that might be needed. I've
also been known to testify if called upon."

Randi felt an instantaneous feeling of relief. The friendly smile and
soft blue eyes chased away the nerves that had been building up over
the past two days. "I hope you'll be able to help us, Mrs. Young."

"Please, call me Harriet. I will be reaching out to your ex-husband
but wanted to meet you first. As you requested, Mr. Beckman has
told me about your marriage with Mr. Cavanaugh. I'm sorry it was so
difficult."

"I just don't want anything to happen to my boys. He says he has
straightened up, but I have my doubts. Two six-year-old boys can be
challenging; I worry he won't have the patience."

"Well, I plan to take it slow. For now, I'd like to spend time with you, let you tell me about the boys and your father. I'll also be talking with their teacher," she looked at her notebook, "Mrs. Spicer?"

"Yes, Ginny and I became friends when I moved here two years ago, and I was so happy to have her as their first real teacher."

"I don't know how much Brad has told you, but I'll be talking with their school counselor and your father. There will also be a home visit just to be sure the boys live in a safe environment. You don't need to worry, I'm sure all is fine. All I ask is that you not coach the boys in any way. After I chat with the boys, I'll be going to Maryland to visit with your ex-husband and his wife."

"They just met Tim for the first time. Last weekend. I haven't even told them he is their father. I don't know what to say. Shouldn't I do that as soon as possible."

"Yes. Especially before I meet them. They need to understand why I'm visiting and asking them so many questions. I have six grand-children of my own. I'm sure they will have lots of questions for me. Many times, children open to strangers they are comfortable with. No matter how close you are with them, they might ask me questions they wouldn't want to ask you. Are they at home now?"

"No. Trevor – Trevor Graystone – a friend took them to their soccer practice."

"And is this Mr. Graystone important to the boys?"

"We've only known him for little over a week. You see, Trevor, ah Mr. Graystone is working on a project for Brina and me. He and I officially met when the boys and I went to Snowridge last weekend. The boys like him very much. All three took to one another almost instantly."

"And is Mr. Graystone important to you?"

"Well, he's working on our firehouse project, but yes, he has become a good friend too."

"I'll probably interview him as well. What do the boys think of him?"

"Oh, they're crazy about him. They're comfortable, relaxed around him. He plays with them, encouraged them to go to the soccer clinic at Snowridge, spent an entire day with us." Randi realized she may be saying too much. "He also owns the resort. Did I tell you?"

Harriet smiled. "I take it their mother likes him as well?"

Randi felt her cheeks flush, then let out a chuckle. "A little."

"That will be another plus for you. If he's as much a part of your family as you say." She added Trevor's name to her notebook. "I'll be visiting with your ex-husband and his wife as soon as I can coordinate things. Since he has never been a part of Scott and Sandy's lives, my first recommendation will be that he have supervised visitations with the boys."

Randi felt a great burden fall off her shoulders. Her greatest concern had been the visitations and had secretly hoped Trevor's suggestion was correct.

"It probably wouldn't hurt for your husband to visit with everyone here in Edmondsville. Maybe he and his wife could attend some family outings?"

"I'll see what I can do." Randi sighed. "First, I need to sit down and have a talk with my boys. This evening."

~~~~~

"**B**oys, we need to talk." Randi settled on the sofa, the boys on either side. Her father and Trevor sat in chairs across the room. After her meeting with Harriet Young in Brad's office, she had called her father, then invited Trevor to join them for dinner when he returned with the boys from their afternoon outing.

Dinner was over, she tried to keep her thoughts organized.

Sandy reached for her hand, gazed at her with innocent blue eyes. "What did we do?"

"Yeah. We didn't mean to push David in the pool."

Randi smiled, gave each a kiss on the top of their heads. "You haven't done anything," she assured them. "And I'm sure David enjoyed being dunked in the pool. No, I need to talk about something else."

She looked across at Trevor and her father.

"Do you remember the man you met at Snowridge the other day. Mr. Tim?"

"The man that doesn't smile?"

Randi's eyebrows shot up as she cast another look at Trevor and her father. She decided her boys were more observant than she gave them credit for.

"Yes. The man that didn't smile. How do I say this? That man's last name is Cavanaugh too. He's your father." She watched the boys process what she'd just told them.

"Our daddy?"

"Yes. You see, shortly after the two of you were born, your daddy and I decided to get a divorce. He moved out of our house; we didn't live together anymore."

She watched Sandy's eyes fill with tears. "But why didn't he visit us?"

"Well, he lived a long way away and was very busy." She never expected them to get upset. Wasn't going to tell them their father had no desire to see them.

"Didn't he love us?" Scott asked anyway, getting upset like his brother.

Randi felt another crying jag coming. She looked across at the adults then hugged both boys close. "Of course, he loved you. That's why he and Miriam want to be a part of your life now. You know how David lives with his Mama part of the time and his Daddy the other part of the time? Mr. Tim, your father, would like to do the same thing."

"Is he going to move here with us?"

"Yeah, what room will he have?"

"No, he won't move here. He will probably come to visit us, but he and Mrs. Miriam won't move in with us. They will continue to live in Maryland, visit us here in Edmondsville. Then, maybe one day, when you get to know him better, you two will go and visit them at their house."

"But what about you? Who's going to take care of you?"

"Who will you live with? You'll be all by yourself."

Randi hugged them closer. She should have known their first thoughts would be about her. "I'll be fine, don't you worry. And it will be a while before you go to stay with them. Until you get to know your father better, he will visit you here and someone, GranPop, me, maybe even Trevor, will always be with you."

She paused a minute for them to digest what she'd told them.

"I also need to tell you that a lady named Mrs. Young will be coming to visit with you. Probably tomorrow. She'll sit down with you, talk to you about all sorts of stuff. I want you two to answer all her questions and tell the truth. She'll be the one to decide how much time your father and I have with you."

"But I don't want to leave you," Scott sobbed.

"No. We don't want to go live with the man that doesn't smile."

Randi's heart ached. Ached for these two little boys who were so confused, would soon have their world turned upside down.

"You two will get to know him better and I'm sure he will smile more. After all," she tickled them, "who wouldn't want to smile at two handsome boys like you?"

Scott and Sandy stared across the room at their grandfather and Trevor.

"Why can't we live with Trevor?"

"Yeah, Trevor always smiles."

Trevor couldn't help but laugh.

"Boys, I would love nothing more than to spend more time with you two but Tim is your father and you need to get to know him better. I'll still be around. In fact," he winked at the boys, "I'll help GranPop take care of your mom."

CHAPTER TEN

R andi watched her sons eat their PB&J sandwiches with Harriet Young at the picnic table in the back yard. The GAL had spent most of the morning with her and her father, individually, and it was now her turn with Scott and Sandy.

Sebastian stood beside her, his arm around her shoulder.

"You were great with the boys last night. I don't think I would have been so nice about Tim."

Randi rested her head on his shoulder. "Dad, he is their father. I can't deny that. And if I'd told them the truth, it would have upset them more. Made it harder for them to understand. Plus, it wouldn't have looked good for me to bad-mouth their father."

"You saying he won't do that to you? Still, you did a good job. We'll get through this. He's going to mess up. You know he will."

Randi smiled. "Let's just hope it's sooner than later."

Sebastian looked outside. "Ms. Young seems like she has a good head on her shoulders. Looks like she's getting on with the boys too. They're both talking a mile a minute."

After her father left, Randi went to her office, studied the catalogs, notes, paint samples spread across the desk. Tried to concentrate on her current project – Carolyn Payne's kitchen. She knew Carolyn loved cooking with her herbs and was googling on her laptop for unique herb planters for the kitchen. She jumped when Marcie spoke from the hallway.

"How's it going? Oh, I'm so sorry. I didn't mean to startle you. I called out but guess you didn't hear me. I know you must be nervous. If it were me, I wouldn't be able to focus on anything."

Randi tilted her head toward the window that overlooked the back yard. "The boys are outside. With Harriet." She sighed. "I'm trying to work on a project; can't say I've accomplished anything. I've pulled up the same picture three different times. Either that's a sign I found what I need, or I've researched the same site three different times."

Marie nudged Randi's mouse. "Let's check your history. Nope, three different sites. I'd say you've found what you were looking for."

Randi continued to stare out the window.

"You know, it's good that you have your desk situated so you can watch the boys while they play, and you work. Love a multi-tasking mom, but I'd be willing to bet in this instance, you're not getting much done. Doing more looking than working."

Randi sighed. "Marcie, I just can't let those boys live with their father."

Marcie crossed her arms beneath her breasts. "You've never talked about your marriage. We've tried to respect your privacy but considering how upset you've been, you can't blame us for wondering. Can you share what happened?"

"Have a seat." Randi invited. "Tim was an alcoholic and the more he drank the meaner he got. He slapped me a few times but after that I stayed out of his way. Then when he knocked me down the stairs,"

"Knocked you down the stairs," Marcie leaned forward, her eyes simmering with anger, "Randi, how is this man still here? Not locked in some jail cell?"

"That's how I managed to get the divorce. My father threatened to go to the police if he didn't give me the divorce. I lived with my parents till the boys were born,"

"But the bastard pushed the mother of his unborn children down the stairs," Marcie interrupted.

"It's history. I've put it behind me. Made a good life for me and the boys. Hadn't meant to tell anyone."

"Does Ms. Young know?"

"Yes, of course. And Brad. I had to tell them when we found out Tim was filing for joint custody. I also had to tell Trevor after he met Tim at the resort, started asking questions. Marcie," Randi looked deeply in her friend's eyes, "please, please don't tell anyone. I don't want to use that unless I absolutely must. Please, can you keep it to yourself for now?"

~~~~~

Harriet Young smiled as she watched the boys climb on the jungle gym. She recalled her six grandchildren playing on the one she and her husband had built in their own back yard. Scott and Sandy Cavanaugh appeared to be happy, well-adjusted little boys and she was sorry to see them in this situation.

They had gotten through the preliminary questions during lunch. Their names, ages, birthday. Favorite toys, cartoons, action figures. Now, it was time to get down to specifics.

"Hey guys, I was wondering, who fixes your meals?"

Both boys stopped and looked at her. "Mommy. Who else?"

"Your GranPop doesn't cook?"

"No, just Mommy."

"Who helps you get dressed?"

"Mommy usually puts our clothes out but we're not babies. We dress ourselves."

"Yeah," Sandy said. "Once she let us dress ourselves."

Harriet smiled. "And how did that go?"

The boys looked at one another and smiled. "At first, she didn't like it. Then she said since we weren't going anywhere, we could keep them on."

"Who plays with you the most?"

"Mommy plays with us sometimes, but she really likes to read us stories," Scott said. "She reads to us every night."

"She taught us to ride our bikes, remember Scott?"

"Oh, yeah. GranPop plays with us sometimes," Sandy added. "And Trevor."

"Trevor?"

"Yeah, he's the bestest. He knows all about Sgt. Slaughter, and Darth Vader."

"And we had a battle with him," Scott announced.

"Oh really? Who won?"

Both boys laughed. "We did."

"Who puts you to bed? Or does Mommy just let you climb into bed by yourselves?"

"Mommy lets us play in the bathtub for a while," Sandy said.

Scott laughed. "Yeah, we have water battles. Then, she reads us a story."

"And then we talk about stuff."

"What kind of stuff?"

The boys climbed off the gym, joined her on the glider. Harriet worried their lives might not be so good after all. "What kind of stuff?" She repeated.

"We talk about what we did," Sandy said.

"What happened in school," Scott added.

"Ginny is going to have a baby. We talked about whether the baby will be a boy or a girl."

"Anything else?"

"Just secrets," Scott said.

"You share secrets?" Harriet asked.

"Yeah." Sandy said. "We even shared one with Trevor."

"Trevor put you to bed?"

"Yeah," Scott said, "one time. We asked him to."

"What did you tell Trevor?"

Both boys spoke at once. "It's a secret."

"You can share it with me." She mimed locking her lips with a key. "I have six grandchildren and they all share their secrets with me. I don't tell their mommies or daddies."

"So," Sandy looked cautious. "You won't tell our Mommy?"

"No, not if you don't want me to."

Both boys leaned forward, each whispered in an ear.

Harriet's heart swelled as she hugged each, desperately hoped they could resolve this situation peacefully for these two adorable boys.

"One last question. If you could have three wishes, what would they be?"

She watched the boys think a minute.

"GranPop take us to play golf," Scott said.

"Yeah, he's always saying we're too little," Sandy added.

Harriet laughed. "Okay, that's one. What else would you wish for?"

Sandy jumped up excitedly. "Cliff and Ginny have a boy. That way we'll have another boy to play with."

Scott nodded in agreement.

"That will be nice. What else?"

"Mr. Trevor visits Mommy more," Scott said.

"Why?"

"Cause he's fun and he makes Mommy smile."

Sandy giggled. "Yeah. And he kissed her too."

Harriet laughed. "Oh, he did, did he? And what did your Mommy say?"

"She just laughed."

Harriet couldn't resist laughing herself. She hugged them a second time. "You know, I've really enjoyed talking to you two. I'm sorry I asked so many questions. Do you have any questions for me?"

"Mommy says Mr. Tim is our daddy. How come he never comes to visit us?"

"Mommy said he lives far away, remember." Scott said.

"That's a good question though. Yes, Mr. Tim is your daddy, and he hasn't been to visit you because he is a busy man. He has an important job and can't always get away."

"Why? David's daddy lives far away but he always comes to visit. And David goes to stay with his daddy sometimes."

"Is that what you two would like to do? Go stay with your daddy some?"

Scott and Sandy looked at one another. "Can Mommy come with us?"

"Probably not. What about if Mr. Tim and Mrs. Miriam came here to visit you? Would you like that?"

"I guess so," Sandy answered.

"Only if Trevor can come too," Scott added.

Harriet smiled. She obviously needed to interview Trevor. "I'd really like for you two to draw me some pictures. What do you say we go inside. I'll talk to your Mommy while you color."

"Yeah," both boys jumped up, raced toward the house.

~~~~~

"**H**ow serious are you about this Trevor?" Harriet asked when Randi set the cup of coffee in front of her.

"Trevor? He's the contractor on our firehouse project. We always seemed to miss one another on the job. Then I officially met him last weekend at the Snowridge. Turns out, he owns the resort."

"So, you've only just met him? Hmm, he has made quite an impression on your boys."

Randi smiled. "Well, he is fun to be with. And took naturally to the boys. He encouraged them to try the soccer clinic at the resort and as a result, they are signed up here with the recreation department. He took them to their practice yesterday so I could meet with you."

"So, you have no problem allowing your boys to go with a man you just met?"

Randi's heart sank. Had she said something wrong? Was this a trick question?

"I, I just met Trevor, yes, but because he has been working on the firehouse project, I feel I've known him longer. And no, I have no problems with Trevor being alone with the boys. He genuinely cares for them as they do him. I do have a problem with allowing the boys to be alone with my ex-husband. It was his decision to walk away from his sons. He has never made any effort to see them. Never called in five years to ask how they were doing, wish them a happy birthday, nothing. They met him for the first time the other day. Trevor knows more and cares more about them than their own father."

Harriet covered Randi's hand. "Don't get upset. I understand completely. I just had to ask. See how serious you and Trevor are. A possible stepfather can sometimes cause friction in custody battles."

"Trevor and I have just met. We're friends, that's all."

Harriet smiled. "I've enjoyed being with you and your two boys today. We talked about a lot of things, and it is very evident they are happy and well-adjusted. You have been the primary caregiver and that's all they understand. I don't want to upset them any more than necessary. I have asked them to draw some pictures for me, but overall, I think I've learned all I need to know.

"I will be interviewing your ex-husband and his wife tomorrow but already feel strongly that the boys should stay with their mother and have supervised visitations with their father. But I would like to see the boys get to know their father a little more. Maybe he will come to Edmondsville for visits? Would you be okay with that?"

Randi had been following Harriet's words very closely but looked away when she suggested Tim and Miriam visit with them. While she didn't like the idea, it would be one way to observe her boys with their father. At least she would be there, see for herself.

"Of course. I'll do whatever is necessary for the sake of my boys."

"Good. And if you'd like to invite Trevor as well, that might be good. Your boys are comfortable with him. Maybe observing him on a friendly basis with their father might smooth the situation."

"Will you be along as well?" Randi asked.

"I can, if you'd like although I feel the boys will tell me any concerns they might have."

~~~~~

"So, how did things go?" Trevor asked that evening. He knew it had been an upsetting day. Marcie had stopped by the job to visit him, rant about the fact that Randi swore her to secrecy.

"If that jerk causes any problems for Randi, I will not hesitate to tell Brina, Ginny, anybody else that'll listen."

The only thing that had calmed her was his promise not to let anything happen to Randi or her boys.

He had texted Randi, offered to pick up some steaks, suggested she invite her father to dinner. He would cook them on the grill.

The boys were once again playing on the jungle gym.

Randi looked at her father. "I guess it went okay. Harriet spent the morning with Dad and me, most of the afternoon with the boys. She was very complimentary about the boys. Says they appear to be very happy and well-adjusted. She's supposed to visit with Tim tomorrow but has already decided that considering he has never been in their lives, he should be allowed supervised visitations until they get used to him."

"Sounds fair," Trevor sipped his wine as he lifted the lid of the grill, poked the potatoes for doneness. "I like her already. What about you?" He turned to Sebastian.

"Humph, she seems like she had a good head on her shoulders. I'd be curious to see how long the asshole keeps his cool with the boys. How quickly they get used to him."

"Harriet said something about inviting Tim and Miriam to some family events."

Trevor shrugged as he flipped the steaks. "Wouldn't hurt. Give everyone a chance to observe everybody. Maybe Cliff and Ginny will do something at the manor house. There's the pool, plenty of open space to ride their bikes, have a picnic."

"Yeah," Randi agreed, "that's what I was thinking. Hope to talk to Ginny later this evening."

After dinner, Sebastian went home, and Trevor cleaned the grill while Randi prepared the boys for bed. "It's back to school tomorrow," she reminded them. "Have to get up early in the morning."

"Can Trevor read us our story tonight?"

Randi blinked. They were so innocent. And trusting. She hoped they weren't going to get a double dose of hurt. First with their father, then with Trevor when he moved on after the firehouse job.

"Sure, can I listen too?"

They chose one of their action hero stories and Randi chuckled as Trevor went a little overboard with some of the narration and dialog. If anything, they had too much fun with the story, too excited to go to sleep.

Once the boys were settled, she walked with Trevor to the door. "Thank you for this evening. You've had as busy a day as I have and still you came to my rescue."

"Anytime. My day wasn't as draining as yours. It was kinda nice to have someone to cook for besides myself. Hope we can do it more often."

Randi smiled up at him. "That will be nice. The boys enjoy being with you."

Trevor reached for her hand, kissed her palm. "How about their mother?"

"Me, too." Her knees wobbled; her breath hitched when his chestnut brown eyes stared at her mouth.

It had been a long time since he'd stolen that kiss from her at the resort. It would be good to taste her again, he thought as he leaned towards her.

Randi held her breath, then jumped.

"Mom," one of the boys shouted. "Can we have some water?"

CHAPTER ELEVEN

Trevor decided to ride around town before heading back to Snowridge. He was glad to be there for Randi, but he needed more clothes too. He'd been looking for Homeless Hal for two days now, decided to make one more swing through town before heading for the mountains.

Duane Peterson had given him a description. Average height, medium build, gray hair; seemed to be somewhat intelligent based on Duane's interview. Trevor figured the old man might be wandering the town now that the streets were bare, people ensconced in their homes.

He saw a lone figure ambling along the sidewalk of Main Street. An old man with his hands in his pockets, meandered past the businesses as if window shopping. He still wore a coat even though the evenings were starting to be warmer.

Trevor parked and headed towards the guy, slowed when they were close.

"Evening," he greeted the man.

The old man slowed, nodded his head but kept walking.

Trevor could see he was nervous. "I'm working on the firehouse project."

"Yeah," the man stopped. "The deputy told me. I've also seen you on the job. Haven't been around there though. Like some people say I have."

"You talked to Deputy Peterson? Hey," Trevor tried to stop the guy when he started to move away. "I believe you. My foreman and I keep a close eye on our jobs, and we've seen no signs of anyone staying on the site. We've had some problems though and I just wanted to ask if you've seen anything suspicious. Where do you bunk down?"

"Got me a little hide-away on the outskirts of town. Near the bypass."

"What about food?"

"Scooter gives me his leftovers. Couple times I've washed dishes for him."

"I might need some help on the job. You interested? Hey," he looked at his watch, "I know it's late, but have you had dinner? I'd like to talk to you about a couple things."

The man gave Trevor a skeptical look. "I ain't had dinner but I don't take handouts either."

"I'm not offering a handout. I just want a little information. I'm sure *White Rose Diner* is still open."

Twenty minutes later Scooter set a burger and fries in front of Hal. "Are you available to work tomorrow?" He asked the old man.

Hal looked up at him and smiled. "If you need me."

"Come by around eleven in the morning. You can take a shower in my apartment upstairs. I have a big function tomorrow night, could use some help prepping." Scooter smiled at Trevor. "He never seems to mind chopping the onions. How's the firehouse project coming?"

"Good so far. About another month or six weeks."

"I know Brina and Randi will be glad to get it done." Scooter said. "Ginny wants to get started on the Children's Museum. You going to do that job too?"

"She's mentioned it, but no plans yet."

"You've had your fair share of problems with the firehouse project," Hal said when Scooter left. "I've heard some of the talk."

"Yeah. That's one of the reasons I wanted to talk to you."

"Contrary to what people say, I had nothing to do with that fire. I was washing dishes here when it happened."

"I believe you, but somebody doesn't want this project moving forward. Do you ever walk that way? See anything out of the ordinary?"

"I enjoy walking at night. At dusk. Usually, it's quiet and most of the walkers are home for the night. Saw a group of kids a few nights ago."

"Kids, huh. Were they anywhere near the firehouse?"

"When I saw them, they were laughing, headed in that direction. One of them carried a bag. Figured it must be beer."

"You know we had a problem with graffiti a few nights ago. Think they might be the culprits?"

"I've seen them before. Probably bored. Need something to keep them busy."

Trevor smiled. He was impressed with the man's demeanor. If he were to meet him on the street, he would never have pegged him as homeless.

"How long have you been homeless? What happened?"

"Almost a year. Retired a few years back and for a while there, life was good. The wife and I took a few trips, daughter was married so we spent some time with the grandkids. Then" He paused, took a deep breath as if to compose himself.

Trevor gave him a moment. "What happened?"

"The wife and I went to bed one night and there was a fire. It was full blown by the time I woke up. Woke my wife, we tried to get out, but the fire was between us and the exit. I called nine-one-one, but my wife disappeared. I searched where I could and finally found her upstairs. She apparently tried to open one of the windows but was overcome by the smoke. The fire crew came and finally got us out but," his eyes filled with tears.

"Your wife died? Did they determine what caused the fire?"

Hal shook his head. "Not for a couple weeks. Some insinuated that it was my fault. I guess because I got out alive. Even my daughter was upset with me. Wouldn't speak to me. Refused my calls. The funeral took almost all I had in savings. Afterwards, I just decided to disappear."

"I'm sure your daughter was just reacting to her grief. Probably having second thoughts now."

"I don't know. She's headstrong. All I know is I couldn't stand the looks. I just walked away. Happened to find an old bike, took the clothes I could salvage and headed up the road."

"You didn't have any money? No savings?"

Hal shook his head. "Paid off the mortgage a few months after I retired. I didn't want to have any bills hanging over our heads. We were living comfortably, had saved for the few trips we planned. But the funeral took all that. I think I had two hundred dollars in the bank by the time everything was done. So, I withdrew that and left town."

"Have you talked to your daughter?"

"Called her once but when she answered, I just couldn't say anything. Miss the grandkids though. They'd be six and nine now. Probably be getting out of school soon."

Trevor thought of Scott and Sandy. How they enjoyed being with Sebastian. He was sorry Hal had been denied a relationship with his grandchildren.

"Been here in Edmondsville for about six months now," Hal continued. "Help Scooter from time to time, do other odd jobs. Discovered I don't really need all that much money when I work for my meals. Got a tent in the woods on the outskirts of town."

"What about this past winter? It was cold.? How did you survive?"

"It was tough. Couple times Scooter let me stay in the kitchen after he closed."

"What if I could offer you a cot in a building."

"I already told you I don't take handouts."

"I'm not offering a handout. Considering all the problems we've had with the firehouse; I need to keep it under surveillance till we get the job done. Stanley, in the garage behind the firehouse said I could set up night watch if I wanted. I'm offering you a cot if you'll keep an eye on the firehouse at night. Don't know if anything else will happen but if it does, I want to find the culprits before it gets worse."

Hal pushed his empty plate aside, wiped his mouth with the back of his hand. "I guess I could do that. When do you want me to start?"

"Tomorrow night. I'll meet you there around seven. And I don't want anyone to know you're doing this. Understood?"

"Not even the Sheriff? I don't want to be accused of trespassing."

"I've already discussed this with Deputy Peterson. You won't have to worry about them."

~~~~~

The following morning, Randi pulled into her driveway after taking the boys to school. Decided maybe she'd give Carolyn Payne a call, try to finish up her project.

She noticed a beige Honda parked in front of the Harper house; thought she knew all the vehicles on their street. Wondered if the Harpers had company. Somebody was sitting in the car. Maybe they were getting ready to leave.

When she checked an hour later, the car was still there. So was the person.

Her heart raced. Was someone casing their street? Many of the people on her street were older but they all kept a close eye on one another. And it's not like they lived in a wealthy neighborhood.

There was only one explanation for why someone would be sitting in their car outside her house. Surely, Tim didn't still have a private investigator on her. He knew where she lived. Had seen the boys. Dropped his little bombshell. Why would he still have someone watching her?

Unless he wanted to see how involved she and Trevor were.

It angered her that someone might be observing her every move. She would not live like this, she fumed. She reached for her cell phone, keyed in the sheriff's department. No sense in dialing nine-one-one when Duane Peterson could take care of things just as easily.

~~~~~

"Caught up with Homeless Hal last night," Trevor informed Duane Peterson at that very moment. The deputy usually stopped by the job each morning. "Said he'd watch the project for me. We're supposed to set up this evening."

"I hate to dump this on you, but we just don't have the staff and unfortunately, it's not that important a case for the Sheriff to put anyone on the case. We drive by whenever we can though."

"That's okay. It'll give Hal something to do. You know, I talked to him; he seems to have hit a run of bad luck. Said something about a fire destroying his home, killing his wife. I'd like to help the man."

Duane shook his head. "You won't believe some of the stories I've heard. The hardest though are the ones involving kids. And their mothers. We have a battered women's shelter on the outside of town, and I've encouraged many that I stumble upon to stay there."

Duane's monitor beeped with a message from dispatch. "Got a call from 1597 Idyllwild Lane. Possible trespassing. She specifically asked for you. Can you check it out?"

Trevor recognized Randi's address, sprinted toward his truck. "I'll be right behind you."

Ten minutes later, Duane pulled up behind the beige car while Trevor parked in Randi's driveway. He remained in the truck, watched Duane talk to the occupant. When the car drove off, Trevor got out, headed to the house.

Randi immediately opened the door, met them on the porch.

"What did he say?" Randi asked Duane when he joined them.

"Said he was being paid to watch your house."

"So, it was a private investigator?"

"Looks like it. I told him he needed to move on and if I heard of his being in the vicinity again, I'd have him arrested."

"Thank you," Randi said and turned back into the house.

"You going to stay with her a while?" Duane asked Trevor.

Trevor nodded. "Thanks. And I'll be in touch about Hal."

Trevor closed the front door, found Randi in the kitchen. She paced between the sink and back door.

"I can't believe he's still having me watched," she fumed. "What does he think he's going to learn?"

"Randi," Trevor tried to interrupt.

"This is the way it used to be. I always felt like he was watching me."

"Randi,"

"I refuse to let him intimidate me," she muttered. "I mean, we've been divorced for five years. I have a life of my own. Don't I?" she exclaimed.

"Randi,"

"He has no right to monitor my comings and goings."

Trevor reached for her, cupped her head in both hands, stopped her rantings the only way possible. With his mouth.

"Trev,"

He kissed her again.

"What?"

Trevor took advantage of her opened mouth and deepened the kiss.

"Hmm," Randi tried to stop him but leaned into him instead. She wrapped her arms around the small of his back and gave up.

Trevor had been craving this meeting of the lips since that kiss on the soccer field at the resort. He deepened the kiss, enjoyed the feel of her breasts pressed against his chest as she hugged him tightly. She was intoxicating. If he kept this up, he'd never get the job finished.

"Whoa," he whispered when he raised his head. Randi's eyes were still closed so he decided to steal another kiss.

Randi was sure she'd died and gone to heaven. Tim had never kissed her like this. She was breathless. Her knees weakened as she melted against him, cuddled closer and hung on as warmth spread through her, thrilled up and down her spine. She could stay here all day, she decided. Then she realized what she was doing, tried to push away.

"Trevor," she mumbled against his lips. "Trevor," she repeated when he continued to kiss her.

Trevor felt dizzy. His heart thumped as his body came to attention, every inch craved her. He heard her voice but didn't want to stop this desire that percolated between them. He felt her hands at his sides trying to nudge him away and jerked, released her to lean against the kitchen wall. He stared down at her, looked as befuddled as she felt.

"You need to get angry like that more often." A smile tugged at his lips. "I've never locked lips like that."

"I'm sorry," she floundered in embarrassment.

"Don't be sorry. I kissed you, remember?"

"Yes, but I don't know what came over me."

"Don't hear me complaining, do you?"

Randi gave him a half-smile, sat at the kitchen table. "I've never been kissed like that."

"Same here. And plenty more available when needed. We'll have to be careful though. If we don't watch it, we'll find ourselves in bed. Not that I hadn't already made that decision hours after meeting you. Just didn't know you offered such potent kisses." Trevor chuckled as he sat across from her at the table.

Randi gave him a nervous laugh. "Two little boys can run interference, create distractions."

Trevor quirked an eyebrow, looked at the clock on the wall and smiled. "Not if they're in school."

Randi gaped. Was he serious? Did he just hint that he wanted to make love to her? Now?

"And we have the firehouse project." He added when she remained quiet. "I might have lots of questions about your office, need to spend some time here discussing them with you."

Randi felt her cheeks blush, her heart swelled. He looked so serious, sincere; she was touched. It had been a long time since she'd flirted with a man. And here she had a very potent one pretty much telling me he was interested.

They stared at one another for seconds. She was tempted to invite him to her bed. He enjoyed her confusion.

So engrossed in one another, they jumped when there was a knock at the back door.

CHAPER TWELVE

"Maybe you need to confront the jerk," Marcie hissed after Randi told her what about the car watching the house. She looked at Trevor. "Maybe you need to rough him up."

"That's all I need," Randi exclaimed as she set three cups of coffee on the table. "Assault charges on top of the child custody situation."

Marcie laughed, covered Randi's hand. "I'm just kidding, you know."

"I know, but I'm mad too. Who does Tim think he is to have a private investigator following me? Like I asked Trevor, what does he hope to gain? Some dirt? I've been the responsible parent. How many men have you seen in my house?"

"Does Harriet know about this?" Marcie asked.

"I'm not sure, but I will certainly give her a call this afternoon. Wait," she paused, raised a finger. "I think she's interviewing Tim and Miriam today."

"Do you have her cell number? Maybe you could text her; she could ask him. Wouldn't that look good in her report?" Marcie smiled smugly.

"Have you given any thought to Harriet's suggestion about a get-together?" Marcie asked after Randi texted the GAL.

"No. Yes. Maybe," Randi sighed. "I just don't know what to do. Are you available?" she looked from Marcie to Trevor. "I just don't want to do it by myself. I need reinforcements."

"Why don't we talk to Ginny and Cliff about doing a picnic at Spicer Meadows? That way they will be outnumbered. Could even invite Brad since he is handling your case. And his assistant, Stacy. I like her."

"Good idea," Trevor agreed. "I'm flexible. Planning to keep my schedule open till we get this project finished. Supposed to have a conference call with the Atlanta people later this afternoon."

"Ginny seemed receptive to it when we talked last night. I'll give her a call when she gets home from school." Randi decided.

Marcie stayed after Trevor left, couldn't help but chuckle when she watched Randi lean forward as if to kiss Trevor, then caught herself.

"Sit down, girlie, we need to talk."

"Talk about what?" Randi asked.

"Talk about you sitting at the kitchen table with a certain hunk in the middle of the morning."

"He, he happened to be with Duane when dispatch relayed my call. Then Duane had to get back to work, and Trevor said he had a couple questions about the job."

Marcie chuckled. "Hmm. And what were these questions? I thought you and Brina had pretty much decided everything."

"Well, you know," Randi shrugged a shoulder, "there are always little things that come up."

"Hmm," Marcie repeated. "You know I had a few seconds to observe you two before I knocked at the back door. Things looked intense if you ask me."

"Oh, all right, yes, things were a little intense. I got upset after Duane left; Trevor helped calm me down." When Marcie remained quiet, she continued. "I was pacing and venting, and suddenly he grabbed me and kissed me. One of those hot, sizzling, melt your bones kind of kisses."

"Wondered when he was going to make a move."

Randi looked down and smiled. "That's not the first time he's kissed me. He kissed me at Snowridge. When we realized Tim and Miriam were watching us across the soccer field. Dipped me back, locked lips. Did it more to rile Tim so it wasn't as sensual as the ones today."

Marcie smiled. "Sensual, huh? And more than one? Better watch out, you know what comes next?"

Randi laughed. Marcie always knew how to relax her. "He had pretty much said as much before you knocked. Can't help but wonder what we'd be doing if you hadn't stopped by."

"Sorry. And with everything that's going on, a good rollicking in the bed would probably do you a world of good." Marcie laughed at Randi's pink cheeks. "Can't think of anything more exciting than planning a seduction." She grabbed Randi's hand and tugged her. "C'mon. Let's go check your wardrobe."

After a thorough search, Marcie stated, "grab your purse. We need to do some major shopping."

~~~~~

Three hours later, Randi was in a much better mood. She and Marcie had hit one of the malls on the outskirts of Richmond and she now had a several new gowns, sexy underwear, fresh supply of makeup and full bottle of her favorite perfume.

Lunch had relaxed her, her purchases excited her. While she waited in the car for the boys to come out of the school, she found herself plotting the big seduction scene.

She'd have him over for brunch. Pick up some bubbly for mimosas, make her egg casserole. Add some Danishes and she'd be set. All she needed was the nerve to do it.

Suppose he couldn't come? Suppose it was too soon?

Maybe he wasn't ready yet.

She jumped when Sandy opened the door, tossed his bookbag on the floor, climbed into his car seat. "Hey Mom, can we stop by the firehouse on the way home?"

"Yeah," Scott buckled himself in. "We did pictures today and drew our avengers. Maybe Trevor can come over for dinner tonight."

"Can I ask him," Sandy added.

Randi smiled. "Sure." Her boys were obviously as smitten with him as she was.

They jumped out of the car as soon as she pulled up to the old building and raced inside. "Trevor," they both yelled at the top of their lungs, "look at our pictures. Can you come over for supper tonight?"

Trevor was looking at their pictures when she caught up with them. Aaron, the foreman was smiling when he left.

"Hey, pretty good guys. You need to frame them. Hang them up. Maybe your mom will put them in her new office." He winked at Randi.

"Can we Mom?" Both boys asked.

"Sure. We'll work on it when we get home."

"Can you come for supper?" Scott repeated.

"Depends on your mom. I need to come back to the job later but should have enough time for dinner with a hot Mama and her ducklings."

"Are you sure?" Randi asked. "Not everyone likes meatloaf."

~~~~~

Trevor brought a bottle of merlot to compliment the meatloaf. He hoped there would be enough left over, he liked meatloaf sandwiches.

After those kisses this morning, he hadn't been able to think about much else all afternoon.

He'd stopped by the *White Rose Diner,* arranged to meet Hal at the garage at eight instead of seven.

When he carried the cot by the garage, Stanley said he had a county vehicle that needed to be finished tonight and would probably be knocking off about that time. Hal could set it up in the office, should have a good view of the back of the firehouse.

Scott and Sandy snagged him for a battle until dinner was ready. They had also drawn more pictures for him to take to the cottage.

"I take it you're feeling better than this morning?"

Randi smiled. "Yes, as a matter of fact. Marcie and I had a good talk, then spent the afternoon at the mall."

"What is it about shopping that is supposed to make women feel better? My sister's always spending my brother-in-law's money. Used to drag me with her when we were younger."

"It's an escape, Trevor. Gives us a chance to focus on something other than what's bothering us."

"And were you successful? Were you able to put the private investigator out of your mind?"

"As a matter of fact, I did. Harriet texted to say she had an interesting visit and would call me tonight. Also texted that Miriam was excited about having a get-together. I thought I'd give Ginny a call this evening."

"I'm sure there's enough to do at Spicer Meadows. I discover something new every morning when I jog."

After dinner, Trevor helped clear the table then played with the boys while she did the dishes.

"Boys, why don't you tell Trevor good night so he can make it to his meeting; then you can start getting ready for bed. You've had a busy day today."

She walked Trevor to the door while the boys dashed upstairs.

"I have a full day tomorrow, need to meet a client. But if you'd like, you could come for brunch on Wednesday," she suggested. "Unless you have other plans."

"Would like that. I also have a busy day tomorrow. Need to run back to the resort for an inspection, do a little research on the project in Georgia."

"You've made a decision?"

"Still working on it but things sound more promising. Just need to check out a few things first. Might talk to you about it on Wednesday if that's okay."

He reached for her hand.

"You know, I might need a boost to help me through my busy day tomorrow." He tugged her closer. Placed her hand on his shoulder.

Randi smiled. "Oh? What kind of boost?"

"This." He pulled her in his arms.

"A hug?" Randi wrapped her arms around his neck. Smiled when Trevor hugged her closer. "Sure, I don't mind helping out."

She saw a sparkle in Trevor's eyes as he moved his hands up and down her back, pressed her breasts against his chest. "I appreciate it," he murmured, stared at her lips. "Oh, and there's something else you could do."

Randi batted her eyes at him. "Really? What?"

"This." His lips covered hers, gently at first, then with more force as his tongue twirled with hers. He inhaled deeply, smelled her perfume, tasted the wine, felt the curves of her body against his as his hands curved around her bottom, pressed her center against his arousal. He ached for her. Kiss followed kiss and she met him with each caress.

Trevor realized he could stay here all night but knew he needed to meet Hal. Tomorrow would be a long one, but he looked forward to Wednesday. Would set aside the whole day for her. Somehow or other, he intended to get her in his or her bed soon.

Randi's heart pounded and her head spun. She'd never been romanced. Tim had never courted her. Simply swept her off her feet then married her before she could have second thoughts.

Trevor was so different. He didn't push himself on her but enjoyed tempting her. And she was certainly tempted.

Her plan to seduce him on Wednesday excited her. They would spend most of the day in bed pleasuring one another. She intended to feed him, charm him, then enjoy him.

Trevor raised his head, gazed at her enticing mouth while his hands massaged her back.

"Tomorrow will definitely be a long one. Believe me when I say I'll be looking forward to that brunch on Wednesday."

He would have kissed her again; except he heard the giggles from the hall. Scott and Sandy peeked around the corner. He smiled, decided to include them in the fun. "Okay boys, do I have your permission to kiss your mom good night?"

"Yeah," they both exclaimed between giggles.

Randi smiled, gave him a quick kiss then handed him his meatloaf sandwich for tomorrow. She laughed when she opened the door and he moaned. "Until Wednesday."

~~~~~

Trevor met Hal and Stanley at the garage. It was a big building with a large waiting room and two sizeable bays for working on the vehicles. The waiting room boasted storefront windows that faced the street. Across the street was a large parking lot, the back of the old firehouse.

Four chairs arranged in front of the windows, faced the long wide big counter that split the room. Customers on one side, staff on the other. There was a small office to the left of the counter. "Don't get in there much," Stanley stated. "Wife usually comes in once a month to do the bookkeeping."

Posters of car inspection reminders, oil and transmission advertisements, and hot rod cars were attached to the cinder block walls. A bulletin board full of fliers reminding everyone of community events hung on the wall next to a coffee station.

"You're welcome to help yourself to the coffee. I think there are some Danishes in the office."

Hal thanked him. "I'll set the cot up in front of the counter so I can keep an eye on things but will store it in the office and be gone before you get here in the morning. Wouldn't look good for people to see me in here."

"Don't worry about that. You might want to lay low till after nine. People sometimes bring their cars by, leave their keys in the night box. Everybody wants to be first in line in the morning."

"I appreciate your working with me," Trevor shook hands with the mechanic.

Stanley smiled. "Looking forward to having something better to look at than the chipping white paint on the back of the old firehouse."

"Yeah," Trevor smiled. "Focusing on the inside now but I have some ideas in mind. Thinking about a small patio with a mural across the back."

Stanley led them into the big bay area. Pointed to the windows midway up the garage doors. "You'll also be able to watch from here. Won't be as noticeable."

Trevor looked out the window. "Duane Peterson said the deputies routinely drive by so we should be covered."

He turned to Hal, handed him the disposable phone. "If you see anything, don't hesitate to call, or text me. It's programmed with my number. Don't try taking them down by yourself. I'll be at Snowridge tonight and tomorrow but will be back on Wednesday."

"Will do," Hal responded.

~~~~~

He stood in the dark, watched from the window at the back of his office. It helped that he could keep an eye on things. It also reminded him every day why they couldn't finish that project.

It was after eight and the contractor just couldn't stay away. He'd watched him pull up, go inside, then leave.

Obviously, they didn't heed his warning.

He hadn't been inside the building but heard that they'd painted over the graffiti. Everybody was talking about the constant problems, wondering if the project was jinxed. He snarled. If they only knew.

He reached in his pocket, studied the key. The foreman had been careless the other day and he'd paid Josh a good fee to have a duplicate made.

He smiled. Now he could get in any time he wanted.

Maybe he'd go now. Check things out.

He stepped outside, walked across the lawn behind his office. He had just crossed the street and was headed down the sidewalk toward the firehouse when one of the deputies drove by. He waved, slowed his pace till the cruiser turned the corner.

He hurried across the street, unlocked the door and stepped inside.

It was dark but he used his small flashlight to walk about. Saw they'd taken out some of the concrete walls, added new ones. He looked at the freshly painted wall. Primed in white, ready for the final coat of paint. Guess they didn't want any reminders.

Studied the hammers, lumber, sheetrock, and tools scattered about each room.

Can't get too much done if they're missing tools, he thought as he reached for a cordless screwdriver and nail gun.

Maybe if their tools started disappearing, they'd give up.

~~~~~

Hal turned one of the chairs around, settled back with a cup of coffee. It was starting to get dark and soon the traffic would die down.

A deputy had just driven by.

He took a sip, then sat up straight. It was dark and the windows on the back of the building were small, but he could have sworn he saw a light. He continued to watch; thought he saw it again.

But after ten minutes, there was darkness and he wondered if it might have been the headlights on the front of the building.

CHAPTER THIRTEEN

Randi checked the egg casserole for the third time then turned the oven off. The fruit salad was in the fridge, crescent rolls keeping warm in the microwave. It was almost eleven and she was jittery. Nervous. What was she thinking? Seducing Trevor Graystone? What if he wasn't interested?

She smiled. What if he was?

She'd been impulsive and bought a dress while in Richmond yesterday. An Aqua blue ruffled and embroidered senorita dress with pale blue eyelet accents. It could be worn on or off the shoulder and she'd tried it both ways. On the shoulder was safe and motherly; off the shoulder was daring and inviting.

It was eleven in the morning, she fumed to herself as she covered her shoulders. Who in their right mind planned a seduction at eleven in the morning? What would Trevor think?

She'd waited until after the boys were asleep to paint her nails; stared down at the soft pink toes that peeked out of the three-inch metallic beige espadrilles. She'd pinned her hair back on one side to show off the silver Carita earrings.

For the first time in a long, long time, she felt feminine, sexy, flirtatious. But what would Trevor think?

He was used to seeing her as the mother of two boys. Dressed in jeans and sweatshirts. Then she remembered their dinner date at the resort, how he had been so complimentary about the outfit Brina, Ginny and Marcie sent her.

What would he say today? She wondered. Would he get the message? Or would he take one look and run the other way?

She jumped when the doorbell rang. Gave herself one last look in the mirror, shifted the top off her shoulders. Took a deep breath then opened the door.

Her heart skipped when she saw he too had taken time to dress for the occasion. He apparently hadn't been by the job yet. His jeans were clean, the white polo shirt freshly pressed, and his work boots replaced by loafers. He looked delectable.

Trevor smiled, handed her a small bouquet of yellow African daisies.

"They're beautiful," she exclaimed nervously, turned and dashed to the kitchen to find a vase.

Trevor closed the door, followed her, appreciated the bare shoulders and long legs as they raced away from him. His nose went up, savored the scent of her perfume, then the aroma of breakfast.

He picked up on her nervousness as he watched her open doors to the cabinets, frantically searching for a vase. Her hands shook slightly when she arranged the flowers, then filled it with water.

"These are so nice," she exclaimed. "It's been a long time since someone gave me flowers. Did you have a good talk with the developers yesterday? What did you finally decide?"

Trevor gave her time to set the flowers on the table then pulled her into his arms before she could do anything else.

"Good morning," He hugged her, waited for her nerves to settle, rest her head on his shoulder.

When he heard her take a calming breath, he leaned back to graze her lips with his.

His easy smile, gleaming eyes, soft voice calmed her. Randi wrapped her hands across his shoulders, leaned into him and allowed herself to enjoy his lips when he deepened the kiss.

"Hmm," he murmured, nuzzled her neck and bare shoulder. "I hope the food is as delicious as you smell and look."

"Mr. Graystone," she leaned back, smiled at him, "are you flirting with me?"

"Damn right. Food smells delicious, the hostess looks ravishing."

"Why don't we start with the mimosas?" She nudged away, headed for the fridge.

"So," she filled the flutes, "did you work things out with the developer?" She asked again. "What did you decide?"

"I offered a counter proposal. Waiting to hear back from them."

He didn't want to tell her part of the proposal involved her. Not until he knew they would consider it.

"How about you? Your client happy with your suggestions?"

Randi spooned some of the casserole onto his plate.

"Yes, she did. It always helps when they can visualize your suggestions. I don't know whether I told you, but I have a computer program that allows me to plug in measurements, doorways, windows, fireplaces, you name it. Then I can play with the design, rearrange walls, change flooring, give them options to consider."

She joined him at the table. "She liked what I put together; said she would take it to her contractor for a quote."

"So, you don't work with a specific contractor?"

"No, for several reasons. Other than you, I don't know that many contractors. And the few I do know, weren't receptive to working with me. I prefer the design side of the business; don't want the client to feel pressured to accept an estimate I might get. That way I'm free and clear, they get what they want."

Trevor grinned. "Now that you know a reliable, professional and fantastic contractor, have your thoughts changed?"

Randi lifted her glass, saluted him. "Depends on the quality work said contractor does with his current project."

"Touché. But you know you're going to be pleased."

"I have to say I like what you've done so far and am even more impressed with the way you've handled all the problems we've had."

"Yeah, well, problems on any job are a given but somebody's still interfering with yours." Trevor frowned. "Got a call from my foreman on my way here. Said they were missing a few of our tools. Planning to meet with him this afternoon to do an inventory, find out what's missing."

"Don't you lock the place?"

"Yeah. Apparently, somebody still got inside. Time to get to the bottom of all this sabotage."

"Trevor, do you normally have this many problems with a project?"

"There are always setbacks. Weather. Theft. Changes in design. That's why I have a lot of patience and good insurance. But I must admit your project has had more than its fair share of problems."

"I'll just be glad when it's finished."

"Trying to get rid of me that quickly?"

"No," Randi stammered, "No. Of course not."

She stood to carry their plates to the sink. Turned, leaned against the sink and shrugged a shoulder. "Just a figure of speech. I've always appreciated how supportive you've been to Brina with the hearings, inspectors, planning. And now that I've finally met you, it has been fun having you around, watching you transform the place."

Trevor stood in front of her, liked the fact that those espadrilles put her eye level with him. Made it easier to look directly into her nervous eyes, brush his lips across her bare shoulders, up her neck while his hands roamed along her back, pressed her against his chest.

"You know I'm just kidding," he murmured in her ear. "Besides, after meeting you and your two boys, do you think I'm going to just leave when this job is done?"

Randi shivered to feel his breath against her ear, felt her knees weaken. "Well," she confided huskily, "you never know."

Trevor raised his head to study her, his hands moved down her back to cup her bottom, hugged her closer to his hard body.

Randi's heart flipflopped when she saw the affection that glowed in his twinkling eyes. Suddenly she was dizzy and light-headed. Longed for the excitement she knew awaited her.

"When I find a woman, who can seduce me with food," his lips skimmed her lips, "her perfume," his nose brushed her neck and shoulder, "her delectable body," he pointedly peeked down at her cleavage, "and sassy tongue, I'd be crazy not to hang around."

Trevor never gave her a chance to respond, simply covered her mouth with his and proceeded to ravish her.

Randi hung on. He tasted of the mimosas; her head was spinning from her own bubbly. She felt his hard chest against her breasts and a warmness between her legs. It had been a long, long time since she had felt like this.

Trevor came up for air.

"This is all I've thought about for the last two days. Do you know how good it is to be able to kiss you and not have to worry about

Scott or Sandy coming in." He cocked his head. "What about your girl friends? Do they make a habit of stopping by during the day?"

Randi smiled. "Sometimes, but I told them I was on a job today."

Trevor gave her a devilish grin. "So, I have you all to myself?"

"At least until I have to pick the boys up from school."

"Then I suggest we make the most of it. Quit wasting time."

He locked lips again.

Randi was nervous, giddy and aggressive, all at once. She met his kisses head on, enticed him to take more.

Trevor leaned down, swept her off her feet. "You're intoxicating," he mumbled against her lips. "Where's the bedroom?"

Randi smiled. "It's the only door on the hall that's open."

He carried her down the hall, stepped inside the bedroom.

"Are you sure about this?"

Randi looked deeply into his eyes and smiled. "Never more certain. It's been so long since a man has made me feel this way."

He set her on her feet, watched as she nudged the elastic shoulders down her arms, stepped out of the dress. He caught his breath, was reminded of the time he saw her in the bikini no larger than the skimpy bra and panties she wore now.

She stepped out of her shoes then reached for the hem of his shirt, pulled it over his head. She stood on her toes to kiss him while reaching for the button of his jeans, lowered his zipper. He inhaled a deep breath, swallowed loudly when she reached inside and caressed him.

"I was wrong," he croaked. "You're more than seductive, you're bewitching."

He quickly stepped out of the jeans and reached for her. Unhooked the front clasp of her bra, ripped the panties aside.

Randi gasped, jerked at the instant orgasm when his hand cupped her center, his fingers stroked the warmness between her legs.

Her head fell against his shoulder as they collapsed onto the bed. She wrapped her legs around him, moved against his arousal and moaned when his kisses moved from her mouth to her shoulder to her breast.

Trevor reached for her hands, shifted them above her head and stared down at her.

"We need to go slow." He slipped inside her, thrust easily and deeply. She was warm, moist and tight.

Randi inhaled deeply, arched back in pleasure, felt like purring. She cupped his face, stared deeply into chocolate brown eyes that almost seemed to worship her. Watched him as he continued to move inside her, hung on when the momentum grew, and they could no longer control themselves.

She felt his pounding heart and heavy breathing when he collapsed atop her. Tightened her legs around him, giddily kissed his shoulder, made her way up his neck. When he raised his head to look down at her, she cupped his face and beamed up at him.

"I take that back. You are a bewitching, provocative, insatiable temptress," he hummed as he felt himself come alive again.

~~~~~

Randi handed him another mimosa, sat Indian style as she faced him while he leaned against the pillow and headboard.

"You had that all planned, didn't you?"

She gave him a satisfied smile.

"Are you saying you didn't have any inkling this might happen? Didn't have plans of your own?"

Trevor chuckled. "I'll admit I was hopeful, but you definitely moved things along."

She glanced at the clock on the nightstand. "Only took an hour."

Her fingers danced up his leg. "And we still have another hour or so if you're interested."

Trevor shivered when the fingers inched past his knee.

"Unless you need to be somewhere," she continued.

He finished the mimosa, sat upright to set his and her flutes on the nightstand. "I'll take morning or afternoon delight with you anytime I can get it."

Randi yelped when he grabbed her feet, flattened her on the bed and covered her.

~~~~~

Twenty minutes after Trevor left, Randi's cell phone rang. She didn't recognize the number just knew it looked familiar. Considering all that had been going on in her life recently, she decided to answer the call.

"Randi, this is Harriet Young. Is this a bad time?"

"No, I have a few minutes before I go to pick up the boys from school. How can I help you?"

"I had my visit with Tim and Miriam the other day and I wanted to run a couple things by you. First, when I got your text, I asked him about that private investigator at your house."

"Oh?" Randi responded.

"Yes. He tried to act surprised."

"I bet he never thought you'd call him out on it."

"No. I let him think that the PI had identified him, and he immediately apologized. Said he'd neglected to pull him off the job."

"I bet. Did Miriam know about it?"

"No, which surprised me. She seemed to be genuinely shocked."

"If her marriage is anything like mine was, Tim is very controlling and non-communicative."

"Hmm," Harriet murmured, "he said he would give the PI a call. Now, the other thing. Do you remember we talked briefly about a get-together so that the boys can get to know their father and Miriam better?"

"Yes. You were going to mention it to him."

"Well, I did. Miriam jumped at the idea and although Tim didn't have much to say, he agreed it would probably be best."

Randi's heart sank. She had hoped that Tim wouldn't want to do it. "He agreed? I'm surprised."

"Well, as I said, Miriam was very excited and after some discussion, he finally agreed."

"Oh, okay. Did they have any date in mind?"

"I know this is short notice but considering we need to get the boys comfortable with their father, I suggested that it be soon. They said they would be available to come this weekend if it was okay with you."

This weekend, Randi screamed to herself. I bet he hopes I'll balk at the idea, Randi decided. "Yes, it is a little short notice, but I think I can work it out. Can I get back to you?"

"Of course. And I'll relay the message to Tim and Miriam."

As soon as she disconnected, Randi texted Trevor. "Can you come to dinner?"

~~~~~

Trevor decided to give his sister another call. Now that he'd heard from Greenwillow, he needed to get a few things straight before pitching his idea to Randi. Chuck, his brother-in-law, was also a contractor and he and Susan had two homes - one in Maryland, another in Georgia.

"Trevor, I was just thinking about you," Susan exclaimed.

"I bet. Been trying to get you all day. Out spending all of Chuck's money?"

She chuckled. "Somebody must do it. I was thinking about your birthday. It's almost here and you don't have much longer on your bet."

"What bet?"

"You know. The one about being married by the time you're thirty-eight."

"I'm working on it." Trevor spoke without thinking.

"Oh? Anyone I know?"

"As a matter of fact, you do. Don't you know Miranda Cavanaugh?"

"Randi," Susan squealed. "Oh Trevor, that's fantastic. When?"

"Hold on. I said I was working on it. We've only just met. Plus, there are a few problems."

"Problems? What kind of problems?"

"Her ex-husband, for one."

"What has he done now?"

"You know Tim Cavanaugh?"

"Unfortunately, I do," Susan groaned.

"Know anything about their divorce?"

"No, not really. Just glad she divorced him when she did. It was so unfortunate that she had to have the babies by herself but she's better off for it. Come to think of it I saw him recently, where was it? Oh, last month, at the Turner's open house. He was plastered as usual. And now that you mention it, I happened to overhear him spouting off something about how cheaply he'd managed to get out of his divorce, married money and now he was working on the child support payments."

"What do you mean?" Trevor interrupted.

"Well, he bragged about how he planned to get joint custody of the boys, then he'd get Randi out of their lives altogether. Wouldn't have to worry about child support."

"Interesting. He's never paid Randi any child support. Supposed to be paying into an education trust for the boys which I understand he hasn't contributed to in over a year."

"That's it," Susan said, "he said something about her agreeing to a Trust Fund for the boys until they are eighteen. Said it's supposed to pay for their college education but by the time they needed it, he'd think of a way out of it. He's remarried, you know. Miriam Ledbetter. Her father owns a computer software company. Nice girl, don't know how she puts up with Tim."

"I met her the other week at Snowridge."

"You've met them?"

"He and Miriam showed up at the resort while Randi was there with her father and the boys. But hearing you, I wonder if it wasn't intentional. He's petitioning for joint-custody and Randi is beside herself."

"Trevor, he doesn't deserve those boys. He doesn't deserve Miriam. You should have heard what he said about her. Said she was cold, couldn't have any children. Admitted that's why he's pursuing joint custody."

"You must have been the proverbial fly on the wall to hear as much as you did."

Susan snickered. "I was standing with my back to him, but he didn't make it hard to hear everything. Like I said, he was pretty much wasted."

"Have you heard anything about abuse? How well do you know Miriam?"

"Vaguely. She moved here a couple years ago. Seems nice though. That's why I was so surprised to read they had married."

"Could you do me a favor? Could you try to get to know her a little better. If he abused Randi, he might be abusing her as well."

"Trevor," Susan exclaimed. "Are you saying Tim abused Randi?"

"You didn't hear this from me but that's why she divorced him. Final straw was when he pushed her down the steps. She was pregnant at the time, almost lost her boys."

Susan gasped, then there was silence. "I will certainly keep my eyes and ears open. Trevor, Tim Cavanaugh is a cruel man. Always had a mean streak. You need to look out for Randi. She, and Miriam, deserve better."

"That's my plan. Hey, I also called to see if you're going to be home next week. I may have to come to Atlanta."

"Bummer. Chuck and I leave this Saturday for two weeks in France. Going to visit the Bordeaux region. But you're welcome to use the house if you'd like."

"You sure? It would only be for a few days. I need to talk to Randi first."

Susan was silent.

"Hello?" Trevor asked.

Susan laughed. "Much as I'd like to win our bet, you couldn't have picked a nicer girl. I'm so happy for you."

"Hey, we're not married. Yet."

~~~~~

Randi was on her way out the door to pick up the boys from school when the flowers arrived. Twelve beautiful apricot-colored roses.

"Oh, my goodness," she exclaimed to Mandy.

"Mom just got the order and as soon as I walked in the shop from school, she asked me to deliver them. I'm supposed to give her details of your reaction."

Randi laughed. "Oh really. Well, you can tell her I am ecstatic, and they are very beautiful. It's been a long, long time since someone sent me roses."

"Mom also said to make note of who sent them. Something about the cute contractor guy?"

Randi looked at the note – *Beautiful flowers for a beautiful lady.* "Yes, I guess this is Trevor's way of thanking me for sending some business his way."

"Wish I had a guy like that," Mandy commented as she turned to leave.

Randi searched for another vase, texted Trevor a second time. "Thank you for the roses. They are beautiful."

"Like the card said," he texted back, "beautiful flowers for a beautiful lady."

Realizing she was almost late, Randi dashed out the door to the school. She wanted to visit a few minutes with Ginny; hopefully discuss a get-together at Spicer Meadows.

She was so glad Ginny had moved up with the boys' class. The school system was trying a new curriculum, assigning the same teacher to the same class for two years. They hoped that this would enhance the children's experience in school. Next year Scott and Sandy would have a different teacher but this year, Ginny would hopefully be able to monitor the boys and prevent this impending upheaval in their lives from affecting their last days in the school year.

Considering that Ginny was now pregnant she wondered if Ginny would return to teaching after the baby was born. She'd been a part time storyteller when she and Cliff squabbled about settling Claude's estate. Then she had stopped the storytelling when she and Cliff were married. Maybe now, Ginny might give up teaching, do the storytelling part-time.

"How are you feeling?" Randi asked when Ginny returned from taking the class to their buses.

"I'm always tired," she collapsed in her chair, "but I'll take that over morning sickness."

Randi smiled. "Yeah, I remember my first three months. I couldn't do anything before eleven in the morning. Saltine crackers were the only thing I could keep down in the mornings."

She glanced at Scott and Sandy who sat at the craft table coloring pictures.

"I know it's early in my battle with Tim, but do the boys seem okay in class? They know Tim is their father but I'm not sure how they're digesting all of this."

Ginny smiled. "If you and Tim can handle this peacefully, they will be fine. It's the ones whose parents are always arguing that I worry about. I have a little girl in my class, Molly, whose parents divorced last Spring. It was difficult at first because the mother was so bitter but in the past year, they've managed to work things out. I did my best to be there for Molly."

"Has Harriet Young been to see you?"

"Yes, she came by this morning. We chatted while the class was out for recess."

"How did it go?"

"Great. Randi, I don't think you need to worry about anything. I've talked with Ms. Young about other cases. In fact, she was the GAL for Molly. Ms. Young is very thorough and fair. She has a big heart and lots of common sense. I've seen her handle cases much more volatile than yours. She was very patient and understanding with Molly and I truly believe she's the reason the family has managed to work through their differences."

"She called me earlier. Said she had a good visit with Tim and Miriam. Said Tim and Miriam were agreeable to coming to Edmondsville for a get-together so the boys can get to know them better. Now, I need to try and plan something by this weekend."

"We haven't been able to get together in a while. Why don't we have a pool party at Spicer Meadows? I've been meaning to invite Trevor; we can include Tim and Miriam as well. Maybe the more we have there, the easier it will be."

Randi felt tears well in her eyes. "Would you do that? For me? I told Harriet I'd try to put something together but,"

Ginny stood, gave Randi a hug. "I will be happy to do this. In fact, Cliff informed me this morning that Pete's flying here Friday evening, so I'd have to do something for him anyway." Ginny laughed. "Cliff always looks for an excuse to cook on the grill."

"I certainly appreciate it. I'll give Cliff a call. Between the two of us, we'll take care of things, you won't have to do a thing."

Ginny laughed. "You won't get any argument from me."

~~~~~

Randi decided to make dinner easy and fixed spaghetti. Couldn't believe that a simple meal would be so confusing. It's not confusing, she scolded herself, you just have too much on your mind.

What happened to her simple, peaceful lifestyle? When there was just her, the boys, her father, her friends? Now, she had not only met a kind, wonderful man, but as of this morning, she was involved with him as well. Memories of Trevor's lovemaking thrilled throughout her body. She hadn't felt this alive in a long, long time.

And just when she'd found a man who interested her, her ex-husband and his wife crawl out of the woodwork to stir the pot. She didn't need Tim breathing down her neck, threatening to take the boys from her. Why after five years, did he suddenly decide he wanted to see them? What was he up to?

Scott and Sandy were coming up on to the end of the school year for goodness' sake. Things are chaotic enough. She didn't need to worry about upsetting the boys more.

Add to that, she now had a GAL, Harriet Young. Who would have thought that she would have some guardian ad litem mediating her relationship with Tim. As if Tim will listen to anything she says.

It seemed she was on pins and needles all the time, looking over her shoulder, wondering when the next blow would come. She was being forced to make plans, include her friends in get-togethers just so her boys could get to know their father. She was thankful Ginny was willing to work with her, but what would they do Saturday? Sit around talking to one another? Swim? Play ball? She needed to talk to Cliff.

And what would Trevor think of all this? Harriet said it might be good to involve him if he was going to be a part of their lives. After this job, would he still be part of their lives? Would he even be interested?

She heard the tap at the back door. When Trevor came inside, she walked into his arms, hung on for dear life.

"You okay? You looked deep in thought when I knocked."

"Yeah, I am now." She smiled up at him, amazed at how just walking into his arms, hugging him brought her instant peace. She lay her cheek on his chest. "Thank you for coming."

"Glad you called." He tightened his hold, kissed the top of her head. "I heard from the developers this afternoon. They liked my idea and I wanted to talk to you about it. I want you to go to Atlanta with me."

CHAPTER FOURTEEN

Randi lifted her head, slid him a guarded look. Did she hear him correctly? "You want me to go to Atlanta? With you?"

"Yeah." He tightened his hold when she started to back away from him. "Just hear me out, okay? If I let you go, will you just sit? Let me discuss it with you?"

Randi stared silently. Sure, she decided. Why not? She should be able to manage a trip to Atlanta with everything else going on in her life, she fumed. But he looked so serious. Desperate. Her heart melted; she nodded her head. "Okay, you have ten minutes."

Randi sat at the table while Trevor paced. "You know I'm all for renovation, right? One of the main reasons I bid for your project is because you and Brina want to take something old and refurbish it. I'd much rather do that in Atlanta. My sister says they've been doing a lot of renovating of old factories in some of the districts. I've been doing some research and found an old cotton mill that's for sale."

"Those mills are pretty big," Randi commented. "Lot of potential, though. Expensive."

"Not if I can talk the developer into channeling their money in that direction. They could put businesses in the main level, housing units in the upper levels. Buildings that size, they could probably get fifty units in each one that could be rented on a weekly basis. In addition to the businesses downstairs."

"I've always wanted to go to Atlanta. Even considered it before I moved here. But it was too big, too competitive for me. Lots of sites though. Georgia Aquarium, Botanical Gardens, Centennial Park, Fox Theatre..." She leaned back in her chair. "Trevor, you might have something. But why do you want me to go with you?"

"I want you to walk through the property with me. Help me check it out. Design it. Sell it. If they like it, then I'll do the construction, you do the interior design and decoration."

"Are you serious? Trevor, it's near the end of the school year. I can't just pull Scott and Sandy out of school."

"I'm not saying you'd have to pull them out of school. It would be just for a few days. We could schedule the trip the weekend before my meeting. I can talk to the realtor, arrange a walk-through, then we could take a couple days to put together a proposal for the developer. With that computer program you have, it should be a piece of cake for you to put something together. I do the construction; you do the decorating."

"I thought you didn't like interior decorators."

Trevor looked shocked. "Who said that?"

"Brina. She said whenever you two discussed the firehouse, you always made a face when she said she wanted to discuss it with her decorator."

"Okay," he sat at the table. "I might have had a different opinion about interior decorating a few weeks ago. That was before I met you." He reached for her hand and smiled. "You and I could make a good team. Will you at least think about it? It might be a long weekend. Four days at the most."

Randi's heart skipped a beat. Could she survive four days alone with Trevor? Just Trevor? No boys, no friends in tow. She hadn't been alone with a man one entire day much less four. She studied him, wondered if he might have an ulterior motive. Not that she wouldn't be interested, but she had to consider her boys, Tim's filing for joint custody. How would that look? Who would she get to watch the boys for that long?

"Trevor, I've got to think about this. I appreciate your wanting my input but I'm also in the middle of a custody battle and I need to think about my boys."

"I'm sure Harriet will take into consideration your work. They don't even have to know you're with me. You could just say that you're looking over a job and leave it at that. Maybe Ginny will keep the boys. Didn't I hear her say something about that the other night?"

"Yeah, but that was for over-night, not four days."

"Maybe she and Cliff might like to try their parenting skills. All you can do is ask."

"Why do I get the feeling that you've already asked?"

"Well, I did mention that I might need your help on a project when I caught her before she left for work this morning. She asked where and when; I said Atlanta, her eyes lit up. Said she would talk to Cliff."

"I bet her eyes lit up," Randi exclaimed.

~~~~~

As soon as the boys were in bed, Trevor reached for Randi's laptop. "Will you at least look at the property?" He pulled up the online listing and they studied the pictures.

"The property is u-shaped with three four-storied brick buildings. Probably takes half a block if not all of it. The back side is open, already has a parking lot. The railroad runs parallel two blocks away making it easy for commuters if they make it residential units. Or travelers if they make it like a resort. Or they could do both. There's a water tower and smokestacks in each building that can be updated to provide water, heat and air."

"Needs a lot of work," Randi studied the images, "but has potential too."

"Nothing that can't be fixed. I'd leave the exterior alone, just do some cosmetic changes around the buildings. I'm sure some of the multi-paned windows will need to be replaced but I want to keep everything as original as possible. I might even be able to replace some of the panes at minimal cost."

He pulled up another picture that showed an open space between the three buildings. "Could put a pool here, make it the courtyard at one end for the housing units, outdoor seating for a restaurant at the other end. The outer windows look over the skyline. In all directions."

"Do they have any pictures of the interior?"

Trevor clicked forward a couple views.

Randi saw large vacant rooms with concrete floors, faded brick walls. "They will certainly lend themselves to the large open rooms people are favoring today. You could even incorporate a kitchen, dinette and sitting area in the room."

"Your idea of the apartment in the upper level of the firehouse made me think about adding loft bedrooms that overlook the open rooms. The ceilings are certainly high enough."

"With a lot of wrought iron," Randi added.

Trevor smiled at the excitement that shone in her eyes. "So, what do you say we talk to Cliff and Ginny?"

"Trevor, let me think about this some. I'm flattered that you'd like me to help but I have a lot to consider. When do you need to know something?"

"They want me to do a presentation week after next. If we fly down the Saturday morning before my presentation, I can arrange to see the building that afternoon. Then we'd have Saturday night, all-day Sunday to put together some ideas, prepare the proposal. My sister and her husband live near there." He didn't say she would be out of town. "She claims she already knows you."

"But I don't know anyone in Atlanta."

"Not Atlanta. Maryland. Susan Mitchell."

Randi's eyes grew large. "Susan Mitchell is your sister. Trevor, if it weren't for Susan, I might not have my business."

Trevor blinked. Susan never mentioned knowing Randi this well. She might be an accomplished businesswoman herself, but his sister never told him about helping Randi start her business.

"She knew I had started my business while I was married to Tim. When the boys were infants, after I moved into my own home, she encouraged a few of her friends to consult with me when they decided to remodel their homes. One referral led to another and the rest they say is history. It'll be nice to see Susan again."

~~~~~

I need help. Anyone available? Randi texted her three friends.

"Busy with a wine tasting," Marcie responded.

"What's wrong?" Ginny texted.

"It's Trevor. He wants me to go to Georgia with him."

"I've got this," Brina texted. Moments later, Randi's phone chimed. "Okay, what's going on?"

"Everything," Randi exclaimed. "As if I don't have enough to worry about with Tim's shenanigans and Harriet Young's recommendation for a get-together, now Trevor wants me to go to Georgia with him."

"I know he's been working on a proposal. And it's more than obvious he is smitten with you."

Randi laughed. She wasn't going to offer that he was more than smitten. "He's looking at an old cotton mill down there. He'll do the construction and renovation, wants me to do the interior design."

"Hmm. And what did you tell him?"

"I haven't told him anything yet. Brina, I'm beginning a child custody battle. How will it look if I went away for a weekend with a man? What about the boys? I've never been away from Scott and Sandy. Never."

"Okay. Sometimes you need to travel to where jobs take you, right? This could be huge for you, and you should be thanking Trevor for including you. I know you're worried about the boys, but I think three women and two men can keep them entertained for a few days."

"But what about Harriet? Tim? You know he'll have a field day with this."

"We don't have to tell them, do we? The interviews are over. Everyone's getting together this weekend. That should satisfy things. You can just slip out of town, enjoy yourself with a good-looking guy, make your proposal, be back before anyone realizes you're gone."

"For four days? It's so deceiving. I just don't want to jeopardize things."

"We'll talk about it Friday night. We won't tell the boys until after Tim and Miriam are gone. Trust me, it'll be okay. Tell Trevor you'll be joining him and plan on having a good time."

~~~~~

Hal paced the front office of the garage, then stopped. It was his third night at the garage, and he thought he saw something at the firehouse. He reached for Trevor's binoculars, looked closer.

Sure enough, he saw some movement, watched what looked like three shadows following the beam of a flashlight. Decided maybe he hadn't imagined those lights the other night.

The shadows made their way across the back of the building, paused, then unlocked the door, went inside.

Hal frowned. None of them looked like Trevor. Or Aaron, the foreman. If it wasn't them, where did whoever it was get a key?

Hal cracked the door, made sure there were no cars coming, made his way across the street. Cars awaiting maintenance were parked in the lot and he quietly, slowly moved between them toward the firehouse.

Ignored Trevor's orders about not going into the building by himself.

Hal crept to the door, breathed a sigh of relief when he saw it was ajar. It creaked at the first nudge then was silent. He leaned down to grab a handful of rocks, slipped inside and listened to determine where the intruders might be.

He heard male voices in the front room, inched closer, saw three bodies huddled around a flashlight that was being beamed in different directions. They looked like teenagers.

"I thought you said this place was being demolished," one of the boys said.

"That's what he said."

"Then what's with all this stuff? They even painted over our artwork from last week."

"Maybe we shouldn't be here," a third voice said.

"It's okay, I tell you. If he says it's okay, it's okay."

Hal knew he wouldn't be able to take the three of them by himself, but he was determined to teach these boys a lesson. He reached in his pocket, tossed a rock across the room.

"What was that?"

"What? I didn't hear anything."

"I know I heard something. Over there."

Hal waited thirty seconds, tossed another rock in another corner. He watched the boys jump, turn towards the noise.

"What was that? Did you hear it?"

"Yeah. Probably just a mouse. You're not scared, are you?" the voice taunted.

"I'm not scared but this place is creepy."

Hal spied a long pipe nearby and a box of supplies. He picked up the pipe, tossed another pebble in the third corner, then nudged the box aside. Had to restrain himself from laughing out loud when he saw all three boys jump.

"I don't know about you," the first boy almost sobbed, "but I'm gettin' the hell out of here."

Hal backed into the darkness when all three boys ran past him.

~~~~~

Trevor had just arrived at the cottage when Hal called from the garage.

"Just scared the shit out of three teenagers that decided to visit the firehouse this evening."

"Teenagers?"

"Yeah. Pretty sure they're teenagers. And they had a key. I watched them sneak across the back of the lot, unlock the door. I snuck over, managed to get inside without them hearing me. One of the boys bragged that he had permission to be there."

"Not from me, he doesn't. My foreman called me to say some of the tools were missing. I'm planning to change the locks tomorrow."

"I couldn't tell, it was dark, but I'm pretty sure these might be the three boys I see walking along Main Street most afternoons. Usually around three thirty. Almost like clockwork now that I think about it. They're also the ones I was telling you about before. Even bragged about doing the graffiti."

"Thanks. I'll have to check them out. Maybe we could use some gofers on the job."

~~~~

Trevor waited in his truck the following afternoon. Just as Hal predicted, he saw three boys ambling along the street. Two were Caucasian, one with blonde hair, the other red hair. The third was a mixed race with black hair. All three were tall and stocky. Probably played football, he decided.

He got out of his truck, walked over to a telephone pole, stapled the flyer to the pole. Made it a point to turn away just as the boys approached.

"Hey, mister," he heard one of the boys call out.

Trevor smiled but kept walking. He didn't want to be too obvious.

"Mister," he heard two voices speak louder.

Trevor turned, watched the three boys approach. "Yeah?"

The red head had the flyer in his hand. "Are you looking for help?"

Trevor nodded. "Trying to finish up a project, need some help in the afternoons. You interested?"

"Well, yeah. What kind of help do you need?"

"Odd jobs. Cleaning around the project, putting tools away, organizing things for the next day."

"How many are you looking for?"

"Two, maybe three." He made it a point to look at each boy as if considering them for the job. "You interested?"

"Yeah," all three boys said in unison.

"Good," Trevor turned, walked to his truck. "Meet me at the firehouse."

He watched them as he started the engine, saw they were huddled together, whispering. Figured they'd show up at the job site or be suspicious and stay away. Either way, he had a description and would be talking to Duane Peterson.

Ten minutes after he returned to the job, the boys ambled through the front entrance.

"Play along," Trevor told his foreman. "I'll explain later."

"So," he reached for his clipboard, "let's get some names." The blonde identified himself as Josh, the red head, Norman and the third, Clay. "How old are you?"

"Seventeen," all three spoke in unison.

"Why aren't you boys working after school? Or playing sports?"

"We played football," Josh explained. "Not interested in baseball."

"And there aren't too many jobs around here," Clay added.

"What year are you in school?"

"Juniors," Norman answered. "Gonna be seniors next year."

"What about your parents? Will they have any problems with you working here in the afternoons?"

All three nodded.

Trevor handed each a form. "I need you to fill these out, have your parents sign off. We'll check into work permits." He turned to his foreman. "This is Aaron. He's going to take you around the site, explain what we're doing. Bring these papers back tomorrow, I'll have a list of things you can start on."

"So, what is this all about?" Aaron asked twenty minutes later. "We don't need any more help."

"We need these boys. They were here on the site last night. One of them had a key to get in. I have reason to believe they may have done the graffiti. Possibly stole the tools too. I'm going to inform Duane Peterson and we'll just keep an eye on them."

~~~~~

He noticed the movement out of the corner of his eye and jumped up when he saw Josh and his friends leaving the firehouse.

What was Josh doing there? Being his usual nosey self? He was always getting into trouble. That's why he had counted on him doing a good job with the graffiti.

But what was he up to now? He couldn't afford to have them on the site. Drawing attention to themselves, confessing to doing the graffiti. Working for that contractor. One thing could lead to another and before long they would know.

Nothing had been said about the missing tools.

Each day he watched them haul stuff out of the building. He'd walked by the back yesterday and there was still a mess there. The pile of scrap materials was growing. Maybe they won't clear the back.

Maybe they won't find out.

CHAPTER FIFTEEN

Trevor watched the teens work. They had been on the job two days now and already he was seeing an improvement in the site. They didn't argue about whatever he had them do. Guessed they were just glad to have something to do. Earning some spending money.

Josh seemed to be the ringleader, so Trevor made it a point to connect with him every day.

"Short work week," he handed each of the boys an envelope, "but here's your first paychecks. What're you planning to do with your hard-earned cash?"

"Going to the arcade later," Josh answered.

"I didn't know they had an arcade in Edmondsville."

"Yeah, in the community center. Not a big one but a bunch of us like to meet there every Friday evening."

"I'd have thought you'd have a hot date."

Josh grinned as he reached for the power tool. "Girlfriend's going out of town with her parents. Me and Clay and Norman are grabbing a pizza then going to the arcade."

"Good that you'll be off the streets. Not getting into trouble like whoever did all the graffiti in here a few weeks ago."

Trevor watched the boy tuck his head. Knew he'd hit home.

"Hey," Josh reached for the power driver. "All your tools have this TAG label on them. What company is that? Never heard of it."

"Trevor Alexander Graystone." Trevor smiled when Josh gave him a puzzled look.

"You have a power tool company too?"

"No. It's my logo. I put it on all my tools so whenever they get stolen, it makes it easier to track them."

Josh looked surprised. "You, you have a tracker on your tools?"

"No. But it has helped to identify my tools whenever they've been stolen. And pawned."

"Sweet." Josh praised.

~~~~~

"Okay, so what's the plan?" Brina asked two hours later. "Has what's-his-name agreed to come?"

Brina, Rafe, Ginny, Cliff, Marcie, Randi and Trevor were relaxing on the patio at Spicer Meadows toasting the beginning of the weekend with wine. The only one missing was Pete, Cliff's friend from California who was due to arrive anytime.

"Yes. Miriam finally called this afternoon," Randi answered. "She was all apologetic; said Tim had been at committee meetings all day. Wouldn't surprise me if he deliberately waited to tell her. He always liked to feel important, used his office to inconvenience people whenever he could."

"What can we do?" Ginny asked.

"You're doing me a huge favor by letting us have it here. I've already planned the menu and if everyone can just be here as moral support, I'd appreciate it. Tim and Miriam should be here around one, I figured we could eat at three. That way, they can leave, get back to Maryland before dark."

"What about Harriet Young?" Trevor asked.

"Oh, she said she could come as well."

Ginny smiled. "I know you don't like having to struggle with all this custody thing, but I think you have a good champion in your corner. Harriet has been more than fair in other instances and prefers to try and fix things peacefully. At least she has in all the cases I've been involved in."

"I'd prefer not having to deal with this problem at all. I just can't understand why Tim is suddenly interested in joint custody of the boys."

Trevor decided not to share his suspicions or what Susan had told him.

"What about Brad?" Marcie asked. "He'd be another body on your side."

"Oh, I forgot Brad. And yes, it might be good for him to observe Tim. See what I've had to deal with."

"And Stacy?" Marcie added. "She came to the wine tasting the other night. All she talked about was how Brad is so different from his father."

Marcie turned to Trevor. "Brad's father is a semi-retired private investigator. Stacy worked for him in Richmond until he decided to close the office. Alex suggested she work out of Brad's office. That way she can help him when he needed her and help Brad as well."

Brina laughed. "Yeah, Brad wasn't too excited about it at first, but I think Stacy's mellowed him a little. She complained about how they've had more than one round whenever she's tried to help him organize and straighten his desk. Called him a pack rat. Said he's always telling her she doesn't need to be such a neat freak."

Ginny sighed. "I just think it's nice that Brad has someone in his life. You know, he hasn't been serious about anyone since Deborah."

She looked at Trevor. "Brina, Marcie and I used to pal around with Brad and Deborah. Her parents were killed when she was young, and she lived with her aunt and uncle. Claude used to talk about how she felt sorry for Deborah and at one point I think she considered adopting her. Like she did Brina and me. But the uncle would never allow it."

"What about the aunt?" Trevor asked. "Didn't she care?"

"I think she did," Brina said, "but Tom was like Tim. Very controlling. For some reason, he kept a tight rein on Deborah. Claude never liked him; always said it was probably because he couldn't control their wild child. She always made it a point to invite Deborah to our sleepovers and parties when we were young but never included Myra."

"He sounds like a nice fellow," Trevor grumbled.

"Oh, we forgot to tell you. The uncle, Tom Marshall, is on the Town Council." Brina said. "He's the one that tried to railroad the project in the beginning."

"And the daughter," Cliff added, "That's Myra White. Another one that tried to derail the project. She tried to smear Brina's reputation at the last public hearing. Then, the next day, Joe Grimes gave us an earful about Myra's childhood."

Marcie snickered. "I never liked her and wish we'd told the town what Brad's Dad had been able to confirm."

"Back to Deborah," Ginny interrupted. "She went to the community college on a scholarship but when it ran out, Tom and Claire refused to help her finish. Claude said she offered to help but Deborah didn't want to impose. She wanted to do it on her own. Wanted to prove to her uncle that she'd do it without his help. She quit school and worked in the library. About that time, we noticed that Brad was spending more alone time with Deborah."

"She was so happy," Brina sighed. "Talked about how Brad was trying to get her to go back to school. We had bets on when he'd pop the question." Brina exchanged looks with Ginny and Marcie. "We thought he'd do it at the Holly Ball, but Deborah disappeared that night. She just vanished in thin air. Nobody has seen her since."

Trevor's mouth dropped open. "She just disappeared. No one tried to find her?"

"Yes. Everyone. The Sheriff, the town, everybody. But it's like she just vanished," Brina explained.

Everyone was silent, reflecting a moment on the young girl who had such high hopes for a future but disappeared instead.

"Does Brad ever talk about her?" Randi asked.

Ginny nodded her head. "He just clammed right up. Went into seclusion for a while. He was supposed to start law school that spring but waited till the fall. Then he went away to school, and we didn't see him for a few years. He came back when he passed the bar, but he wasn't the same."

"I had no idea," Randi sobbed. She reached for her phone. "We've got to do something. How about if I text Brad and Stacy both now. Do we want them to know we're match-making?"

"If it was me, I'd want to know." Cliff said. "At least let him be prepared."

Scott and Sandy raced through the patio just as Randi finished talking with Brad, told him she would be calling Stacy to come as well.

"Dudes," Trevor exclaimed. "How about you two riding home with me and I'll help your mom get you ready for your beauty sleep."

"We don't need no beauty sleep," Scott joked. "That's for girls. And sissies."

"Maybe, but you need to rest up. You've got a busy day tomorrow."

"What?" Sandy asked.

"Your father is coming to visit. Remember?" Randi said.

Trevor smiled. "Yeah, you need to rest up so you can wrestle with your dad."

Randi smiled at the group when Trevor grabbed the boys like sacks of potatoes, headed for his truck. "Somehow I cannot imagine Delegate Tim Cavanaugh on the floor wrestling with his sons."

~~~~~

"So," Trevor pulled her into his arms when she joined him in the den, "the boys are in bed. It's just you and me." He hugged her close. "Have you decided about Atlanta?"

Randi looked up at him. She knew he was anxious to know.

"Well, I talked to Ginny. She said she and Cliff would love to keep the boys. And I'll agree to go if we leave Saturday morning, get back by Monday evening."

Trevor smiled. "I'll take any free time I can get. We'll be busy though. So, you don't have to worry about me seducing you the entire time." He kissed the tip of her nose. "Just part of the time."

Randi linked her arms behind his neck, beamed up at him.

"Trevor, thank you for being so patient. This is all so new to me. I've never had a man in my life since Tim."

Trevor cocked an eyebrow, squinted down at her. "As far as I'm concerned, Tim doesn't qualify."

"He wasn't like that at first. Maybe some of it is my fault."

Trevor cupped her face between his hands, stared hard into her eyes. "None of what happened is your fault and I refuse to let you believe that. For all you know, he may have been that way before you met him. You just didn't find out until it was too late."

Randi covered his wrists with her hands. "I know. But it happened. And he gave me two wonderful little boys."

"That's the only thing he gave you and he doesn't even deserve them. Wish I knew why he's suddenly interested in them."

"Don't know and don't care. I'm just grateful that I have you in my life now and that the boys are crazy about you." She stood on her toes to touch his lips with hers. The kiss deepened and Randi realized Trevor was slowly, carefully backing her down the hall.

"Trevor," she murmured against his lips.

"Hmm?" He answered while he turned her into her bedroom.

She giggled. "What are you doing?"

"Seducing you."

He pushed her onto the bed, then followed to land on top of her.

Randi had a moment of trepidation. The boys were across the hall. What if one of them should awaken and find them? She knew the boys liked Trevor but what would they think if they found him in her bed?

The concerns quickly dissipated as Trevor continued to kiss her, his weight moving suggestively above her. This man is too potent, she thought to herself.

Trevor himself couldn't seem to get enough of her. He grazed her cheeks, moved on to her small, pointed chin, down to her neck where he inhaled traces of her perfume. Searched for those secret erotic places he had discovered the first time he'd made love to her. He felt her squirm beneath him and raised his head to be sure she wasn't having second thoughts.

"You okay with this?"

Randi kept her eyes locked with his as she unbuttoned the top buttons of his shirt, nudged the material aside to explore his neck, trailed her feet up his pants legs.

"You realize we have a few too many clothes on," he teased.

Randi smiled as she tugged his shirt from his jeans, slid her hands inside to squeeze his cute butt. Suddenly they were both wiggling out of their clothes.

Trevor caught a whiff of the roses; spied them on her dresser and smiled.

"You know, red roses are supposed to mean love but those orangey, peach roses caught my eye." He lay on his side next to her, skimmed his fingers from her neck, between her breasts, down to her flat stomach. "I googled it to see what that color meant. Said they express fascination. I remember thinking they are perfect for you."

Randi moaned when his fingers went lower.

"You definitely captivate me." He moved over her. "Bewitch me." He grazed her cheek and neck. "Arouse me." He slowly slid inside her.

~~~~~

Trevor didn't stay long. Knew she worried about what the boys would think if he stayed overnight. Said he'd see her bright and early the next morning. Would help with the get-together wherever he could.

He decided to drive by the firehouse on his way back to the cottage. It was late and most of the houses on the way into town were dark. He approached the center of town and found empty sidewalks. Store windows were dark, streetlights dimly lit Main Street. Side streets were also lit and with all that had been going on at the firehouse, he appreciated that the town had replaced the light near the firehouse. It lit the front of the building, the light at the garage behind the firehouse offered semi-lighting of the back.

He approached the site and thought he saw a shadow. Looked again but saw only a bush. He turned at the corner, drove past the garage, decided to swing around the block to be sure no one was lurking in the shadows.

All looked okay when he drove by a second time, but figured he'd check with Hal in the morning.

~~~~~

He stepped out of the shadows when Trevor drove by. Annoyed that he had reacted so rashly, worried about being caught on the street. There was no law against anyone walking after dark.

He'd just reached the back of the firehouse when he heard Trevor's truck then saw the approaching headlights. Had just enough time to duck behind the bush. He decided to stay where he was and smirked when he saw Trevor drive by a second time.

When he was sure the coast was clear, he stepped out, headed for the back door. He'd just check to see how much had been done. See if there was anything he could do to hamper their progress.

He aimed his key for the doorknob, but it wouldn't fit. Reached for his flashlight to be sure he was aligning it correctly, and it still wouldn't fit. Anger roared through him. They had apparently changed the locks he fumed.

He looked at the back window, saw they had replaced it with a sturdier one. One that wouldn't be as easy to break without making a lot of noise.

He couldn't ask Josh to do anything without making him suspicious.

He aimed the flashlight across the back of the lot. Saw the shadow of the scrap pile, could see that it had grown.

They were obviously making progress inside.

CHAPTER SIXTEEN

"When you finish checking the bastard out, you can hand me the salt and pepper," Cliff stated. He'd been watching Trevor watch Randi's ex-husband for ten minutes. Ready and waiting for something to happen.

Trevor grinned. No sense arguing. He was pretty sure everyone there was on pins and needles. Waiting for the other shoe to fall. He took a swig of beer.

"I'm sure Randi appreciates you and Ginny agreeing to this."

Cliff shrugged as he flipped the steaks. "Randi's done all the work. Said it was a celebration of our news as well. Wouldn't let anyone to do anything. Only allowed Marcie to provide the wine."

Trevor felt like he was watching a play. It was a cool Saturday afternoon. The sun was bright, blue skies dotted with what looked like white puffy cotton balls. The sun's rays shimmered off the pool. It was a little cool for swimming, but Cliff had started preparing the pool for the summer.

Beneath it all, tension simmered.

Randi was nervous. Running herself ragged. Dressed in a jean skirt and apricot colored tunic top, she'd probably been up since the crack of dawn. The boys bragged about how they had helped her make brownies. He'd make it a point to be sure she had a large glass of wine when the evening was over.

He knew Marcie was fuming. She was dressed in jeans and a black tee shirt with *Wine Diva*, sequined across the front. She might be flirting with Pete, the guy from California but she never kept Tim out of her sight.

Brad was quiet. Considering all Randi had told him about her marriage, Trevor was sure the lawyer was trying to put things in perspective to better prepare his case. He kept an eagle eye on Tim and the boys.

Brina and Rafe had just arrived, full of apologies but he was sure he knew why the newlyweds were late. He wouldn't mind another one on one with Randi.

Ginny, Miriam Cavanaugh and Harriet Young chatted while setting the table. Ginny was her usual quiet self; Miriam was nervous being overly friendly while keeping an eye on Tim; Harriet just observed.

Pete seemed to be the only one that was enjoying himself. Cliff had told him that Pete owned a winery in California but hadn't told Marcie yet. He enjoyed teasing and arguing with her when they discussed her wine ideas. Maybe Pete did sense Marcie's fury, Trevor decided, as he seemed to be going out of his way to keep her distracted.

Tim just sat in his chair while Scott and Sandy talked non-stop, trying to engage with the father they never knew. He wore khakis, a navy polo shirt, expensive watch and loafers. Looked thoroughly bored.

Trevor recalled his conversation with Susan and watched Tim's every move. Noticed the man's hands sometimes shook, wondered if it was nerves or if he needed a shot of bourbon. He acted like the bored, irritated teenager assigned to baby-sitting.

Trevor tried not to laugh as he watched Tim get a dose of fatherhood.

He also worried what the boys' lives would be like if Tim got custody. What little he'd heard so far, Tim's answers were curt, single-syllable and non-interested.

Trevor grinned when Cliff cleared his throat. "Is it that obvious?"

Cliff laughed. "You've hardly taken your eyes off Randi since Tim and Miriam arrived."

"She's running herself ragged," Trevor defended himself. "And for what? The prick doesn't deserve any of this. Look at him, he sits there, no expression, no conversation; it's plainly obvious he'd much rather be somewhere else. The boys try to talk to him, he answers in monosyllables."

Trevor paused, came to attention when he saw Tim ball his hand into a fist.

He and Cliff watched Tim snatch his sunglasses from Sandy who had innocently picked them up to try them on. Sandy immediately had a hurt look on his face.

Trevor locked eyes with Brad who shook his head.

"Why don't you go relieve the jerk," Cliff suggested.

"Not a bad idea," Trevor responded. "What better way to earn extra points since Harriet just observed it too."

Trevor exchanged looks with Rafe, reached for the soccer ball and kicked it out into the yard. "Dudes, why don't you show me some of what you've learned at soccer."

"Yeah," both boys hollered.

"Coach says we just have to keep our hands off the ball," Scott explained as he kicked the ball to his brother.

An expert with playing against his nieces and nephews, Rafe joined them and before long it was the big guys versus the little guys.

Harriet sat in the chair next to Tim. "Hope you're enjoying your time getting to know your boys."

Tim nodded, then frowned when Miriam joined them.

"Aren't they so cute?" Miriam crooned. "Can't wait to have them come visit us in Maryland."

"Do you have any plans?" Harriet asked.

"Plans?" Tim asked.

Harriet smiled. "Yes. Like going to the movies? Eating ice cream. You know they like anything that has to do with action figures."

"Miriam can arrange all that," he shrugged a shoulder. "I'll be busy with meetings."

Harriet turned to Miriam. "Summer's coming. Maybe by then the boys will be familiar enough with you, they can spend a few days with you."

Miriam beamed. "That would be wonderful."

"Might be better to do weekend visits for a while," Tim stated.

~~~~~

Trevor grabbed the beans, followed Randi inside when she started clearing the table. He set the bowl on the kitchen counter, grabbed her before she could return outside.

"Trevor," she sighed, started to push him away.

"Wait up. Take a minute. Breathe. It's almost over. You're doing great."

Randi looked up at him, sighed again and rested her forehead on his shoulder. "This has been so hard. Miriam's all excitement, Tim's all gloom and doom. Harriet is observing, the boys are full of it. Not sure how much more I can take."

"You're doing fine." He rubbed his hands up and down her back. "Food was good, boys are behaving, everyone, except Tim seems to be happy." He hugged her closer. "If Tim wants to be an ass, let him. Just remember we'll have next weekend in Atlanta."

"Shush, I haven't had a chance to tell the boys yet." She lifted her head, smiled up at him. "Ginny's excited though. Making all sorts of plans. Wants to take them to the Children's Museum."

Trevor smiled, kissed the tip of her nose. "While Mom is busy in Atlanta working."

They both turned when Tim stepped into the kitchen and glared at them. Randi started to pull away but Trevor hugged her closer and smiled.

"Just thanking the little chef," he kissed her lips.

"Doubt that Cliff will appreciate that comment." Tim sneered.

"Doubt Cliff will appreciate what?" Cliff asked, following Tim into the kitchen. "All I did was flip the steaks. Good job, Randi," he congratulated her as he set the cooking tongs in the sink, gave her a kiss on the cheek.

"Yeah, Mom," Scott and Sandy carried the left-over napkins and eating utensils to the table. Since Trevor was still holding their mother, they each gave them both a hug around their waists before racing back outside.

"Guess Miriam and I need to be heading out," Tim announced when Ginny and Miriam strolled in with more leftovers.

"Oh, that's a shame," Ginny commented. "I had thought we could take a ride around the place. Visit Lariat's grave. See some of the beautiful countryside."

Tim frowned. "Lariat?"

Ginny stared at him, a shocked expression on her face. "Yes. You know, the triple crown contender about fifteen years back? Spicer

Meadows is where he was born. Claude Spicer trained and groomed him here." She smiled. "He was such a beautiful horse."

"Oh, I think that would be lovely," Miriam gushed, then backed away when Tim gave her a scouring look. "Oh, I'm sorry. I just thought you would like to spend more time with the boys."

"I also have an early committee meeting in the morning." He extended his soft hand to Ginny. "Thank you for a delicious meal but we'll have to pass this time."

~~~~~

"Can you believe the nerve of the man," Brina exclaimed as Tim drove down the driveway. "Such an asshole. Can't give Randi credit for anything." She cringed when she turned and saw Harriet. "Sorry. But it's true."

"Well, I'm certainly not going to pass up a chance to ride the territory." Marcie announced. She looked at Pete. "How about you handsome? Are you up to riding the horses? Ready to check out the competition?"

Marcie smiled when everyone was silent.

"Oh, come on, I'm not stupid." She pinned Pete with her eyes. "I googled you the second time you visited. Peter Evans, owner of *Hideaway Winery*. Why do you think I've baited you so much?"

She turned, headed for the stables.

Pete grinned. "Woman after my heart," he sprinted after her.

"Can we ride?" Sandy called out to Marcie.

Marcie turned, looked at Randi. "Only if it's okay with your mother. You can ride with me, Scott can ride with Pete."

Both boys raced to their mother's side. "Mom, pleeeeezze?"

"You have to sit very still," Randi ordered when everyone followed Marcie and Pete to the stables.

As soon as Scott and Sandy were seated on the horses with Marcie and Pete, Cliff, Ginny, Brina and Rafe loaded up into Cliff's jeep. Brad and Stacy said they'd follow in Brad's vehicle.

"Harriet?" Randi asked. "Would you like to join us? I'll be glad to drive the Escalade if you'd like."

"No, no," Harriet waved her hands. "I really need to be going anyway. My daughter is having a surprise birthday party for my grandson this evening and I promised I would help her with the decorations. Probably should have been there thirty minutes ago."

She didn't add that she'd almost left earlier but was glad she stayed and witnessed Tim's performance in the kitchen.

Harriet took Randi's hand and smiled. "I want to thank you for a wonderful time. It's obvious you put a lot of thought into this, and I appreciate your hard work."

"Thank you. Ah, before you go, I need to tell you that I will be out of town next weekend. I need to go to Georgia. With Trevor. To bid on a project in Atlanta. But Ginny will be taking care of the boys," she quickly added.

"I don't want you to think you have to give up your life just because Tim is seeking joint custody. If he and the boys were more familiar with each other, I'd suggest that they might spend the weekend with him but after what I observed today, he is nowhere near ready to be their father." She looked at Trevor. "I'm sure this job will be an important one and I encourage you to get back to a normal life. You need to earn your living as well."

"Thank you," Randi said. "You don't know how much better that makes me feel."

Harriet gave Randi a hug and smiled. "I don't think you have anything to worry about."

~~~~

"**D**id you see the way Tim treated Miriam while they were here?" Randi asked Trevor as they headed out in his truck to catch up with everyone. "I mean, she's so timid. Almost afraid to be with him but scared to be away from him too."

"Did he always talk down to you like he did her?"

"Not at first. Only after he got elected and our marriage had started going downhill."

By now, they had caught up with the rest of them at the family cemetery. Ginny bent to weed around Claude and Alexander's graves.

She glanced up when Randi and Trevor stepped through the gate.

"You haven't been introduced to the members of Spicer Meadows' family, have you?" Ginny called to Trevor.

"Claude and I traced the genealogy of the family, discovered there were lots of girls and only one surviving son for each generation. We also wondered if the family had been cursed as the mothers died in childbirth after giving birth to the sons."

Ginny stepped to the far side of the cemetery. "Almost all the Spicer men were active in the military and the community. This is Gerald Spicer. He immigrated to Virginia from Ireland at the age of eighteen, built the two-story log cabin over there in the woods. He planted tobacco and became established in the church.

"His son, Gerald the second continued to develop the farm and served in the House of Burgesses. Gerald's son, Clifton, fought in the French and Indian war, then built the Manor house when he returned home."

Ginny moved to the next row of tombstones. "This is Clifton's son, Clifton the second who worked the farm but also trained horses. That's how the family got into the horse business.

"His son, Clifton Gerald trained in the military and served as a Confederate officer in the Civil War. He also had to rebuild the manor house after the war when the Union soldiers almost destroyed it.

"Clifton Gerald the second was Claude's father. He was a strange man. You'll notice he has the biggest marker, and his two wives are buried on either side of him. He had one son – Clifton Gerald the third – then another son Alexander and four daughters, Claude being one of the daughters.

"Claude's father bragged that he had somehow escaped the curse until his oldest son was killed aboard the Lusitania in nineteen fifteen. There is a second Clifton Gerald who is buried next to his second wife. He was born in nineteen thirty-seven and named Clifton Gerald the third in honor of his firstborn.

"There were no more Spicer males in the family until my Cliff was born thirty-two years ago."

Ginny pointed to Claude's headstone. "This is Claudette Spicer. She was Clifton Gerald the second's oldest daughter after Alexander. For the longest time, everyone thought Claude was Cliff's great aunt, but we learned last year that she is really his grandmother. You see, she fell in love with Quentin O'Malley before World War II. It's a long story but Quentin went off to war and was injured. Claude had Cliff's father the same day her stepmother had another girl. Claude's father was so distraught, he made Claude give up her baby, claimed him as his son Clifton Gerald the third."

Trevor shook his head. "Quite a story." He looked at Cliff. "I'm sure it was a shock."

"Yes," Cliff sighed heavily, "at first but it also explained why Claude made herself so much a part of my life." He looked at Ginny. "I used to come here in the summers, worried the hell out of Ginny. When I had to return to settle Claude's estate, things started unraveling. Claude stipulated that we both administer her estate and marry within a year of her death. Claude became foster parent to Ginny and Brina late in life; I think she always knew I was in love with Ginny."

"And this baby?" Trevor nodded at Ginny's stomach.

"Will not be Clifton Gerald the fifth," Cliff quickly answered. "We're still working on that."

Ginny took Scott and Sandy up the hill to visit Lariat's grave. The triple crown contender had put Edmondsville on the map and was like the mascot for the town. Streets were named after him.

Trevor knew they planned to name the firehouse complex *Lariat Square* once it was finished.

"Trevor, if you don't mind, I'd appreciate it if you could look at the original home-site." Marcie pointed to a cabin tucked just inside some trees at the far end of the field.

"I know it's a long way off the main road, but the soil is good back here. I think Pete even agrees with me on that. In addition to planting grapes in these back fields, I'm hoping Cliff and Ginny will let me do some renovations to the original home site, make it the tasting room."

"She doesn't want to take my word for it," Pete complained.

Marcie glared at the winemaker. "You?" She poked a finger to his chest. "The guy who couldn't be honest with me from the beginning."

"I was just having fun," Pete defended himself. "I wanted to see how determined you were. Didn't want to sway you either way."

Marcie winked at Trevor. "You might know about grapes and winemaking, but Trevor is the construction expert."

Trevor headed across the field. He'd let them catch up when they stopped arguing.

It was a small lot with trees that had apparently grown up when they moved to the bigger manor house. He looked back at the cemetery.

Knew in the old days, family cemeteries were located off in a distance so family could visit with ancestors whenever the mood struck.

Trevor decided it would add a little charm to the exterior. Especially if they spruced up Lariat's grave up on the hill. The horse could be part of the purpose of the winery.

Marcie and Pete joined him as he stepped towards the cabin.

"I know it needs a lot of work," Marcie said, "but I'm hoping you'll think it is worth it."

"Yes," Trevor agreed, "but nothing a little upgrading and renovating can't take care of." He stepped inside, studied the exposed ceiling joists. "Considering the age, everything looks pretty solid."

"There are only two rooms. And they're both small. But I was wondering if it would be possible to take part of the interior wall out and make it one large tasting room."

Trevor checked both sides of the wall. "No reason why it can't. Not like you'll have a second floor. And any needed support for the roof can be provided with columns." He looked up. "The exposed beams will give it a little more character."

Marcie hid her pleasure behind the hands that covered her mouth. Her eyes sparkled as she stared from Trevor to Pete and back to Trevor. "Are you sure?"

"It's doable, yes," Trevor assured her. "Clear the front for a parking lot."

"Add onto the back, make it the operations center for the winery." Pete added. "Maybe even replace part of the back wall with glass so customers can see the winemaking in action."

Tears glistened in Marcie's eyes. "You don't know how happy this makes me. A winery and tasting room here; new wine shop in town. I can't wait."

CHAPTER SEVENTEEN

R andi was busy preparing an invoice when her phone rang. Caller ID registered a number she hadn't seen in a long, long while. She wondered what Tim's next bombshell would be and was surprised to hear Miriam's voice.

"I wanted to thank you for the wonderful visit the other day. Your boys are just adorable. I enjoyed watching them play soccer with Trevor and the other gentleman. I'm sorry, I'm not good with remembering names. Tim is always fussing at me about that."

Randi chuckled. "That's okay. That was Rafe. He has ten nieces and nephews, so he's used to playing with the boys. I think he also coached some a few years ago. This was before he met Brina."

"I'm sorry we couldn't stay for the tour of Spicer Meadows. I would have liked that. I'm sure it is very beautiful."

"Maybe another time. I'm glad you were able to make the trip to visit with us." Randi didn't add she was just as glad it was over. "The boys haven't stopped talking about you two," she lied.

Miriam laughed. "You know, I don't get out as much anymore. All those tests and treatments tired me so much. Being depressed didn't help much either. I've also been having headaches," she paused, "I don't mean to bore you with my problems. I just wanted to thank you for a nice visit."

"Maybe now that the tests are over, you can enjoy life again," Randi encouraged Miriam. "You and Tim can start making plans. Go out more."

"Oh, he still goes out. Almost every night he has a meeting or function he needs to attend."

"And he doesn't ask you to go with him?"

"Oh, no. He says I would be bored to tears. And after all the testing, disappointments, he said I should take my time, stay at home more."

Randi was concerned. When she was married to him, he always nagged her to go out with him. He stopped when she got pregnant. She wondered if Tim was drinking again.

"Miriam, is Tim okay when he gets home from these meetings? He used to drink a little too much but said he had quit. He hasn't started again, has he?"

"Well, most of the time when he gets home, I'm already in bed. Although he did say that these meetings and events are often boring; he sometimes needs a drink to get through them."

"But you've never been around him when he comes home? When he drinks?"

"No. Randi, you have me worried. If you don't mind my asking, why did you and Tim divorce? Was his drinking a part of it?"

How much should she tell Miriam, Randi wondered? "I, uh, I guess you could say we drifted apart. He spent most of his time away in meetings and when I fell,"

Randi heard Miriam gasp. "You fell?"

"Yes. I was pregnant with the boys at the time. Spent over a month in the hospital. Like I said, I guess we just drifted apart." How do you tell a man's wife that he abused his first wife?

"I'm so sorry. I'm glad it didn't affect your pregnancy. You know, Tim wants to run for governor and realizes he needs to improve his relationship with your boys. That's why he has taken such an interest in them; wants to share custody."

"Miriam, I can't deny Tim that right, but I also need to think about my boys. They are very important to me. I'm sure they would love to get to know their father better. Let's hope we have a smooth transition and the two of you can have them for extended amounts of time."

"Yes. Me too. And I hope we can keep in touch."

"You're welcome to call me anytime. I see you're using the land line but if you text me your cell number, I will be happy to add you to my contacts."

"Oh, I let Tim talk me out of keeping my cell phone after we got married. Said I would get all sorts of phishing calls by being married to him. Did you have that problem? Did you have a cell phone?"

"Yes. I did then, and still do. I need it for my business."

Randi was concerned that Tim might be isolating Miriam for some reason.

"Miriam, I don't want to intrude on your marriage with Tim, but would you do something for me? Would you please consider getting a cell phone? It can be a disposable one. Now that you are getting more active, I think you'll enjoy having it again. You can call your friends, meet them. Plus, you never know when you might need one for an emergency. You don't even have to tell Tim if you don't want, that's up to you. But I really hope you will get one. And when you do, you are more than welcome to call me. Anytime. We don't have to tell Tim about any of this."

"That is so sweet of you, Randi. I will certainly think about it. And if I do, you will be my first call. Thank you."

~~~~~

Randi stopped by the wine shop before she had to pick up the boys from school. Marcie had just restocked the shelves and was ready for a break. Suggested they relax in the tasting room.

Randi always enjoyed being in the tasting room. Marcie worked hard to give it the homey feeling. The bar was large enough that small groups could stand around it while they sampled her wines. Pictures of vineyards hung on the walls behind and on either side of the bar, so you felt like you were in the middle of wine country. A wine barrel with artificial grapes draped over the top stood in a corner. Next to the barrel was a small electric heater that always gave her the warm cozy feeling. Regardless of weather, Marcie always had the flames reflecting.

Marcie had offered her a sample of a pinot grigio label she was thinking about adding to her selection of wines.

Randi appreciated the hints of apple in the wine. "Did you watch Miriam much this weekend?"

"Not really, I watched the snake more. The boys were all over him trying to play and it was obvious he wanted to be somewhere else."

The corner of Randi's mouth quirked up. "You noticed it too? That's why Trevor distracted them with the soccer ball."

"Tim's such a prick; I don't see what you saw in him," Marcie held her glass to the light, studied the pale straw color. "But Miriam seems nice enough. Why are you asking?"

"She just called me. To thank me for the invitation this weekend. And the more we talked, the more I worry about her. Marcie, she doesn't have a cell phone. She let Tim talk her out of it. I mean, who doesn't have a cell phone these days? He's isolated her from her friends; I'm worried she might be having the same spousal abuse problems."

"Well, now that you mention it, I did notice her flinch a couple times. Remember when she asked Sandy what kind of ice cream he liked. Tim glared at her, and she flinched like she was worried she said the wrong thing. What kid doesn't like ice cream?" She added another sample of wine to their glasses. "Now that I think about it, Ginny said she saw him grab Miriam's wrist, squeezed it. Do you really think he might be abusing Miriam?"

"I'm not sure. Apparently, she's not around him when he's drinking because he doesn't take her to his social events. She said she's usually in bed when he gets home, so she's not exposed to his temper. But it could be a matter of time before something triggers him. I worry for her, and for Scott and Sandy. I don't want them hurt."

"Maybe she's aware but doesn't want to admit it."

"Well, she did ask why we divorced, and I had to tell her. Nothing specific, only that we drifted apart. And then I ended up telling her about falling down the stairs."

"What did she say?"

"She was shocked. Sorry it happened. Glad the boys weren't hurt. Tim apparently hasn't told her. That's when I suggested she get a cell phone. Hinted she didn't even have to tell Tim about it."

"Do you think she'll get one?"

Randi shrugged a shoulder. "Have no idea. But I hope so. Maybe I'll ask Harriet how her interview with them went. She may have picked up on things."

"Good idea," Marcie agreed as she screwed the top on the wine, stored it in the wine chiller next to the bar. "Now," she rested her elbows on the counter, gave Randi a smug smile. "I'm more interested in your plans for your up-coming weekend with Trevor?"

Randi shook her head. "It'll be a working weekend, remember."

"Doesn't mean you won't be able to enjoy each another. I believe I noticed you two have already enjoyed each other."

Randi felt warmth on her cheeks. Marcie knew of her plans to seduce Trevor; just wasn't aware she'd accomplished her mission.

"We're staying with his sister. Can't do too much when other people are around."

"Really?" Marcie's eyebrows shot up. "Huh. I could have sworn I overheard Trevor tell Pete his sister was going to be in France with her husband for the next two weeks."

~~~~~

"So, is your sister excited that we're coming to visit this weekend?" Randi asked later that afternoon.

The boys had asked to stop by the firehouse on their way home from school and were helping Josh and Clay put tools away.

Trevor frowned. "Who said Susan was going to be there?"

"You did. Didn't you?" She lowered her voice. "You said your sister had a house there."

"Yes, but I didn't say she would be there."

"Trevor, I know you said she would be there. I'm self-conscious as it is going away with you but now to learn that Susan won't be there, I'm worried. I don't want people getting the wrong idea and I'm not sure I want to just take over someone's house while they're away."

"We won't be taking over. We'll be working, remember. Besides, she has a pool and I've missed my evening laps." He leaned closer to her ear. "It'll give me another chance to see you in your bikini."

Trevor let out a breath when Randi punched his hard stomach.

"You've never seen me in my bathing suit."

"Oh, but I have." He gave her a half-smile, his eyebrows waggled. "Remember when your father invited me to dinner that first night? We were talking in my office when he invited me. I saw you playing with the boys. That's when he told me you were his daughter. I'd already met you earlier, remember, and there was no way I was going to turn down a dinner with the lady in unit thirty-eight."

Once again, Randi felt her cheeks pinken.

"So, don't forget to pack your lavender bikini. Took my breath away when I saw you get out of that hot tub." He chuckled when her mouth fell open.

"Trevor," she exclaimed a little too loudly. All the boys looked their way.

Trevor smiled, spoke loud enough for everyone to hear. "All I said is you deserve a night off. I need to head back to Snowridge for a few days. Check on Max, put out a few fires there. Just thought I'd bring a pizza by before leaving."

"Yay, pizza," Scott and Sandy cheered.

~~~~~

Trevor stopped by the garage before heading back to Snowridge. It was late but he'd helped Randi put the boys to bed, snuck a few kisses after assuring her that Susan was excited about them staying at the house.

Now, he wanted to talk to Hal. Even picked up another pizza for the old man.

"Nothing exciting has been going on around the job site during the day. How about the nights?" Trevor leaned back in one of the chairs, stretched his legs out, crossed his ankles.

Hal bit into a slice of pizza, enjoyed the blend of sausage and pep-peroni. "Quiet at night too. Didn't I see you drive by the other night?"

"Yeah. Thought I saw something, but it turned out to be nothing."

"But it was something." Hal stated with a half-smile. "I saw you drive back around so I figured I'd keep an eye out. Sure enough, a few minutes after your second drive-by, a shadow stepped out of the bushes. I couldn't see who it was, but I watched him try to unlock the back door. Guess it's a good thing you changed the locks.

Hal took another bite. "Didn't get a chance to sneak up on him though. When he couldn't get in, he didn't hang around long."

Trevor let out a harsh breath. "Well, it couldn't have been one of the boys. They were there when Aaron and I changed the locks."

"No, this one was lankier. Probably older; didn't move as agilely as the kids."

"Haven't seen him since?"

Hal nodded. "Been watching, but all has been quiet the past couple days. Are you sure you want me to keep watching?"

"Yes. Unless you need to be somewhere else. We're almost finished the job and I don't want anything else to happen.

"I'm heading back to Snowridge for a few days then I need to go to Atlanta this weekend. I'll feel better knowing you're keeping an eye on things. But if anything happens, don't hesitate to call me."

CHAPTER EIGHTEEN

Randi felt like a kid on her first vacation without her parents. She already missed the boys but was excited to be getting away too. She hadn't flown much, not even with Tim so the thrill of takeoff and landing excited and unnerved her at the same time. The thought of flying five hundred miles per hour was bewildering.

She'd never been on a private jet, either. The Learjet was white and sleek with its T-tail, sharp nose and wraparound windshield. Five small windows graced each side.

It was family-owned by Trevor and his brother-in-law Chuck. "It was really Susan's idea. She uses it the most. And I'll never tell her this, but it has come in handy for Chuck and me many times."

"Gives this guy a steady income," Trevor joked as he introduced Randi to the pilot, Mark Fisher. "He's been flying exclusively for us these past five years."

"You did get a good nights' sleep, right?" Randi might have been teasing but she was serious too.

Mark was old enough to be her father, but he smiled, replied politely. "Yes, ma'am."

Trevor grinned. "Now that you're assured about our pilot's mental condition, I guess we can get started?" He reached for Randi's hand, led her up the narrow steps.

Randi was sure she had wandered into the world of luxury. She caught the aroma of the ecru upholstered leather seats with armrests, heard soft music piping throughout, stepped upon lush beige carpet, and admired the glow of the wood veneer cabinetry. She took a deep breath and smiled.

Mark followed them inside, turned to the cockpit. "Should be ready in about five minutes."

Trevor led Randi towards the first seating area. Four seats faced each other conference-style, two on each side of the aisle, a window for each. "The seats also recline."

He led her toward another area where a long leather sofa on one side faced two more seats with windows. "This area can be sectioned off if you want." He pointed to the pocket doors tucked in the dividing wall. "The sofa opens into a bed, comes in handy for long flights."

Beyond the sofa lounge area was more cabinetry in a semi-kitchen with countertop, sink, microwave, and mini fridge.

"Can't really cook a gourmet meal but many a snack has been prepared here. Also, good for popcorn while watching movies." He pointed to the flat-screen TV mounted above the seats, across from the sofa. "Don't know whether you noticed, there are smaller TVs in the conference area up front. Even cup holders."

A lavatory boasting mirrors, high gloss walnut woodwork, marble countertops and pewter hardware was at the far back.

"Trevor, this is so nice," she whispered. "I've never seen so much luxury."

"It's not cheap but it beats waiting in the lines, going through security in the airport."

"Time to buckle up," Mark's voice sounded over the intercom.

Trevor led her back to the front. "Do you need me to sit next to you? Hold your hand?"

Randi made a face at him. "I think I can handle a simple takeoff." She sat, buckled her seatbelt.

Trevor decided to sit across from her. He enjoyed watching her awe. It still amazed him that less than a month ago he didn't know this woman existed. Then she literally fell into his arms, and he'd been smitten ever since.

He recalled how his heart had almost stopped when she'd greeted him at her front door in the tight black capris and royal blue shirttail hem shirt. The capris made her legs look longer, the shirt with the cuffed sleeves and stand-up collar added a touch of crispness to the outfit. He studied the smoky blue shoes with the wooded heel and lacing on the back when she crossed her legs, turned to watch the takeoff.

"Takeoffs and landings are actually a lot smoother than the commercial planes," Trevor assured her as he buckled in. "There's also a pull-out table we can use once we're in the air."

"This just gets better and better," Randi gave him a lopsided grin.

She'd already decided it was going to be a working weekend. They'd arrive in Atlanta about ten, pick up the car Susan had left for them, then meet the realtor at eleven. Of course, it depended on traffic. She had heard that a simple five-mile trip might take an hour. They planned to walk around the old mill, take some pictures, do measurements, then spend the rest of the day and all-day Sunday working on the proposal.

Right on time, they landed in the smaller airport near Atlanta International. Randi made it a point to compliment Mark on his piloting skills.

Her day of luxury continued when Mark handed Trevor the keys to a lean, black Cadillac CTS SUV that was parked near the hanger. The interior oozed extravagance with tailored gray seats and burgundy accents as well as the Cadillac signature interior lighting.

She chuckled when Trevor clicked the remote and the car started. With two little boys, she'd decided against that option with her Escalade. But it was cool to see it work.

"It has a Wi-Fi hotspot if you need to charge your phone." Trevor mentioned as he headed towards the interstate. He keyed in the realtor's cell number; told him they would be at the site within the hour.

~~~~~

The streets leading to the mill were hundred-year-old brick. Revitalized businesses lined the narrow avenue as Randi watched shoppers walking the street, perusing the store fronts, or enjoying brunch at intimate café sites.

"This seems to be an old section of the city. I like the brick paving and the aged exteriors."

"Yeah, the brick paving continues just past the mill." Trevor pulled over in front of a large three-storied brick building with long narrow windows that seemed to stretch for to the skies.

Randi counted ten sets of windows on each side of the entrance to the foundry. She walked to a corner of the edifice and counted twelve windows with a boxed section midway between them that probably housed stairs between the three floors.

Someone had gone to the trouble to protect the integrity of the manufacturing plant by boarding up the windows on the lower level.

"Those can be removed once we start the construction," Trevor announced.

"How many buildings did you say this includes?"

"Three. This one in front and then one on each side at the back with a big court area in the middle. I figured you could put a pool or courtyard there."

"Well, I have to say the pictures don't portray the magnificence of these buildings. I can't wait to see the inside."

"Here comes the realtor now," Trevor extended his hand to a stocky, middle-aged man with wiry red hair who introduced himself as Don Murray.

"So glad you are considering doing something with this site. This used to be one of the thriving business sections of the city. The mill closed about ten years ago. City council has been hinting about having it condemned, demolished for a parking deck."

Trevor smiled. "Well, Ms. Cavanaugh and I prefer to revive and renovate. If the inside is as good as the outside, we hope to put together a proposal that will save the building."

Don pulled out a big ring of keys, located the one that had been marked for the front door. They entered a spacious, square room that could easily be converted into a lobby. Debris and broken glass scattered across the floor, graffiti on the walls.

"When they realized some transients had broken in," the realtor explained, "they boarded up the lower windows."

Don stepped away, led them into a massive open area that appeared to be the guts of the mill. Randi smelled the concrete dust of yesteryear, heard the silence of emptiness with the distant sound of traffic and a train. She looked up, appreciated the simple design of the wrought iron railing.bordering the top two floors that looked down upon the open area.

Trevor had already studied the site online, but Randi was right, the pictures didn't portray the expanse or magnificence of the building. He watched her turn in a complete circle, her eyes wide, lips parted as she stared in awe.

"Oh, Trevor," she whispered. She reached for his hand, squeezed it with excitement.

"My grandmother used to work here when the mill was in its heyday," Don commented. "She'd describe all the belts, pulleys, spindles and looms that were in this open area. Said they used to have to wear masks because of the dust and ear plugs because of the noise. I guess the upper levels were for inventory?" He wondered. "The large windows would be opened for circulation."

Don led them to the far end of the room. "There are dumb waiters, this was before elevators, so we'll have to use the stairs. There's a lot of cast iron because of the fire risk," he added as they made their way up the metal stairs.

When they reached the second level, Randi went to the railing and looked down at the main floor; then turned and leaned back some to look up at the third floor. She pulled a tape measure out of her pocketbook. "Can we take some measurements?"

She imagined adding a long wall three-quarters of the way from the outer edge, with doors to hotel rooms. The aisle would look down on the businesses below.

She walked over to the windows. Despite their grimy dirty panes, they offered a splendid view of the city.

She brushed her hand against the brick wall. "A fresh coat of paint will add so much charm to the rooms. Clean the windows, some will probably need to be replaced."

She stared at the floor. "Should do something about the concrete floors but it's doable, right?" She looked at Trevor who nodded.

Don took them on a tour of the other two buildings which were duplicates of the main building. Randi and Trevor measured sections, counted windows to determine how many rooms would be possible. Trevor also did a brief sketch of the basic layout so Randi could put together a scaled model.

They stood outside in the large open space between the buildings, studied the exterior walls for cosmetic work. Stared up at the walls of windows that loomed over them. Randi gave Trevor an appreciative grin.

"You were right. This place has so much potential. I can feel it. It's almost like those walls are trying to tell us something."

Trevor thanked the realtor, confirmed the asking price.

"Ms. Cavanaugh and I will be putting together a proposal and hope to be in touch."

Trevor suggested they walk the couple blocks to the revitalized area, have lunch in one of the sidewalk cafés. After ordering a cobb salad for Randi, Reuben sandwich for himself, they sat back to watch the world go by.

"I was serious what I said about the building. I felt as if those walls were talking to me. Pleading with me to dress them up, make them worthy of a place for people to come to live and play. Did you feel it too?"

"Didn't hear any voices or feel any vibes but I agree, it deserves a second chance. The structure is sound. There's minimal damage to the concrete floors. Certainly, nothing a little sprucing and upgrading can't take care of. You really liked it?"

"Oh yes. My mind's already envisioning ideas."

The waiter brought their bottle of wine. Trevor raised his glass to hers.

"Here's to an interesting partnership. Your ideas, my skills. *TAR Associates*. Trevor and Randi," he explained when she frowned.

Randi laughed. "Well, I think that sounds a lot better than RAT – Randi and Trevor." She tapped her glass to his. "You sure you're up to this?"

"Can't wait."

~~~~~

Randi yawned when they headed out of the city. "Whew, with two rambunctious boys, I'm not used to having so much wine in the middle of the day."

Trevor smiled as he maneuvered onto the interstate.

"This might be a working weekend but who said you can't enjoy it too? Probably take twenty minutes to get to the house. Go ahead and take a nap if you need to."

"And miss all this excitement? I've always thought Atlanta was an exciting city." She beamed at Trevor. "Thank you for inviting me along and to look at the site. Were you serious about a partnership?"

"Of course. I watched you as you walked over the property. We share a mutual passion for architecture and design, and I can see us working on this as well as other projects. You know, I'm all for preservation and I think you share the same vision. We can certainly give it a try."

Randi stared at the man sitting behind the wheel. Wondered why she hadn't met him so many years ago. Tim may have given her Scott and Sandy, but he never admired or praised her the way Trevor did. Instead, Tim had belittled, downplayed her success.

"Thank you," she whispered. "You don't know how much your confidence means to me."

Trevor gave her a puzzled look. "Tim never encouraged you?"

Randi nodded. "He was so wrapped up in his own career."

She rested her head against the seat, stared out the window.

"You know, Miriam said he's planning to run for governor. I'm willing to bet that's why he is pursuing this joint custody. He's not really interested in the boys. Only how it would reflect on him by not having them in his life."

Trevor reached for her hand and kissed it. "I have to say, I questioned his motives but had no idea he had such grand political aspirations."

Trevor took the exit, navigated past malls, fast food eateries, industrial complexes and housing developments. The further they travelled the larger the subdivisions. He turned into a brick entrance, crossed a narrow bridge, passed what appeared to be a gated clubhouse.

Maneuvering down quiet streets, Randi observed the houses, and lots got larger. Acreage separated houses so that no house was on top of one another as in most subdivisions. Here there were mansions with manicured lawns and expensive cars.

Randi gave a nervous laugh when Trevor turned into a paved drive that circled in front of a stone residence. Villa came to mind.

"You've never told me what Chuck does for a living. He obviously does very well to be able to afford a Learjet, Cadillac SUV and house like this."

"He and Susan are financial advisors. They work with several major corporations and have done very well for themselves. Susan always jokes that she helped Chuck start the business now advises him on how to spend his money."

"Sounds like my kind of girl," Randi chuckled.

Trevor touched an icon on the dashboard screen and Randi watched the garage doors slowly slide open. He parked beside a black Escalade.

"They left this one at the hanger for me. I'll leave it there for when we get home from their trip."

Trevor disengaged the security system, unloaded the luggage, entered a large Florida room that looked over the pool in the back yard. He left their luggage inside the door, took Randi's hand.

"Let's take a walk."

He opened the sliding doors to the large, paved patio that spread across the back of the house. Offered an option to enjoy the outdoors on a beautiful afternoon such as today. An outdoor living area with lounge sofa, end tables and chairs were arranged outside the windows to the den.

The main kitchen extended to the outdoors with a grill and combination countertop and bar beside it. If you didn't want to eat at the bar, there was a large table with benches for large family or company events as well as a smaller café set for more intimate seating.

Adirondack chairs surrounding a firepit polished off the far end of the patio.

Trevor led her down some steps toward the sparkling water of the inground pool. Bright blue edging shone through the crisp clear water. LED lights were arranged in and around the pool. Randi was sure they offered a romantic glow at dark. More Adirondack chairs and tables with umbrellas were arranged throughout the pool area.

"Trevor, it's so beautiful here. This place is like an interior decorator's dream come true. Has all the ideas in one place." She looked beyond the pool.

"Look," she exclaimed. "There are also tennis courts. Wow, if I had a place like this, I'd never want to leave."

Trevor smiled.

"The pool is lit at night. I thought maybe we could take a swim later." He put a hand around her back, pulled her into his arms. "You did bring the bikini, didn't you?" He asked before his lips covered hers.

CHAPTER NINETEEN

Randi tried to focus on preparing a salad but kept looking outside, watching Trevor at the grill. After a quick tour of the house, they had returned to the patio to toss around ideas for the project.

The plan was to enjoy a relaxing dinner, fine-tune those ideas and spend the day tomorrow developing them. Trevor had yet to pressure her into deepening their relationship. Other than the kiss near the pool, he hadn't made any moves towards intimacy.

She on the other hand, had plans of her own. She smiled as she thought about the bikini, she wore beneath her favorite denim shirt style maxi dress. It was comfortable for working and presentable should anyone stop by the house. It also buttoned down the front and would be easy to unbutton, step out of when she tempted him for a swim.

She put the salad in the fridge, prepared the asparagus for grilling. A relaxing dinner with stimulating conversation followed by seduction in the pool. Sounded like a plan she decided as she replenished her cabernet then took the bottle out to the patio to fill Trevor's.

"You know," she handed him the asparagus and sat at the bar, "if I had a house like this, I'd never want to leave. I can't imagine Susan travelling as much as she does."

"She blames their travel on the business and takes advantage of every opportunity to go anywhere new. But she's also told me every time she comes home, she appreciates it more."

Trevor closed the grill, joined her at the bar.

"So," he sipped his wine, "you could get used to a house like this?"

"What woman wouldn't," Randi exclaimed. "And I'd love to see Susan, compliment her on her decorative eye. This house has certainly given me ideas to share with my clients."

"The steaks should be ready in a few minutes. What do you say we add the asparagus to the grill, light some candles and watch the sun go down while we eat?"

Fifteen minutes later they were doing just that.

The rosy horizon reflected across the lake on the back side of the property. When they strolled down to the bank earlier, Randi had noticed that several of the other homes had piers with boats. She saw the lights of one of the boats as it slowly coasted through the water.

Rather than a pier, Susan and Chuck chose to leave six large oak trees across the back of their property. They not only provided shade in the late afternoons but an impressive backdrop for the setting sun.

"You know, I really like your idea about renovating the mill better than creating another resort. I hope Greenwillow Associates will agree. That's an unusual name. Where did that name come from, anyway?"

"Kevin Green and his wife Willow Banks were good friends with my parents. They started the Investment company thirty years ago. They have three kids, about my age, that serve with them on the Board.

Kevin and Willow plan to retire in the next three years and this project is supposed to be their swan song. A legacy for the kids to take over.

"Kevin came to me with this idea after he and Willow stayed at Snowridge. I like his idea and want to help him, but I've never wanted to duplicate my resort. At least not here in Atlanta. That's why I've put a lot of thought in it; feel this will be a better investment of their money for this location and provide stability and longevity for the kids."

"Good idea." Randi lifted her wine to him. "We need to incorporate as many businesses as possible into the plan. Make them see the potential and services people will want to live with or travel her for. You know, make the entire project like a small community. Who wouldn't want to live where almost everything is at your fingertips? That seems to be the trend of today's millennials."

"Yeah. I think I like your idea of creating the mall in the lower levels and making the upper levels of each building different. Hotel rooms in the main building, apartments in another and vacation rental units in the third."

Randi smiled. "When I do the sketch, I want to put names on each of the stores so they can visualize the possibilities. You know, like Marcie's Wine Shop, Ginny's Bakery, Cliff's Music Store? And sketch wine bottles, pies and cakes and musical instruments in the front windows. I think if we offer as many possibilities as possible – bookstore, coffee shop, candy shop, antiques and collectibles, travel agency, small grocery store, for instance, the better they can envision the feasibility of the project."

"Don't forget the restaurants. Fast foods for those who are on their way to work or want something quick. A sports bar would be good for those – residents or visitors – who are looking for casual dining and the finer restaurants for those who want more intimate settings. With

three buildings, they could offer more than one of the sports bars and
upscale restaurants."

"With a food court," Randi added, "maybe in the main building."

Trevor stared at her, then asked, "Do you think you can put all this
together in time?"

Randi smiled. "Sure. Once I plug in the logistics, measurements, it's
a matter of deciding square footages, then sectioning off the different
stores. Once we come up with the design for a hotel room, unit and
apartment, we can section those off, determine the number of each.
That's where you come in. You know the necessary materials and basic
costs for that. I really like the high ceilings, think we can make the
units, rooms unique."

She leaned back in her chair and sighed. "Tomorrow's going to be
a full day."

Trevor pushed his plate away, topped off their wine to empty the
bottle and nodded towards the pool.

"What do you say we give the boys a call then make use of this time
and enjoy ourselves."

"Good idea," Randi reached for her cell phone, dialed Ginny.

Trevor glanced at her dress and noticed that a couple buttons had
come unbuttoned while they ate. He smiled when he glimpsed the
lavender material.

She put the phone on speaker so the two of them could talk. While
the boys rattled on about all they had done, Randi caught Trevor
staring at her dress and smiled. As the conversation wound down,
she stood and unbuttoned more buttons. Watched Trevor take a deep
breath when she stepped out of the dress.

"Looks like you already had a plan," he uttered huskily when the
call ended.

Randi smiled. "I was a girl scout and *be prepared* was our motto."

Trevor swallowed; his eyes feasted on the curves of her body. He'd already seen her naked but tonight was different. She was more seductive. More alluring. More enticing. His desire for her flickered to life.

He stood and reached for her, pulled her into his arms.

Randi smiled, watched him as she brushed her hands up his arms, roamed the firm muscles, swept along his shoulders and thru his hair. She pulled his head down for a kiss.

Trevor gathered her close, deepened the kiss, his blunt fingers splayed the bare skin of her back, pressed her closer to his fevered body. As the kisses became more passionate, he leaned down, lifted her in his arms. Carried her towards the pool.

"Aren't you going to change?" Randi asked when he set her on her feet, pulled his shirt over his head.

"Why bother when we've got the whole place to ourselves?" He stepped out of his shoes, unbuttoned his jeans. "And don't think you'll be keeping your suit on either."

Randi backed away from him. "Trevor, we can't swim in the nude," she proclaimed. "What if people see us."

"Look around. Do you see any houses?" He unzipped his jeans.

"But how do you know someone won't be watching from the woods?"

Trevor stepped out of the rest of his clothes, tossed them aside.

"Who cares. If they can manage to get past the security – which they can't – then I guess they deserve a peek."

He grabbed her, fell backwards into the pool.

Randi yelped when they landed in the cold water, came up gasping.

"Trevor Graystone," she tried to reprimand him, but his mouth covered hers and they went under again.

She threw her head back and laughed out loud when they came up a second time. "This water is so cold," she shrieked as she wrapped her legs around his waist, spread her arms wide.

Trevor's breath quickened; he was speechless. He was struck by her natural beauty. Wet hair was plastered around her face, the moonlight shimmered off her bare shoulders.

"I've never heard you laugh like that." His lips curved into a smile. "I like it. Want to hear it more often."

Her eyes blazed with desire when she stared into his, overwhelmed by his straightforward sincerity, adoration, longing. Lowered her head and kissed him.

"Let's have some fun," he said as his hand skimmed her back, un-hooked the top of her bikini. Since he held her against him, he was pretty sure she didn't realize it was undone.

"Didn't I see you playing Marco Polo with the boys that afternoon at the pool? Before we officially met."

Randi frowned. "Was my father in your office that day?"

Trevor nodded as he reached for the tie behind her neck, slowly untied it. "We'd already sorta met, remember? You literally fell into my arms earlier that morning."

"Only because you scared me."

"I watched you step out of that hot tub and couldn't keep my eyes off you. Your father pointed you out and I had to turn away for fear he would see the lust in my eyes."

"Stop. You're just saying that" Randi laughed, nudged away from him. Her eyes opened wide when she felt the cool water against her bare breasts, her top floating away from them. "Trevor, you did not," she exclaimed.

"What do you say we play a little Marco Polo? If I win you shed the rest. If you win, I put mine on."

"You don't have your suit."

"Whatever," he shrugged a shoulder, gave her a wolfish smile. "I don't plan to lose. What do you say?"

"Okay." She grabbed the top and tossed it out of the pool. Quickly moved away and smiled. "You go first."

Trevor put a hand over his face and smiled. He'd give her a few seconds, then he'd pounce.

Since he was the better swimmer, Randi tried to put as much distance between them as possible. She was sure he wouldn't play fair.

"Marco," he said menacingly.

"Polo," she answered in a normal voice, quickly realized her mistake when he lunged toward her. She managed to dodge him, swam further away. When he called out again, she answered more softly.

Trevor laughed but didn't move.

"Do you know how sexy that sounds?"

When he called out again, as softly as she, she crawled to the right before answering. Trevor anticipated her move, successfully grabbed her ankle as she tried to swim around him. She squealed as he yanked her into his arms for a kiss.

Randi went under, managed to slither out of his grasp.

"My turn," she laughed when she surfaced and jolted away from him, daring him to pursue her.

Trevor gave her a smirk, floated backwards while he waited for her to close her eyes.

Eyes closed; Randi listened for any sudden movements. She was sure he wouldn't play fair. "Marco."

"Polo." Trevor responded quietly.

Randi frowned. It was different when the shoe was on the other foot. He spoke so softly she couldn't decide which direction to turn. "Marco," she repeated.

"Polo," Trevor chuckled to her right. When she quickly reached out, she came up empty.

"Almost got you," she warned. "Marco," she murmured, then gasped when he answered next to her ear. Her eyes flew open, and she saw that his face was inches from hers.

"You peeked," he threatened softly. "And cheaters pay dearly."

Randi laughed. "I don't think so." She tried to paddle backwards, then yelped when he once again snagged her foot and pulled her towards him.

He went under and she felt both of his hands grab her bikini bottoms, jerked them down her legs. He surfaced with a smile on his face, her suit dangling from his finger. Holding it out of reach above her head, he tossed the suit in the direction of her top. The other hand streaked down her lower back to pull her against him.

Randi felt more brazen without the suit. She wrapped her legs around his waist, brushed her breasts against his chest.

"Hmm," Trevor hummed when his hands cupped her bottom, nudged her against his arousal.

They briefly studied one another, aware that the playfulness had been replaced by passion before his lips covered hers.

When Randi rocked against his length, Trevor moved his fingers between them to stroke her. She arched back, almost moaned at the sudden flurry of pleasure that surged throughout her body when his fingers entered her.

"Look at me," he whispered as he continued to fondle her. "I want to watch you go over."

She raised her head, stared into his eyes and caught her breath when the orgasm coursed through her until he could hold it no longer and he penetrated her.

Mesmerized, Randi held on as the water swirled around them with each powerful thrust. She cried out in euphoric bliss then collapsed against him as he emptied into her.

Randi rested her cheek against his shoulder. She was unable to move and still held him inside her. She felt his heart pound in time with hers, listened to the water slap between them with each deep breath he took.

"That. Was. Amazing," she sighed.

Trevor chuckled. "Yeah, I don't think I'll ever be able to look at that maxi dress the same way either. Do you realize how seductive you were when you unbuttoned that dress and stepped out of it?"

Randi giggled, started to push away but his hands held her in place. Still reeling, she hugged him with her legs but fell back, her head and arms floating above the water. The night air felt cool on her exposed breasts until his mouth closed around one. She felt him come alive and limply rested on water when he took her for another ride.

~~~~~

She watched him while she rested in the lounge chair beside the pool. After their lovemaking, Trevor wanted to do his laps. She said she'd rest, then go inside.

The sun had long since disappeared, but the soft lights and moon reflected on the water.

He'd told her to check the long tub near the chair and she'd been surprised to discover lush towels and robes inside. She snuggled in the bright blue robe while watching his muscular arms propel him through the water. No wonder he stayed so fit she thought. Between early morning jogs and evening swims. Her body still tingled from their lovemaking.

Tim never made her feel this special. Not even when they were first married. It suddenly occurred to her that she was so grateful she and Trevor had found one another. Fate seemed to have brought them together and she decided she could get used to having a man like Trevor in her life for a long, long time.

She smiled, grabbed her bikini, and headed towards the house. Maybe she needed to make this night more memorable.

~~~~~

Trevor caught a glimpse of her leaving during one of his strokes and saw her heading for the house. He was convinced more than ever fate had brought her to him. It amazed him that they had managed to miss each other all those months he was in Edmondsville but stumbled upon one another at Snowridge.

The more he was around her and her boys, the more he wanted her in his life. This afternoon he realized they had the makings of a strong partnership. He just needed to move slowly. He didn't want to scare her away. Didn't want her to think he was downplaying her own business. She had worked hard to develop her business and there was no reason they couldn't mesh their professions.

Yes, he had to admit he was glad he had run into the little lady in unit thirty-eight. He intended to become an important part of her life and could get used to having her in his life for many years to come.

~~~~~

Randi smiled as she entered the bedroom. Crisp and the old world came to mind the first time she entered the room. They had opened the windows and the breeze billowed through the hand smocked sheer organdy panels. The white woven cotton quilt trimmed with ruffles of light cotton sheer glowed from the light of the lamp that resembled toughened acanthus leaves on a square pedestal.

The weathered French styled headboard mounted on the wall had once been a panel from a winery with the hand carved ivory clusters of grapes and blooms. Three rows of beige, blue and brown pillows were arranged across the head of the bed with an antique ivory bench at the foot of the bed.

The European touch continued with the chandelier that hung over the bed. The center was of twisted hand-carved wood with curved arms for candles and wooden grape clumps hanging around the center.

She stared into the floor to ceiling framed mirror that leaned against the wall. Her crinkled white chiffon gown with soft orange and red hibiscus buds in the pattern may not be as seductive but she liked it anyway. The white satin neckline and ruffled hem made her feel feminine.

She caught movement behind her and saw Trevor watching her from the door.

"I'm sorry I don't have anything more seductive, but I haven't had a need for anything sexy for many, many years."

"You're sexy in anything you wear," he murmured as he moved into the room, stood behind her. She shivered when he softly brushed his hands up her arms then across her shoulder while his lips teased her neck.

"Why don't you let me get a quick shower and show you how sexy you are."

Randi smiled. "I'll be waiting."

Trevor took a quick shower, smiled when he saw she had pulled the quilt back, waited for him in bed. He climbed in, reached across her to turn the light out and saw that she was sound asleep.

CHAPTER TWENTY

Randi awoke early the next morning and was immediately disoriented. This wasn't her bedroom. She felt warmth, turned her head to see Trevor sound asleep beside her. Then she recalled where she was, how she had promised to wait up for Trevor. Her plans for seduction were her last thoughts before falling asleep.

She slinked out of the bed, grabbed the maxi dress and headed for the bathroom to change. She'd get started on the plans and let him sleep.

She would like to have sat on the patio near the pool but wasn't sure what would happen if she opened the door. Didn't want to start the day setting the alarms off.

Thirty minutes later, she was hard at work at the dining room table when a mug of coffee suddenly appeared next to the laptop. She looked up, smiled at Trevor when he settled in a chair across from her.

"You're up bright and early," he noted.

"Unfortunately, when I have a new project, I can't think of anything else. Sorry. You were sleeping so soundly; I didn't want to awaken you."

"That's okay." He leaned back in his chair. "You were sleeping pretty soundly when I came to bed."

She cringed. "Sorry. I don't know what came over me. Must have been the wine. It certainly wasn't the company," she teased, took a sip of the coffee. "How did you know I like a little cream in my coffee?"

"Observant like that," he tilted his head slightly, his eyes sparkled over the rim of his cup when he took a sip.

"Well, thank you." She looked at her laptop and the paperwork spread across the table. "I've been plugging in the measurements and was just getting started on putting a plan together. What do you say I throw some breakfast together and you can tell me your ideas?"

Trevor nodded as he gathered her notes and laptop, headed for the patio.

Fifteen minutes later, she joined him with a plate of muffins and fruit. "That was so considerate of Susan to leave a supply of food for us. Hope you don't mind a simple breakfast. I can fix more if you want." She freshened his coffee. "I really wanted to come out here to work but was worried I'd set the alarms off."

"Only if you'd come in," he explained.

"So," she reached for a spiced muffin, "any thoughts on the project?"

"Yeah, but you look like you're itching to tell me yours. Let's start with you first."

"I think it would be best to keep the design simple, use what we have, dress up the interior. Make everything structurally sound. Play up the wrought iron railings inside."

Trevor nodded in agreement.

"Build walls three-quarters the way across the upper two levels to allow for living space. The long windows can be the focal point of the individual units. Entrances will be from a walkway that looks over the mall below. I'm assuming you'll have to install support beams, but they can be incorporated in the design of the mall."

She showed him a sketch of a bookstore.

"Various square footage sections could be available for the retail stores on the main level. You know some businesses won't need as much space as others. Here's a sketch of the exterior of a bookstore, another with the shelving and reading areas. There could even be enough room for a little coffee shop.

"Like I said last night, I should be able to sketch storefronts of a few more shops and what I don't get finished, we can include a list of possible businesses so they will get an idea of the magnitude of the project." She stopped to take a breath. "Sound good so far?"

Trevor nodded in agreement.

"Will you be able to put together an estimate of the construction costs? Necessary equipment, utility work? I know it will be very preliminary for now, but you should be able to give them an idea, right?"

"Rough estimate, yes."

She poured them more coffee. "So, what do you think?"

"I like it. I recognized a lot of potential in the building, and you've pretty much homed in on my thoughts."

"Where do you want to go from here? Divide the square footage to determine the number of stores we can accommodate? I can work on a few more sketches while you calculate the logistics?"

Trevor stood, kissed the top of her head, settled beside her. "Sounds like a plan."

They spent over an hour discussing the best layout for the retail stores. Once a preliminary blueprint of the design was decided, Trevor grabbed his calculator and clip board, settled at another table to do his calculations.

They had already decided the units in the two back buildings would be better suited as apartments for purchase or rent. Or vacation units available on a weekly or monthly basis. Of course, the *Green Willow* Board would make the final decision.

Randi began designing the living quarters on her laptop. She'd already researched another mill and planned to incorporate the best features for their project. The main rooms would be large and open with plenty of space for living, socializing. More than likely, there would be support beams that could be painted to match the walls or covered to make columns.

She inserted large sofas, ottomans, recliners to create a lounge area that faced the long windows. Being the focal point of the room, the windows could be left bare or shaded with blinds, depending on the tenant. Maybe Trevor could install fake fireplaces with gas logs.

Spacious kitchens were sectioned off in one corner with counters, sinks, stoves, refrigerators. Cabinets above the counters offered shelving as well as space for microwaves or wall ovens. Dishwashers as well as washers and driers could be installed below the counters.

Large or small dinette areas would be an offset of the kitchen. Like the windows, this area could be elaborate or simple, depending on the occupant.

Front doors opened to a short hall with rooms on either side which could be used as bedrooms or office space.

At the end of the hall, before entering the larger room, she inserted a wrought iron spiral staircase on the left. The high ceilings were perfect for a loft that could be a spacious master bedroom or guest bedroom. The loft area looked down over the living area from a railing.

Bathrooms would be available on both levels and could be as intricate or Spartan as the owner wanted.

The hotel rooms in the main building followed the same design with wrought iron railings that overlooked the retail stores on the first level. She envisioned the rooms being on a smaller scale, more like suites and adjusted the scale to accommodate a small seating area, kitchenette and bathroom. King size beds would be available in both the main room and a separate loft that overlooked a railing from above.

Just as the long, tall windows were the central point of the living units, she added a large majestic circular wrought iron staircase at the far end of the mall that whipped around to the second and third levels. Elevators would be installed to make the building handicapped accessible. And for more convenient movement from side to side, she added a single walkway from one side to the other at the middle of the building. She smiled as she embellished the walkway with decorative wrought iron railings and tile flooring.

She also added above ground garden boxes for flowers and shrubs.

When her stomach growled, she looked over at Trevor, wondered if he was having as much luck as she was and found him leaned back in his chair, hands behind his head, watching her.

"What?" She asked.

"Do you believe in fate?" His voice was low, husky, his eyes caressing her. "Do you wonder if we were meant to meet on that dark winding road at the resort? Especially after missing each other so much of the time in Edmondsville."

Trevor watched puzzlement etch her face as she pondered what he asked. Being so wrapped up in her career and sons, he wondered if she even considered the possibility of another man in her life.

"I, uh, I don't know. To be honest, after Tim, I had no desire to be around men. I decided to focus on raising my two boys. Figured maybe something might develop when they were older."

"Then Brina decided to renovate the firehouse," he said. "I distinctly remember seeing the ad for that job. The words 'renovation' caught my eye. I didn't do anything about it at first but when I saw the ad for a second time, something made me pick up the phone, give her a call. It was a cold November day when I met her at the firehouse."

"She had called me to meet her there, but I couldn't get away. The boys had a program at school."

"I liked her idea but had a lot on my plate with Snowridge. I was pushing myself to get as much construction under roof as possible so the crews could work inside during the winter months. Then when it looked like that was going to happen, I stumbled on my notes and contacted Brina to see if she had found a contractor."

Randi smiled. "I remember when she called me. She was so excited. You were the only contractor that showed any real interest and when you didn't get back to her, she was really discouraged."

Trevor smiled. "She kept telling me she had a partner, but the partner never seemed to make the meetings on time. When she said her partner was an interior decorator, I just laughed. That may be when I expressed my feelings about your profession."

"I really did try to make the meetings," Randi defended herself. "Either the boys, my father or a client always managed to interfere. Several times I arrived just as you were leaving." She giggled. "That's why I always joked about your cute butt."

"I thought the same thing when I saw you walking away from me in that grocery store. And thanked my stars when I found you hiking on the side of the road twenty minutes later. Then when you literally fell into my arms the next day, I was hooked. And when we officially met and I realized who you were, I knew it had to be fate."

"Maybe you should thank my father. He's the one who pushed me to go to Snowridge with him."

"I certainly will. You and your boys have certainly livened my life these past few weeks. And now, with us working on this project, I can't help but see the possibilities."

Randi moved to settle in his lap. "You mean you might be able to work with a crazy interior decorator after all?"

"I mean," he wrapped his arms around her, kissed her along her neck. "I am realizing I can work with you. I want to work with you." He unbuttoned the dress and kissed beneath her chin. "We share the same philosophies," he unbuttoned another, kissed the exposed cleavage. "I've liked all the ideas you've had so far." His lips moved back to her chin. "We can make it a fixer-upper partnership." His mouth closed over hers.

Trevor raised his head, stared into her eyes. "What do you say we take a break, go inside, and authenticate this partnership. Confirm our commitment and then celebrate with some bubbly and lunch?"

"Sounds like a plan, to me. Just not naked in the pool."

"That's for tonight."

Randi laughed when Trevor stood, carried her inside.

~~~~~

"You know, half the day is gone already," Randi said from her side of the bed as Trevor filled her glass with more champagne. "Good thing Susan thought to stock the champagne in the chiller. Much as I enjoyed sealing the deal, we still have a lot of work to do."

"Already trying to get the upper hand?"

"Whatever it takes. The sooner we get the proposal finished, the sooner we can try the pool again."

"Is this the way you manipulate Scott and Sandy? Bribe them?"

Randi laughed. Sipped the last of her wine, then straddled him.

"Whatever works," she stated as she took his wine flute, set it on the nightstand. Brushed her breasts against his bare chest as she moved to kiss him. "You just lay back and relax. I'll see if I can add some benefits to the deal."

"I like the way you negotiate."

She gazed into his eyes while her fingertips glided down his body, past his stomach, inches from his fullness growing harder by the second. Her nipples brushed against his chest as she leaned forward to brush her lips against his lips, then moved on to his neck and shoulders to follow the path of her fingers.

When Trevor reached for her, she captured his wrists, held them out to his side, made seductive moans as she continued her journey of his body.

Unable to contain himself, Trevor grabbed her hips, helped her mount him. He was sure he heard her purr when she threw her head back, rocked back and forth.

Yes, he thought. This was one partnership he intended to keep for life.

~~~~

Hundreds of miles away, in Edmondsville, Josh knocked at his uncle's office door. Wondered why he had summoned him today of all days. It was Sunday, for cripes sake. Did he ever take a day off?

First thing that stuck him was the shades were drawn, made the room darker. The desk was cluttered with stacks of papers. He would have thought an accountant would be a neat freak, but what did he care.

He'd never really liked his mother's older brother. Uncle James always thought he was better than everyone else. He was an accountant. So what?

"You asked me to come by?" Josh asked.

"Yes." The old man leaned back in his chair, glared down his nose at him. "I understand you're working on the firehouse project."

Josh shrugged his shoulder. "A little. Trevor pays us to clean up. Put stuff away. Get things for them. Why?"

His uncle hooked hands across his stomach. "Just wondered how the job was going. That's all."

"Should be finished in a couple weeks." Josh recalled an earlier conversation with his uncle, couldn't resist asking, "why did you tell me they were going to demolish the building? If Clay and Norman and I knew that we wouldn't have messed the place up."

"Your Uncle Tom told me," James snarled nonchalantly. "Guess he was mistaken."

Josh stared at his uncle. "Well, the pay is good. In fact, Trevor is paying me extra to check on the place while he's away. I don't want him to think I wasn't doing my job, so I need to head on over there."

"Sure," the old man shrugged, sat upright in his chair, returned to his paperwork. "If you need any extra cash, just let me know. Oh, and don't forget to lock the door behind you on your way out."

Josh shook his head as he turned to leave, noticed some objects in the corner between the file cabinet and the wall. He started to ask his uncle about them, saw he had been officially dismissed as his uncle was studying the paperwork.

Josh moved slowly towards the door but frowned when he gave the corner a closer look. He'd learned a lot about tools since he started working for Trevor. If he wasn't mistaken, that was a nail gun and cordless screwdriver.

His uncle shuffled papers. Why would he need tools like those in his office?

When Josh looked closer, he recognized the familiar red TAG label on the equipment.

CHAPTER TWENTY-ONE

G inny parked in front of the *Children's Museum* and led the
boys inside. They had a half-day at school, and she was almost
as excited as they were to be here. Her very own Children's Museum
was the next phase of the firehouse project. She brushed her hand
along her stomach. Maybe when the baby was born, she would work
on that full time. What better way to take your child to work?

She had already talked with the franchise owners here and they were
excited to branch out. She planned to take notes today while the boys
enjoyed themselves.

Raised beds lined the entrance with Spring Garden vegetables. She
had Scott and Sandy identifying the asparagus spears, red and white
radishes, stalks of artichokes and mustard greens that they had studied
in her class.

As soon as they entered the large facility, she immediately had second thoughts about bringing them by herself. People – adults, staff,
the public – and children were everywhere. She bought their tickets,
made their way toward the depository of fun exhibits. Scott and Sandy

were excited, had talked all the way into the city about the different areas they wanted to visit, play in.

She held their hands, reminded them they needed to stay close. "There are a lot of people here today and I don't want anything to happen to you. Okay?"

Both boys immediately headed for the mechanic station where they looked under the hood of a play car, changed the miniature play tires, fastened, and refastened the license plate.

"We need to be sure the inspection sticker is good." Sandy announced. "Remember when Mom got a ticket because hers was bad."

"Yeah, where do you change the oil?" Scott asked Ginny.

They decided to go to the Diner next. Each sat at one of the five tables, played with the juke box then moved to the replica of a counter with child size stools. They took turns taking orders with several of the other children.

Ginny laughed as they ordered cheeseburgers and fries and pizzas.

While they played, she studied the sections, made mental notes of other stations she would like to have in her own children's museum. There was the bank with a miniature teller window, ATM machine and play money to count.

The news studio had a child size news desk, control panel, and sports backdrop. Even a working camera where they could pretend taping each other at the news desk.

Ginny knew she wanted an Art Studio where children could paint pictures then hang them to dry. And a theater with a ticket booth, lighting box and dressing room with a trunk full of costumes. She was all for anything that stimulated a child's imagination.

They were headed toward the mock Grocery Store when Ginny looked over, thought she saw Tim Cavanaugh. She immediately checked on the boys, looked back to find he was no longer there. That's odd, she thought. Surely, he wouldn't be here of all places.

She gave the boys a list of groceries to look for and was headed for the observation seats designated for parents when Tim suddenly appeared beside her. He was apparently taking the day off as he was dressed casual in khakis and a white shirt.

"Tim," she exclaimed. "This is a surprise. I thought I saw you earlier. What brings you to the *Children's Museum* in Richmond?"

"I talked to Randi about coming to visit and she said you were bringing them here."

Ginny beamed. "Yes. And they're having a fantastic time. Did you bring Miriam with you?"

"No. I just thought I'd try spending a little time with them by myself. You don't mind, do you?"

"Of course not. I think it's wonderful that you're taking the time to get to know your boys." She spotted them in the grocery store and laughed. "They're doing a little grocery shopping right now. We plan go to the bank next. Problem is, there are so many children here. Let me go get them."

Ginny turned back to the store, frowned when she couldn't find the boys. She hastily searched for red heads, hoping they would be conspicuous, but there were no redheads in sight. She dashed closer, ran among the children but could not find them. She turned to enlist help from Tim, only to find he was no longer there.

"Oh my God," she exclaimed, where were the boys.

She searched the area more closely, then moved frantically throughout the entire building. She dashed to the front desk to see if a concerned parent might have found Scott and Sandy, taken them there. She described the boys and the clothes they wore, asked if they had seen the boys leave with anyone.

Four from the staff immediately started searching the crowd. They had just regrouped with no sightings when one of the teen volunteers returned from her lunch.

"Wait," she replied. "Did you say they were twins? Wearing navy and white shirts? I think I saw them on my way out to lunch. Yeah, I saw them leaving with a woman."

"A woman," Ginny exclaimed. "I saw their father but not his wife. Was she tall? Slender? Have dark hair?"

"Yeah. She had each of the boys by the hand and was talking to them the whole time they walked out."

Ginny panicked. "You've got to call nine-one-one. This is a possible child abduction. I talked to their father right before they went missing. Please, we need to get an amber alert out on these boys."

Ginny grabbed her phone, called Cliff. "Please, you need to come to Richmond. The boys and I were here at the *Children's Museum* and suddenly Tim appeared out of nowhere. He distracted me, I lost sight of the boys and when I turned around Tim was gone too."

"What was he doing there?" Cliff barked.

"I asked him the same thing," Ginny felt a need to defend herself. "Tim said he had called Randi and she said we were here. Cliff, a volunteer saw the boys walking out with Miriam. After Tim told me she didn't come. What if they've kidnapped the boys?"

"I'll call the others and we'll be right there."

"Please hurry."

~~~~~

Ginny was talking with the state police officers when Cliff, Brina and Rafe arrived. She ran into Cliff's arms. "I'm having the hardest time convincing them the boys should be with me. I've been trying to call Randi but she's not answering her cell phone. Cliff, how could

Tim do this to us? And if Randi said it was okay, why didn't she call me?"

"Ma'am," one of the officers interrupted. "It's not that we don't believe you. We need to be certain they are supposed to be with you."

"But can't you do an amber alert anyway?"

"We've got everything set up, just need verification from their mother. She's their sole guardian, right? You said their father had supervised visiting rights."

"Yes," Cliff answered. "Her ex-husband has recently started joint custody proceedings but Miranda Cavanaugh, their mother, has sole custody." Cliff turned to Brina. "You've got Trevor's number. Can you give him a call?"

"On it," Brina stated as she reached for her phone.

"Trevor," she exclaimed seconds later. "Hey, is Randi with you?"

"Yeah. We just finished the presentation, why?"

"We're here with Ginny at the *Children's Museum* and we think Tim has kidnapped the boys."

"He what," Trevor growled. "What is he even doing there? Here, here's Randi."

"Brina?" Randi asked. "What's wrong?"

"It's the boys. Ginny brought the boys to the *Children's Museum*. They'd been here a while, then Ginny saw Tim. While he was talking to her, Miriam apparently lured the boys out of the building."

"Tim was there? Miriam? Miriam took the boys," Randi's voice broke with concern. "Oh my God," she stammered, "have you called the police? Issued an Amber Alert?"

"That's what Ginny has been trying to do but the police want to be sure she is supposed to have them. Here, the policeman wants to speak to you."

Randi gave the officer a moment to identify himself.

"You have got to find my boys," she pleaded. "Their father is Tim Cavanaugh, and he is not supposed to be around them without supervision. Harriet Young is our GAL if you need to verify this. Please, please get an amber alert started. I have no idea why he should want to see my boys now. Or what he might do."

"Mrs. Spicer has given us a description of the boys and what they are wearing. As well as what Mr. Cavanaugh was wearing. She said he is a Delegate. From Maryland?" When Randi confirmed it, he continued, "we can go online to get a picture of him. Do you know what kind of vehicle he drives?"

"I can give you that information," Randi heard Cliff say. "Black BMW. Not sure of the license plate. Did you notice, Rafe?"

"No but I think it was personalized."

"Ms. Cavanaugh, I think we have enough information to get an amber alert issued. One of our officers will get in touch with your local authorities who will more likely contact Mrs. Young. Do you know approximately when you will be home?"

"Trevor?" Randi turned to Trevor; her eyes wet with tears. "How soon can we get home?"

"Plane's ready. Three hours at most."

"And where will you be?" The officer asked after hearing Trevor's response.

"They'll be at Spicer Meadows," Cliff responded. "I'll give you the address once you finish talking with Randi."

~~~~~

Miriam reached in her pocket for her cell phone when Tim stopped to get gas. She had been concerned after her phone conversation with Randi, decided to get one. Now, she was glad she'd decided not to tell Tim.

It bothered her that Ginny didn't come out of the museum with him. She worried more when Tim abruptly told her to shut up, ordered the boys to get in the car, buckle up. When they complained that he didn't have their car seats, he once again demanded that they buckle in. They had been quiet ever since.

She was shocked when the amber alert was broadcast on the radio; turned to check on the boys, to see if they understood what was happening. Her heart wrenched when she peered into their wide, frightened eyes.

She watched her husband study the fuel pump, discreetly dialed nine-one-one.

"Nine-one-one, how may I help you?" the responder answered.

"Please, you've got to help us," she turned to face the window, tucked the phone against her shoulder. "My husband has kidnapped us, and I'm worried about the boys."

"Can you give us a location?"

"No, not really. All I know is we're past Fredericksburg. Just got off I-95 to get gas. Oh," she exclaimed, "he's finished pumping gas. Please, you've got to find us."

"Ma'am, leave your phone on. Hide it but leave it on. We should be able to track you if your phone is on."

Miriam tucked the phone between her and the console seconds before Tim settled behind the wheel. "Tim," she touched his arm when he started the car. "Don't you think we should stop and get the boys something to eat."

"I don't have time for that."

"But Tim, I'm sure Scott and Sandy are getting hungry. Probably need to go the bathroom by now. They're already upset, please don't make this more difficult. Look," she pointed a finger, "there's a McDonald's up ahead."

Miriam turned to look at the boys, tried to smile. "Wouldn't you two like a happy meal?"

She turned back to Tim. "You can even get a burger. Eat it on the road if you want. Just let me take the boys in to the bathroom while you order. Maybe you can let us out near the door then go through the take-out line. You won't even have to get out of the car. I'll meet you outside."

Miriam worried Tim wouldn't pay attention to her but mentally sighed in relief when he turned into the fast-food parking lot. He stopped by the door, told the boys to unbuckle and make it quick. Miriam grabbed the phone and got out. She steered the boys inside frantically searched for the restroom sign.

"I need you boys to go with me to the women's bathroom. Please. I'll lock the door and we won't let anyone come in except the police. Okay?"

Scott and Sandy nodded with watery eyes, followed her into the restroom. She locked the door, reached for her phone.

"Are you still there? Did you hear?"

"Yes, ma'am," the dispatch officer answered. "And you did great. We think we have a location and have dispatched some local authorities there. You just stay where you are until your husband is apprehended."

Miriam collapsed on the floor, hugged each boy to her side. "We're going to be okay," she sobbed. "You'll be with your mommy soon."

~~~~~

The flight felt like it took forever, the road to Spicer Meadows seemed endless. They landed in Richmond in record time; Trevor raced up I-95 toward Edmondsville.

"Should be another fifteen minutes." He looked over at Randi who had been silent since landing. She had paced on the plane, worried out loud about what Tim might do with her boys, called Ginny twice. He pulled off the exit.

"Give Ginny another call. It's been over thirty minutes since you talked. Maybe there's been a development."

"My phone's almost dead," she complained. "Thank goodness, we're almost home. Ginny," she exclaimed, "hey we're almost there. Have there been any developments?"

"Yes," Ginny sobbed in relief. "Yes. They apprehended Tim about thirty miles North of Fredericksburg. Duane Peterson called to say he was on his way to get the boys. Randi, I am so sorry this happened. I should have been more careful. I'm just glad they found the boys."

Randi reached for Trevor's hand and squeezed it. "Ginny, it's not your fault. It could have been me. I just wonder how Tim knew I was going to be out of town. And that you would be there. Did Duane say when he might be back?"

"No." Then Ginny laughed. "He said he would try to give the boys something else to remember this night for and would probably run the blue lights all the way home."

Everyone was at the manor house when Randi and Trevor arrived fifteen minutes later. All looked exhausted but happy.

Ginny greeted them at the door. "Duane just called; said he had the boys. They were upset and confused but otherwise okay."

"Did he say anything about Tim? Or Miriam?"

Cliff nodded. "Just said he'd tell us when he got here." He exchanged looks with Trevor and Rafe. "I don't know about you, but I could use a drink. What about you two?"

"Lead the way," Trevor responded.

"Are you okay, Ginny?" Randi asked, concerned that Ginny looked exhausted; knew Ginny had been nervous the entire time. "This hasn't affected the baby, has it?"

"No, but I've just experienced a mother's worst nightmare. I'll probably never let this child out of my sight."

"Honey, it wasn't your fault." Randi hugged her friend. "And it could just as easily have been me. I'm just sorry Tim put you in that situation. And Miriam? I find it hard to believe she went along with it."

"Well, I can't imagine how Tim's going to talk his way out of this," Marcie fumed. "Oh, I called Brad. Figured he should be here. I hope that's okay."

Randi smiled. "Probably for the best. Especially since he's representing me. And he can talk to Harriet."

"So?" Brina asked as they settled in the den. "While we wait, maybe you can tell us about the trip."

"The trip was great. We worked hard, put together the presentation and are almost certain they like the idea. If so, Trevor will start on the project as soon as the property is purchased. I'll also be involved as I'll be doing the interiors. I'll probably have to go to Atlanta some but thankfully, the boys will be out of school by then."

"And won't let me babysit them ever again," Ginny sighed.

"Stop it," Randi scolded. "I'm not going to let you blame yourself." She looked out the front window, saw the blue lights coming up the drive. "I guess Duane wasn't kidding. Here they come."

Everyone rushed outside to greet the boys. Randi fell to her knees, hugged both boys who literally flew into her arms. "I am so glad you two are okay. I hope your father didn't hurt you."

"He was mean." Scott sobbed.

"He didn't hurt you, did he?"

"No," Sandy hiccupped. "Just yelled at us. Wasn't going to let us eat."

"But Mrs. Miriam talked him into stopping at McDonald's. Then we went inside, and she locked us in the bathroom."

Randi looked up at Duane who nodded. "Yup. Let's go inside. I think one of the boys said he was hungry, but I couldn't go through the drive through with my lights going. They said they'd have a PB&J sandwich here."

"Yeah. Can we?" Sandy asked.

While the boys ate their sandwiches in the den in front of the TV, the adults congregated in the kitchen.

"Please don't tell me Tim sweet-talked his way out of this." Randi almost pleaded.

Duane laughed. "Not this time. When I got there, he was hollering from the back seat of the cruiser."

Everyone laughed. "What about Miriam?"

"She was standing by another cruiser talking to the officers. She asked me to tell you how sorry she was about all this. She thought Tim wanted to take the boys and Ginny out to lunch. Didn't know what he'd planned until he returned without Ginny, ordered everyone in the car.

"I talked to the officer in charge who said Tim will be charged with kidnapping, child abduction and child endangerment since he didn't have the proper car seats.

"Even Miriam is claiming she was kidnapped. The officer said Miriam helped them to find them. Called nine-one-one from her cell phone, talked Tim into stopping for something to eat, then locked herself and the boys in the bathroom until the police got there. She even made the officer identify himself before she would open the door."

"You know, she called me the other day," Randi sighed. "Asked me all kinds of questions about my marriage to Tim. I think she was already having regrets, getting suspicious of his behavior and when she told me she didn't have a cell phone, I told her she needed one. I'm so glad she took my advice."

"Well, I think things have finally caught up with your ex-husband," Trevor announced. "And nipped any political aspirations he had planned for his future.

CHAPTER TWENTY-TWO

The following day Trevor asked Randi and Brina to meet him at the firehouse for a semi-final walk-thru. "You know, we're coming down the home stretch with the project."

They were seated on inverted five-gallon buckets. Ten gallons of different color paint were spread across the room. The crew would be painting the newly sheet-rocked walls the next day. Boxes of laminate flooring were stacked in the main room; would be installed the day after that.

Trevor leaned back against the wall, crossed an ankle on his knee.

"Have you two given any thoughts to doing anything with the back of the building? Right now, it's an eyesore with a parking lot and not so pretty view of Stanley's garage.

"Plus, Randi's office looks out on a trash pile. I have the boys clearing the debris, but what do you think about putting in a patio? We could put down pavers, enclose it with lattice fencing to block the view of the parking lot. Add a couple tables, chairs, hanging plants.

Give you another place to meet with clients or just enjoy lunch outside on a clear day."

Brina tilted her head as she gave it some thought. "I hadn't really thought about that. We've been so focused on just getting the building done." She turned to Randi. "What do you think?"

"I like it." Randi smiled, then frowned at Trevor. "How much will it cost?"

"Haven't figured it yet, but I can make it worth your while."

Brina snickered. "A man after my heart. Although I don't think it's my heart he's thinking about," she teased.

Randi punched her friend, turned back to Trevor. "How long will it take? How complicated will it be? Will it be finished in time for the Grand Opening?"

Trevor shook his head at the barrage of questions. "Well, for starters, we'll need to clear it." He grabbed his clipboard and pencil. Drew a long line with an opening for the back door. "The back wall is long enough you could have a mural painted on the cement blocks. Maybe a racetrack, horses racing since this is Lariat's hometown."

He drew a table and chairs. "You could put the patio on one end and balance it with a deck off the loft at the other end." He stopped, looked up when Josh stumbled into the room.

"Finished clearing the pile already?" Trevor saw the boy was white as a sheet and jumped up. "What happened? Did somebody get hurt?"

"No," Josh croaked, "but you gotta' come see it."

"See what?" Trevor tossed the clipboard onto the floor, followed the boy outside. Found Clay vomiting off to one side, Norman on his knees by the mound of trash, staring straight ahead as if in a daze.

"What happened?" Trevor ran to Norman's side.

Norman pointed to the big pile of dirt that had grown up over the years. The boys had already tossed the scrap lumber from the job into the dumpster, had started on the matted weeds that had been flattened by the scrap wood.

"We started pulling the brush away and there were lots of weeds. Clay grabbed a bunch and," Norman paused, "and then we saw that." He pointed to a bare spot in the dirt.

Trevor knelt, examined it, saw what looked like a worn burlap bag. There was a hole in the bag where Clay had pulled away the tough grass. Trevor gently brushed away a little more dirt with a finger, saw what looked like a small hand. A small human hand.

He raised a palm toward Randi and Brina, motioned them to stay where they were. Saw that his foreman had followed them outside. "Aaron, see if you can find Officer Peterson. Don't say anything. Just ask him to come to the site."

Aaron saw the bones, nodded and raced away.

"Randi. Brina. I think you two need to stay over there. Don't come any closer."

"But what is it?" Randi took a step forward. Trevor motioned again for her to stop.

"I'm not sure. But I don't want to do anything else until Duane gets here." He turned to study the teens who were obviously in shock. "You three, go inside. Chill up in the loft for a while. I won't be long, but I don't want you calling or texting anyone about this. Understood?"

The boys nodded then stumbled inside.

Trevor stood and walked to the two women. "Don't get upset but I think we have a body buried there. I'm going to get a tarp to put over the site for now. Why don't you wait inside till Duane Peterson gets here? We're going to have to halt the job while the authorities identify the body, cause of death."

Aaron returned within ten minutes with Duane Peterson. Trevor took the deputy to the spot, lifted the edge of the tarp, gave him a chance to observe for himself.

"Are you thinking what I'm thinking?" Trevor asked. "Do we have us a body? Could this be why someone doesn't want us to finish the job?"

Duane nodded. "Looks like it. We don't have a medical examiner, though. Sheriff's going to have to bring someone in." He checked his watch. "It's getting late in the day. We can make a few calls, but it'll probably be morning before anyone can get here."

Duane looked at Trevor. "Who found it? You?"

"No. I had the boys clearing back here; they found it. Understandably, all three are upset. I had them go up to the loft till you or I could talk to them. Aaron," he turned to his foreman, "would you go check on them?"

Duane looked at Randi and Brina who had huddled near the back door of the firehouse, shook his head. "This project just gets more and more bizarre by the day." He stepped towards them. "Let's go inside."

Everyone returned to Brina's make-shift office, stood in silence.

When she realized the time, Randi grabbed her cell phone, called Ginny.

"Hey, we've had a problem come up at the firehouse and I was wondering if you could take the boys home with you."

"Sure. Is everything okay?"

"I'm not sure."

"Tell her we need to have a group meeting at her house. This evening." Trevor suggested.

"I heard that," Ginny said. "Did something happen?"

"Yes. No." Randi huffed, wiped damp hands along her jeans. "But Trevor's right. We need to meet. There're a few things we need to take care of, but if you could get in touch with Marcie, Rafe and Cliff, we need to meet this evening."

Randi pocketed her phone, leaned against the wall next to Brina.

"The Sheriff's on his way," Brina whispered.

"Don't know how long the body's been there but have you had any missing persons lately?" Trevor asked Duane.

"Not really. None while I've been here and that's going on eight years. Of course, it could be from outside the area."

"Based on what little I could see, I'd say it's female, a child or small man."

"Yeah," Duane agreed. "You sent your crew home, right? Why don't we go talk to the boys till the Sheriff gets here? Probably should arrange for some counseling for them. More importantly, we don't want anybody saying too much about this yet."

Trevor and Duane spent twenty minutes with the boys.

"Do you know what it is?" Josh asked.

"We're not sure, yet." Duane answered. "It could be an animal for all we know."

"But it looked like a hand," Norman contradicted.

"Yeah, but we need to let the medical examiner verify that."

"Boys," Duane sat in the floor with them. "I need you to help me here. Until we know more, we need to keep this quiet. People might get upset; some might snoop around the site. If the media finds out, it could be a real circus. That's why I'm asking you not to talk to anyone about this. I know it'll be hard not telling your parents, but we can't go public with this. Not yet."

He handed each of the boys a piece of paper. "If you need to talk to anyone, don't hesitate to call me."

~~~~~

Sheriff Matthews determined there was nothing they could do until he secured a medical examiner.

"I'll be staying here tonight," Trevor decided. "I need to meet with Randi, Brina and her friends this evening but will come back to safeguard the scene."

"I appreciate it," the Sheriff said. "I don't have the manpower for round the clock security. I'm sure if we pile some of the scrap wood on top of it, it will be okay, but I appreciate your staying here too. I just don't want word to leak out before we've had time to determine whether these are human bones and if so, who it could possibly be." He looked at Duane. "We'll make some calls, be here as soon as we locate someone to study the area."

Trevor followed Randi and Brina to Spicer Meadows after he and Duane covered the tarp with some of the brush so no one would notice the disturbance in the earth.

"Do you really think it's a body?" Randi asked later that evening.

Trevor nodded his head. "We didn't want to upset the kids but that's what it looks like."

"I can't believe that someone would just bury a body behind the firehouse," Ginny exclaimed.

"And who could It possibly be?" Marcie asked.

~~~~~

The following morning, Randi fixed two egg sandwiches, a thermos of coffee and a Danish for Trevor. As soon as she dropped the boys off to school, she headed for the firehouse. He's tired, she thought to herself when she saw his blood-shot eyes, sluggish movements.

He took a bite of the sandwich. "I talked to Aaron last night, suggested he and the guys work on one of the other projects until we get this taken care of. Then Sheriff Matthews called to say the state medical examiner's office is sending someone first thing this morning. I was on my way to clear the brush before he gets here."

"You're tired." Randi said, brushed a hand across his shoulders. "Finish your sandwich and I will help you," Randi said. "Did anyone come around last night?"

"No. Hal is still holed up in the garage, so he was my backup. He came by when he saw my flashlight, so I had to tell him I was staying on the job. Didn't tell him why though." He leaned his head against the wall behind him. "Came back this morning, said he didn't see any activity outside all night."

Randi shivered. "Let's just hope we can take care of this quickly."

Duane arrived mid-morning with a stocky man with salt and pepper hair, carrying a small bag that reminded Randi of a doctor's medical bag. His name was Gil Fitzgerald and he walked around the site then knelt to examine the bare spot.

"Looks human alright. Will know better when we clear the rest of the mound."

Trevor knelt beside him, and they meticulously removed weeds, clumps of dirt. The more debris they removed, the more burlap they uncovered. Two hours later, they had completely uncovered the bag, carefully cut it down the center to peel it back and had an entire skeleton laying before them."

"I'll take over here." Gil advised.

When Trevor couldn't do much more, he headed inside to Brina's makeshift office to catch a couple hours sleep on the cot Hal had brought over from the garage.

Randi and Brina unlocked the front door, found him sound asleep.

"He looks exhausted," Randi whispered to Brina. They tiptoed through the building, found Duane talking with Gil Fitzgerald in the back.

"How's it going?" Brina asked, took in a deep breath when she saw the skeleton.

"We've cleared the bulk of the pile, Gil's almost finished clearing the dirt from around the bones."

Randi blew out a breath. "Do you have any idea about who it might be?"

"Not yet," Duane said. "Won't be able to do that until we have a name and some DNA to compare it to. That's why we need to review the missing persons cases."

"I just feel so bad for whoever it is." Randi sighed. "Somewhere, a family is missing a loved one."

Brina stared down at the bones. So small, she thought as her eyes travelled up the body from the feet to the skull. She saw something shining near the skull. "What's that?"

"I was just getting to that," Gil announced as he carefully brushed more dirt aside, reached for the loose object. He heard Brina's loud gasp, looked up to see the color drained from her face, her hand over her mouth.

"Brina?" Duane touched her arm. "Are you okay?"

"Brad," Brina turned, raced through the firehouse. "I need to find Brad."

~~~~~

Stacy had just settled at her desk when Brina and Randi entered Brad's office. She smiled. "Hey girls, how's it going?"

"Is Brad in?" Randi interrupted her. "Brina needs to talk to him."

"Sure," Stacy jumped up. "I think he's working on an email. Let me check." Stacy returned moments later. "He says to come on back." She touched Randi's arm when they stepped forward. "Is Brina okay? Can I get you anything?"

Randi nodded. "No, but thanks."

Brad stood as soon as he saw how upset both women were. "What's happened?" He looked at Randi. "Has Tim done something else?"

"No. No, it's not me. Brina needs to talk to you though." She looked at her friend. "Do you need me to leave?"

"No." Brina reached for Randi's hand before she turned to Brad. "Brad, we need to talk."

When he saw her eyes fill with tears, Brad guided Brina toward the sofa. "You're scaring me. What's wrong?"

A tear streaked down Brina's cheek. "Didn't you give Deborah a locket?"

Brad's head jerked in confusion. "Yes. I gave her one after we'd been dating a few months." His mouth curved into a smile. "My Mom had shown me the one my father gave her before he left for World War II. She used to talk about how it comforted her while he was away. I decided to give Deborah one till I could afford a ring."

Randi's heart swelled, felt tears in her own eyes when she realized why Brina was upset.

"What did it look like?" Brina asked.

"It was shaped like a heart, had a rose engraved on the front of it. I remember talking about how important my mother's locket was to her. We laughed when we put small clippings of our hair together inside. Brina, why are you asking about this now?"

"Brad," Brina whispered. "There has been a development at the firehouse. You need to come with me."

"Brina," Brad stood when Brina jumped up. "You're scaring me. What has happened?"

"Please," she pleaded, "just come with me." She pulled him behind her.

"Stacy, I need to go with Brina and Randi. I'll be back as soon as I can."

Brad followed the women around to the back of the firehouse. Gil had brushed the last of the dirt away from the body.

"Mr. Fitzgerald," Brina asked. "Have you been able to uncover all of the locket." When he nodded, she continued, "Could you show it to Brad?"

Gil stood, handed the clear sample bag that contained the necklace to Brad.

Brina sobbed when Brad stared down at it, then held it to his heart. Looked over to see the small skeleton.

Trevor immediately put two and two together, wrapped his arms around Brina and Randi. Hugged them to his side. He watched the man who had become a friend grieve for someone he had lost.

Brad fell to his knees, lightly touched the bones of the hand he had often held over ten years ago.

"Deborah," he whispered. "My Deborah."

CHAPTER TWENTY-THREE

Randi prepared pastrami on rye sandwiches, Stacy heated the chicken noodle soup and cut up fruit, Cliff hunted up the chips and beer while Rafe opened a second bottle of wine. Trevor was due back any minute from taking the boys to stay overnight with their grandfather.

Ginny, Brina, Marcie and Brad huddled in the den. Brad was quiet, heart-broken, everyone was in shock.

Sheriff Matthews didn't want to go public yet, so Deborah's bones had been discreetly removed to Richmond. Gil Fitzgerald had also taken the locket with him, hoped to get some DNA to further verify it was Deborah.

Spicer Meadows seemed the logical place to regroup but once there, everyone sat in silence. Reeling from the discovery at the firehouse, reliving the grief all over again.

On the verge of tears, Ginny reached for Cliff's hand when he settled beside her. "Who could have wanted to hurt Deborah?" She spoke softly. "What could have happened?"

Marcie was thoughtful. "Do you suppose something happened at the library? Could she have witnessed something? Was the Director carrying on a secret love affair she wanted no one to know about? A patron stealing books on how to make bombs?"

Everyone half-smiled at Marcie's ridiculous queries.

"Deborah loved working at the library," Ginny disagreed. "Enjoyed helping people." A tear streaked down her cheek when she looked at Brad. "Did you know she was saving her money to move out of her aunt and uncle's house?"

Brad silently nodded his head.

"She told me she'd talked to the Turner's about renting their garage apartment." Ginny continued, looked back at Marcie. "No, I don't think it was something at the library."

"I know. I know," Marcie sighed. "It's just that she was so happy that night. Remember?" She studied her friends through glossy eyes. "Said she felt like Cinderella all dressed up, riding in the limo, dancing with her prince charming." She turned to Brad. "I think she suspected that you were going to finally ask her to marry you."

Brad sat on the edge of the sofa, his elbows on his knees. His shoulders drooped as he hung his head.

Finished with the food preparation, Stacy sat beside him, silently rubbed a hand up and down his back.

Brina paced the room. "I was probably the last person to see her alive. We were outside, on the stoop, cooling off." She stopped to look at Brad. "I remember teasing her that her cheeks were flushed because of you, not the dance. I should have been more insistent that she come back inside with me."

"She wouldn't have run away, would she?" Rafe asked, then raised a hand in defense when Brina stopped in her stride, glared at him. "Just asking, honey. Was she depressed? Worried? Hiding some deep dark secret?"

"No," Brina answered curtly, peeked at Brad. "She was happy, Brad. Excited that you were starting law school."

"Rafe might not be too far off though," Marcie interrupted. "I sometimes thought Deborah was hiding something. Felt sorry for her. I mean, who wouldn't? Living with that bitch, Myra. There was always some craziness going on in that house." Marcie snapped her fingers. "Do you suppose Myra could have done something to her?"

Brina recalled the nasty comments Myra had made about her at the public hearing. "I saw Myra when I returned to the dance," Brina huffed. "As much as I'd love to point a finger at her, she couldn't have done it."

"Deborah was always talking about how Myra would pitch tantrums," Brad spoke for the first time.

"Do you suppose she knew about Myra's abortion?" Cliff asked. Everyone turned to him. "Think about it. If it weren't for Joe Grimes hearing about it from the medic that took her to the hospital and then him telling us, no one would have known about it. Was the family crazy enough to get rid of Deborah because she knew?"

"Let's hold that thought," Brina suggested, "even though I don't think it has much merit."

"She did have secrets though," Brad continued. "There were several times she would be in a deep thought, preoccupied. I asked her to tell me, but she wouldn't. Just said it was nothing."

"Then what could have happened?" Ginny sobbed. "How did she just vanish into thin air? We searched for days; she was right there! Why didn't anyone find her?"

"I had already bought her ring," Brad said. "Planned to propose during the last dance that night. Had already talked to the DJ about closing the evening with her favorite song. I was going to get on one knee and ask her." His throat tightened as a sadness tore at his chest. Stacy hugged him tighter. "Now I wish I'd proposed sooner. Maybe she would have stayed by my side the whole evening."

Everyone silently stared at their friend, jumped when Trevor and Randi joined them from the kitchen.

"Let's hope Gil Fitzgerald can shed some light on what might have happened," Trevor commented after everyone had settled in the den after trying to eat. "They can do so much with forensics now."

"It's so tragic and I feel for all of you," Randi whispered, "but at least you now have some closure."

"Do you think this might be why we've had so many problems with the project?" Brina asked Trevor. "Someone didn't want us to find her body?"

"Probably." He looked at Brad. "Brad, I'm very sorry about what happened, but until we have some answers, there's nothing more we can do right now." He rolled his shoulders, massages the back of his neck. "Maybe we need to call it a night. All of you, especially Brad, need to come to grips with everything, take some time to grieve again, come together in the morning."

"Everyone is welcome to stay here tonight," Cliff announced. "We certainly have enough rooms."

Brina looked at Brad. "I think that's a good idea. You don't want to be alone tonight."

~~~~~

Since Scott and Sandy were staying with her father, Randi accepted Trevor's offer to stay with him at the cottage. So much had happened since their trip to Georgia. She promised to be over first thing the next morning to help fix breakfast.

"I feel so sorry for Brad," she murmured when Trevor opened the door to the cottage for her. Turned into his arms when he closed the door behind them. "I know this is all so new to us, but I don't know what I'd do if something happened to you."

Trevor hugged her when she sobbed.

"Me either." He kissed the top of her head. "You or the boys. It's hard to lose anyone you love." He rested his hands on her shoulders, nudged her away, stared down at her. "But we're going to get to the bottom of this. Soon."

~~~~~

"I'm sorry I snapped at you," Brina apologized as she and Rafe undressed. Since their marriage weeks ago, they often slept in the nude so tonight wouldn't be any different.

"Honey, I understand. But I think we need to consider that there may have been something bothering her. Something else going on in her life. Someone certainly had a secret they didn't want her exposing."

"She was an orphan like me," Brina pulled the spread back, climbed into bed. "Claude wanted to adopt her, bring her here to live with Ginny and me but her uncle wouldn't allow it. I know Deborah always felt like an outsider. That's why Ginny and I tried to include her in everything we did."

When Rafe settled beside her, she snuggled into his arms. "Rafe, she didn't deserve what happened to her. She was finally finding some happiness," she sobbed. "Who could do such a thing."

Rafe let her anger turn to sorrow. Cry the tears she wouldn't release earlier.

~~~~~

"What's wrong?" Pete asked as soon as he heard Marcie's voice on the phone. "You're upset. I can hear it in your voice."

Marcie couldn't sleep, needed someone to talk to. Pete was the first person to come to mind and for once, she was thankful for the three hour time difference with the West coast.

"It's Deborah."

"Who's Deborah?"

"A friend. She disappeared ten years ago. We think we just found her remains behind the firehouse."

"You found a body at the firehouse?" Marcie heard the disbelief in his voice.

"Yeah. Behind the building. Trevor was having it cleared for a patio and the teenage boys helping him on the job found her."

Pete was silent.

"They uncovered a burlap bag, then discovered her body. It hasn't been confirmed that it's Deborah, but Brad recognized a locket that was with the body. We'll know more tomorrow."

"How is everybody handling it?"

"Brad is heart-broken, of course. Ginny is sad. Brina's angry."

"What about you?"

"I'm in shock. I can't understand why someone would harm that sweet, sweet girl. Pete, Deborah and Brad were going to get married. Brad planned to propose that night at the dance," she sobbed.

Pete let her talk over an hour. Gave her the time to reminisce.

As soon as she said good night, he made another call for a flight to the east coast.

~~~~~

"I'm going to have to call the school in the morning. Ask them to get a substitute," Ginny decided as she brushed her hair.

Cliff watched her from the bed. "Not a bad idea. Maybe you can blame it on morning sickness."

She smiled at him from the mirror. "Haven't had too much of it lately but that's a good excuse." She set the brush down, headed for the bed.

When she had settled in his arms, Cliff extinguished the light. She sometimes talked better in the dark.

"Cliff, why would anyone want to harm such a sweet, sweet girl?"

"There are a lot of crazies out there."

She reached for his hand, rested it on her stomach. "Deborah once told me she wanted to have four children. Two boys and two girls. And she was going to shower them with all the love her aunt and uncle never gave her."

Cliff hugged her in silence.

"She said Brad was trying to talk her into going back to school but she wanted to get married and have children. Said she'd wait. Go back to school when the children went to school. Who could have been so mean?"

~~~~~

Stacy knocked softly at Brad's door. They might not always agree, but he was hurting, and she wanted to comfort him.

"Are you okay?" She asked when he opened it.

"I don't know," he turned to sit on the side of the bed. "I'm numb. Sad. Angry. Upset, you name it. It's all like a dream to me."

Stacy leaned against the closed door, watched him. He was still dressed in his pants and shirt from work.

"It's been so long but not a day has gone by that I don't think about her. Couldn't understand why she'd disappeared like she did. When we never found her, I wondered if I did something that drove her away. Did I say something? Should I have proposed sooner? Now," he grimaced, threw his hands in the air, "it seems she was never far away."

Stacy moved to stand in front of him. She nudged between his legs, opened her arms, cuddled his head against her breasts. Held him close when he wrapped his arms around her, and the tears came.

She kissed the top of his head, brushed her fingers through his hair.

"Tell me about her," she whispered.

CHAPTER TWENTY-FOUR

Trevor was sweeping the concrete floor when Duane arrived early the following morning. He arose early for his daily jog, left Randi in his bed with a note that he would be at the firehouse. Suggested that it might be good if everyone stayed at Spicer Meadows a while longer. He'd be in touch as soon as he knew something.

"Heard anything?" He asked the deputy.

"Just got the call. Gil spent most of the night working on it. Confirmed that it was Deborah Gilman. Her arm was broken, she apparently died from a blow to the head. Also suspects asphyxiation but that might be a little hard to prove."

"Now we need to find out who would do something like that and why."

Duane nodded his head in agreement. "Haven't talked to the Sheriff yet so until he gives the word, we'll keep this under wraps. If you think the project was jinxed and compromised before, wait till the media finds out about this. Everybody will be here."

"Do we have to go public?"

"Until the Sheriff gives the go-ahead, no. The culprit must be someone local; I'd like a little more time to investigate it."

They heard a noise behind them, turned to find Josh standing in the doorway.

"Are you okay?" Trevor asked.

"Not really," Josh sighed. "Me, Norman and Cliff, we haven't slept too much. We holed up in my room these past two nights. My parents keep asking if something's wrong, but we haven't said anything. I'm supposed to be in school but came here instead. Do you know who it is?"

"Deborah Gilman," Duane answered.

Josh's mouth fell open and all color drained from his face. Both men reached for him when his knees buckled, and he almost collapsed. They helped him to sit on one of the five-gallon buckets.

"Did you know her?" Duane asked. "Did you know Deborah Gilman?"

"Yeah. She lived with my aunt and uncle. I remember she disappeared a long time ago. That body was Deborah?" He asked. "I remember my mom was really upset. Cried a lot. She liked Deborah and often asked her to babysit me."

"What were you? Five? Six?" Trevor asked.

Josh nodded. "I always thought she was cool. Used to take me to the ballpark. I was in little league; she'd help me hit the ball off that baseball tee."

"Do you remember whether Deborah ever seemed to be upset or depressed?" Trevor asked, recalling their discussion from last night.

"No. She was always in a good mood." He paused. "Well, except when we had these family get-togethers on Sunday. Then she was quiet. I always tried to get her to play with me, then she'd be okay."

Duane pulled out his notepad. "Who would be at these family get-togethers?" he inquired.

"Me, my mom, Dad. Uncle Tom and Aunt Claire. Myra. Uncle James, he's my mom's older brother."

"Do you recall anyone that might have given her a hard time?" Duane asked.

"No, not really. I don't think she was crazy about Uncle James though. Nobody really likes him. He thinks he's better than everyone else."

"This Uncle James," Duane asked. "Is that James Marshall? The CPA?"

Tears filled Josh's eyes when he nodded his head in agreement. "Is it really Deborah? Do you know what happened?"

"It looks like there was a blow to the back of her head."

"You mean like someone really meant to hurt her?" Josh asked.

Duane nodded.

Josh felt sick in his stomach. This was his first brush with death. Never knew anyone who died. Much less been murdered. Visions of his smiling babysitter flit through his mind. Why would anyone want to hurt her, he wondered, then bury her so no one would find her. He sat upright as he recalled seeing Trevor's tools in his uncle's office and turned toward Trevor.

"Do you know my uncle? Would you have lent him any of your tools?"

Trevor frowned. "No, wouldn't know the man if he walked up to me."

"Those tools that were stolen; was it a nail gun? Cordless screwdriver?"

"Yeah. Why?"

"I saw them in my uncle's office the other day. I know they're yours. They had your TAG label on them."

~~~~~

"**W**e think we might have a lead," Duane told the group when he and Trevor met with everyone at Spicer Meadows an hour later.

"Who?" Cliff asked.

"James Marshall."

"Tom Marshall's brother?" Brad asked in shock.

"Why?" Ginny and Brina spoke at the same time.

"Turns out Josh Stevens knew Deborah." Trevor explained. "He came by the firehouse this morning. When we told him who it was, he almost collapsed. His mother is James and Tom Marshall's younger sister. Josh said Deborah used to babysit him."

"Yes, I remember," Marcie affirmed. "Deborah was always talking about him. Used to take him to the ballpark."

"He mentioned that" Duane stated. "He also said Deborah didn't like going to the Marshall family get-togethers. Said he thought his Uncle James made her uncomfortable."

"Can't say that I'm crazy about him myself," Brad added. "I've had a couple clients complain about him. Asked about some legal advice. But why do you think he might be connected to Deborah?"

"Josh said he saw some of my missing tools in James Marshall's office."

"Also turns out James Marshall told Josh and his friends the firehouse was being demolished. That's why they went there, painted the graffiti on the walls," Duane continued. "Josh also remembers seeing Mark Smith leaving his uncle's office one afternoon."

Brina gasped. "He knew Mark Smith?"

She remembered the day she saw Mark at the hospital. He had been so apologetic. Later, she'd learned he had died. That was the same day

Duane called her about the brakes on her car. "The same Mark Smith we suspected tamper with my brakes?"

Duane nodded.

"But how is all this related? What makes you think James Marshall had something to do with Deborah?" Ginny asked.

"James Marshall is brother to the family that raised Deborah. Josh seemed to think she didn't like him. There may be a reason. He may have done something. Add in the fact that Marshall knew the Smith kid, baited Josh to trash the firehouse, stole some of Trevor's tools. I think Marshall has a vested interest in wanting to see the firehouse project shut down."

"And I have an idea how we can find out." Trevor announced.

~~~~~

Trevor, Cliff, Rafe and Brad sat at a table in the *White Rose Diner*. They had talked to Scooter who confirmed that James Marshall always ate lunch in his diner every Tuesday and Thursday. Ordered a club sandwich, fries and chocolate cake like clockwork.

Being as it was a Thursday, the men decided they'd have some lunch at the Diner.

Wendy, the waitress had just set four beers in front of them when James Marshall strolled in, sat at his usual table which happened to be next to theirs.

Trevor sat closest to Marshall. They wanted to be certain Marshall heard every word of their conversation.

Moments later, Pete sauntered in and joined them at the table. "The girls told me you were here."

"Yeah," Cliff jumped up to give his friend a chest bump. "When did you get in town?"

"Had a few days, thought I'd spend them with Marcie. How's the project going?" Pete asked Trevor.

"Great. Heading down the home stretch. Interior is just about completed, flooring is going down today, have the final inspection next Monday. I talked Brina and Randi into putting a patio across the back and we'll be starting that tomorrow. Next week this time, the job should be finished, and I'll be back at Snowridge."

"And the girls will be planning their Grand Opening," Cliff added.

Brad sat where he could observe Marshall. He watched the man's head jerk up when Trevor commented about doing the patio and gave a thumb up that he'd taken the bait.

"I need to talk to Randi about her ex-husband," Brad said. They didn't want to elaborate too much on the firehouse, so he talked about the only other thing he knew to talk about.

"I hope he's still in jail," Trevor grumbled.

Rafe chuckled. "I can see him trying to use his political position to weasel his way out on bond."

"Oh, he tried," Brad affirmed. "But considering the kidnapping and child endangerment charges, the judge wouldn't consider it. I think his arraignment is scheduled for next month. Probably be several more months before it goes to trial."

"Randi will be glad to hear that," Trevor commented. "She's been concerned he'll somehow get off."

"She doesn't have to worry about anything. Considering the spousal abuse and kidnapping charges, he'll probably never be able to see the boys. I understand Miriam has already filed for a divorce and will be testifying against him."

"What about his delegate seat?" Rafe asked.

"Next year is an election year; I doubt anyone will back him much less vote for him."

Wendy brought their orders. When she stopped by James Marshall's table, he asked her to box his lunch, stated he needed to get back to the office.

"Eat up, boys," Trevor rubbed his hands together. "It might be a long night."

~~~~~

The women refused to stay at the house, let the men have all the fun.

"It could be a long night," Rafe stated. "A long, cold night."

"We'll wear our long johns," Brina retorted. "There is no way I'm going to miss out on tonight's excitement."

Trevor had piled brush and lumber over the site, so it looked like nothing had changed. He and Randi hid at the far corner of the firehouse, behind the two propane tanks he'd had installed. They sat on a blanket, watched through the lattice panel.

"You need to think about the baby," Cliff had said but Ginny refused to stay home.

The lights were still on at Marshall's office so Cliff and Ginny were parked in the bank parking lot within sight of the office; said they would text everyone when he left.

Brina and Rafe hid behind a clump of bushes ten yards away from the brush pile; Marcie and Pete waited inside one of the cars parked in the parking lot behind the firehouse.

Brad and Stacy watched from inside the garage with Hal. Trevor thought it might be best not to let Brad get too close to Marshall if he showed up.

Duane waited inside the back door of the firehouse, prepared to arrest Marshall for trespassing once they caught him searching the pile.

It was almost eleven o'clock and Randi's toes were starting to get numb. She was worried it might have all been in vain until her phone vibrated.

He's on the move.

Trevor nudged her moments later, squeezed her hand as they watched a shadow come around the far corner from down the street.

The shadow slowly crept across the back of the building. Randi thought he carried a small shovel. As he advanced into the pitch blackness, she saw the beam of a flashlight highlight the brush pile. Randi almost gasped out loud when he set the flashlight on the ground, stepped into the light.

They watched Marshall kneel, push some of the brush aside. As he nudged more and more of the debris aside, Trevor stood to shine his LED spotlight on him. Rafe did the same from their position and Pete turned the car lights on him.

"Need some light?" Trevor asked.

Marshall jumped up, shocked at being caught. He turned to run but Duane stepped out of the firehouse and tripped him.

CHAPTER TWENTY-FIVE

It was almost midnight when Duane Peterson escorted James Marshall into the small interview room at the Sheriff's office. The room was sparse with a table, three chairs, cream color cinder-block walls with exception of the two-way mirror on one wall. A camera affixed to the ceiling at one corner of the mirror, blinked, recorded everything.

The small observation area on the other side of the mirror was standing room only as everyone prepared to watch the interrogation.

"Care to tell me why you'd be digging behind the firehouse at eleven o'clock at night," Duane asked.

"No law against it," Marshall responded huffily. He was angry. Annoyed that he'd been caught, resentful that they would suspect him of anything, infuriated that he was still handcuffed, being questioned like a common criminal. "Where's the Sheriff? I don't have to answer to you."

"You were trespassing," Duane ignored the man's outburst.

Marshall jumped up; his chair crashed against the wall behind him. "I don't have to put up with this. Take these handcuffs off me or I'll-"

"Or you'll what?" Sheriff Matthews entered the room carrying a box. "I'll tell you what you'll do." He set the box on the floor, out of Marshall's sight. "You will have a seat. Answer our questions." He relaxed in the chair next to Duane. "Continue, deputy."

"Did you lose something?" Duane asked. "Do you always carry a shovel with you?"

"I thought I saw something when I walked by earlier today." Marshall settled in his chair. "I wanted to check it out."

"It's dark. Why did you wait so late?"

"I was working late. Almost forgot," he answered nervously. "Remembered when I left my office."

"Why didn't you say something to Trevor Graystone?"

"Why should I?" He grumbled. "He's just the contractor."

"Maybe but given that there have been so many problems with the firehouse project, if you saw something, you should have told him."

"I'll remember that next time," Marshall responded testily. "Now that I've explained why I was there, I'll be going."

"Do you know Mark Smith?" Duane asked before Marshall could stand.

"No."

"He was seen leaving your office a few days before he was killed."

Marshall jerked in surprise. "In that case, I may have done some taxes for him. I have so many clients, I'll have to check my records."

"Or could he have done some work for you?"

"Where are you going with this? I told you I didn't know the kid."

"Have you ever been inside the firehouse after hours?" Duane moved on.

"No. Why would I? As far as I'm concerned, it's unsafe. Should be demolished."

"Like you told your nephew? Josh Stevens?"

Marshall looked anxiously at the mirror, up at the camera in the corner. "I don't know what you're talking about."

"Are you saying that you didn't tell your nephew the firehouse was due to be demolished?"

"I, I might have mentioned it," Marshall answered nervously. "The Town Council discussed that at one time."

"That was last year. Before Brina Hollingsworth, excuse me Brina O'Malley, expressed interest in refurbishing it. You spoke to your nephew a few weeks ago. After the remodeling had started" Duane pushed harder.

"Look, my nephew may have overheard me talking to his father. Are you going to take a teenager's word over mine?"

"Back to my original question," Duane challenged, "Have you ever been inside the firehouse after hours?"

"I said no," Marshall exclaimed in outrage.

Sheriff Matthews reached down, set the nail gun on the table. "Do you know what this is, Mr. Marshall?"

"I'm not into construction," the CPA fidgeted.

"It's a nail gun. And this," he set the screwdriver beside it, "is a cordless screwdriver. Have you ever seen them before?"

Marshall clutched the side of the table, answered testily, "I told you I've never seen them."

"That's funny," the Sheriff continued, "we found these in your office. Can you tell us how they got there?"

Every muscle in Marshall's body tensed. "What are you talking about?"

"I'm saying we received an anonymous tip that these tools were seen in your office. Don't worry, we got a search warrant." Sheriff Matthews assured Marshall. "We found these tucked away in a corner."

"You can't have found those in my office," Marshall barked, "I've been there all day."

The Sheriff smiled. "While you were trespassing at the firehouse, we were examining your office. Didn't take us long to find them."

"Do you know Deborah Gilman?" Duane asked.

Marshall cast another look at the camera, then the door as if he considered making a quick escape. "Of course, I knew Deborah Gilman," he snapped. "She lived with my brother and his wife. Why are you asking?" He demanded.

"We understand she complained about you." Duane knew he was stretching the truth but suspected he knew why Deborah might have been uncomfortable around the old man.

"About what?" Marshall snapped. "The little tramp was always complaining."

Brina, Ginny and Marcie gasped out loud. Trevor, Cliff and Rafe restrained Brad when he almost charged out of the room. Randi covered her mouth as her eyes filled with tears.

Everyone immediately suspected the worst.

Duane's expression hardened. "Why would you refer to Deborah as a tramp?"

"Because she was always spreading her legs for anyone interested."

"How would you know?" Duane badgered.

"Because she baited me," he blurted. "All but asked for it."

"Asked for what?" Duane hounded. "Are you saying you raped Deborah Gilman?"

"Of course not," Marshall exclaimed. "It was consensual. But she's gone. Disappeared ten years ago. What difference would it make now?"

"We found her," Duane stated.

"You couldn't have - "

"Couldn't have what?" Duane challenged.

"You couldn't have found her. She's dead."

"That's correct," Duane retracted. "We found her remains."

"But, how do you know it's her? It could be anyone."

"It has been verified that the remains are those of Deborah Gilman. Why were you behind the firehouse?" Duane repeated. "Prepared to dig in the exact spot we found Deborah Gilman? Did you put her there?"

"I don't know what you're talking about."

"You claim you didn't know Mark Smith, yet he was seen leaving your office. You claim you've never been inside the firehouse, yet tools that were stolen a couple weeks ago were found in your office. You claim you didn't tell your nephew the firehouse was being demolished, yet Josh tells us something different." Duane pumped the questions. "Your credibility is slipping Mr. Marshall. Why were you at the firehouse? Did you know Deborah Gilman was buried there?"

"Of course not," the man exclaimed.

"Do you typically walk late at night?"

"I live two blocks over. I work late several nights a week so yes; I sometimes walk late at night."

"Were you working late on Friday, December tenth, ten years ago?"

"How the hell would I know?"

"That's the night Deborah Gilman disappeared. I understand the whole town looked for her. I talked to Sergeant Barlow. He was working security the night of the Holly Ball. The night Deborah disappeared. When she wasn't found, he made detailed notes about the evening in case something should develop."

Marshall was visibly shaking.

"Are you sure you didn't see Deborah Gilman that night?"

"Okay. I might have seen her when I walked home that night."

"Which is it? Did you or did you not see her?"

"I saw her. She was standing on the exit landing outside the Town Hall side doors. She was drunk, started yelling at me. Came at me. Fell down the concrete steps."

"You are saying she was drunk? Brina O'Malley was the last person to see her, and she never said anything about Deborah being drunk."

"And you believe her? For all you know, the two bitches might have been arguing and the O'Malley woman pushed Deborah down the steps."

Rafe wrapped an arm around Brina's shoulders when she stepped toward the door.

"Which is it, Mr. Marshall? Did Deborah Gilman threaten you or did Brina O'Malley push her down the steps?"

"Okay. I may have gone up the steps to talk to her. But she tripped. And fell. I swear, she fell down the steps and I couldn't wake her up."

"Why didn't you get help?"

"Because I knew they'd blame me. I left her at the bottom of the steps and ran home. Figured someone would find her."

"That's not what Sergeant Barlow says. He said he remembered coming out to do another patrol, saw you putting something in the trunk of your car. You drove away towards the firehouse. Shortly after that, Deborah was reported missing, and everyone was searching for her."

"The Sergeant is lying," Marshall sputtered. "I was nowhere near the Town Hall."

"Again, Mr. Marshall, your credibility is slipping. Deborah Gilman was killed from a blow to her head. Did you argue with her? Strike her? Then bury her at the firehouse?"

"I'm done talking to you. I want my lawyer," Marshall shouted.

"I think that's a good idea," the Sheriff interjected. Nodded his head at his deputy.

Duane Peterson stood and stepped around the table. "James Marshall, you are under arrest for the murder of Deborah Gilman."

Everyone could have heard a pin drop in the observation room after Duane finished mirandizing the old man.

Brad collapsed against the wall behind him. "I don't know what lawyer he'll call. I'm the only one in town and I'll do everything I can to help the county prosecutor."

"I can't believe he actually raped her," Ginny sobbed. "Why didn't she say anything?"

"He may have threatened her." Brina said. "Told her no one would believe her."

Marcie dropped into one of the chairs. "Do you think she fell? Or did he knock her down the steps?"

"Guess we'll find out soon enough," Trevor answered.

Duane came into the room. "The Sheriff's taking over. My suggestion is that all of you go home, get a good nights' sleep. Thank you for your help with apprehending him quietly." He looked at Brad. "I never knew her, but I am sincerely sorry for your loss. Hopefully, you, all of you, can now have some closure."

~~~~~

Trevor's alarm sounded but he shut it off, turned over and reached for Randi. She squeezed his hand when it rested against her breasts.

"What time is it?" She groaned.

"Six."

"I need about four more hours sleep," she moaned. "I also need to get to my father's house, get the boys ready for school."

After James Marshall's confession and Duane's suggestion that everyone go home and get a good night's sleep, no one argued. All headed to their respective houses. Their own beds.

Since the boys were with her father, Randi didn't hesitate when Trevor suggested she stay with him another night. The last she remembered they had both collapsed on the bed. She was sure she fell asleep as soon as her head hit the pillow.

Today was another day and she needed to check on her friends. Last night had awakened so many memories, she was sure the grieving would start all over again. They would have to plan a memorial service.

When she started to pull the covers back, Trevor hugged her closer.

"I need to get the boys."

"Another few minutes won't hurt." He tightened his hold. "Other than being tired, are you okay?"

"I think I'm better than my friends," she sighed. "Today is going to be another long one. I want to do something to help ease the pain."

"Time will be the best thing. Maybe Duane will call with more news. I'll stop by the Sheriff's office on my way to the job."

The briefing didn't come until later that evening when everyone had gathered at Spicer Meadows. Duane reported that Marshall had finally confessed to murdering Deborah Gilman. He also admitted to raping Deborah when she was sixteen.

"We could charge him with contributing to the delinquency of a minor, but the murder charge will keep him in jail the rest of his life."

~~~~~

"**S**o much has happened this past week, I'm hesitant to be excited," Randi said the next evening. She stared out the window. They had just finished dinner; her father was with the boys in the backyard. Trevor sat at the table.

"You know," she turned to look at Trevor, leaned against the counter, "they say things happen in threes. Tim is finally out of my life and thankfully, the boys don't seem to have suffered from his scare. We've solved the mystery at the firehouse and although it has revived old memories, I'm sure everyone will be back on track in the coming weeks. Now, I worry what else could possibly happen."

"Well, we still have our contract to negotiate," Trevor stated. "I heard from *Greenwillow*. They voted to accept our proposal. Now you and I need to negotiate our contract."

"Contract?"

"Yeah. I stopped by Brad's office. To check on him, ask him to put something together for me."

He handed her two sheets of paper.

"Mighty short agreement for going into business together," Randi said as she sat at the table.

"Read it," Trevor encouraged her. "Tell me what you think."

"The name of the corporation shall be TAR, Inc." she read out loud. "I'm assuming that's Trevor and Randi?"

He nodded.

"It says you are party one, I'm party two," she continued.

Trevor nodded again. "There's also a little line beside each of the items. You need to initial each one if you agree."

"Okay. Party one and party two will merge their business knowledge and experience, work together for the common good of the community." She smiled at him. "I guess I can agree with that."

He handed her a pen, she initialed it.

"Contribution. Party one will provide all necessary equipment and staffing to construct safe and up-to-standard projects. Party two will provide all necessary intellect and creativity to accomplish final design."

"Okay. I guess I can agree with that. You provide the muscle; I provide the fluff." She initialed the condition.

"Ah, here's the catcher." She smiled at him. "Ownership. Party one and party two shall have fifty percent vested interest in said corporation." She looked at him. "Not going for the sixty, forty? I guess I can agree with that as well." She initialed the paper, took a quick glance at the second page.

"No peeking," Trevor warned.

"Decision making. Party one and party two must agree one hundred percent to all projects."

"In other words," Trevor added, "all projects need a unanimous vote of two."

"Okay," she initialed the line, "I can agree with that."

She moved to the second page.

"Hmm. Dispute resolution. If party one should disagree with decisions made by party two, all negotiation shall be conducted in bed."

Randi took in a sharp breath; her eyes grew wide in shock. "Trevor," she exclaimed. "Seriously? You had Brad put this in writing!"

He gave her a straight face. "Keep reading."

"If party two should continue to disagree with party one, party one shall provide flowers and any other enticements not to exclude more resolution in bed. Trevor, I cannot believe you had Brad put this together. I'll have to think on this one a little longer." She put a question mark on the line.

"Terms," she continued reading out loud. "Party two must marry party one within two months of the closing date." She looked up at him. "What? Really? Trevor, are you serious?" She chuckled. "At least Cliff and Ginny had one year."

"I drive a hard bargain."

Trevor slid out of the chair, kneeled in front of her.

"Randi Cavanaugh, we'll be finished with the firehouse project in the next week, but I want you to be a part of my life for an eternity. Will you to marry me?"

Randi stared at him. He looked so serious. So handsome. So focused. How could she say no?

"Yes." She cupped his face and kissed him. "I will marry you for an eternity."

Suddenly there was a loud cheer from the back door as Scott, Sandy and her father barged into the kitchen.

"Did you know about this?" Randi asked her father who smiled.

Both boys jumped on Trevor's back.

"Does this mean you and mommy will be getting married?" Scott asked.

"You made our secret come true," Sandy exclaimed.

"What secret?" Randi asked.

"When we were in the mountains, we asked Trevor if he'd be our dad," Sandy said.

"Then when he picked us up from school yesterday, he said he needed to talk to us man to man," Scott added. "Said we had to give him permission to marry our mommy."

"Well, I'm glad you approved," Randi exclaimed.

EPILOG

I t was a magnificent June day. Summer Solstice. The whole town had waited on the courthouse lawn while Randi and Trevor exchanged vows inside the centuries old brick building. Judge Reamy allowed the women to spruce the courtroom with candles and flowers. The glow of the candles reflected off the wooden walls and pews, the luscious scent of gardenias filled the air.

It had been a beautiful occasion. Trevor looked immaculate in his dark suit as he stood next to the justice of the peace. Randi was exquisite in her ivory silk tea-length dress. Ginny, Brina, Marcie and Stacy sniffled, Cliff, Rafe, Pete and Brad smiled when Scott and Sandy, looking handsome in their miniature suits led Sebastian and Randi into the building.

It had been an emotional ceremony when Trevor and Randi exchanged their vows. More sniffles were heard when Trevor included the boys in his vows, accepted them into his life, promised to love them as his own.

Everyone cheered when Trevor and Randi stepped outside the courthouse as husband and wife.

The reception and another ceremony followed at the firehouse where everyone gathered for the Grand Opening of *The Row* in *Lariat's Plaza*.

"Happy?" Trevor kissed Randi on her cheek.

"Couldn't be happier. But we still have one more thing to do, right?"

Trevor smiled, reached for her hand, and then attempted to get everyone's attention.

"Randi and I want to thank everyone for coming out for our wedding and the Grand Opening of *The Row*. But we have one more little ceremony we'd like to share with everyone."

He looked at the twins. "Scott, Sandy, can you two come over here?"

The boys were so small, Trevor lifted them onto a small stage he had built for this special occasion. The boys stood tall with their extra three feet in height but looked out at the crowd, worried expressions on their faces.

"No, you haven't done anything wrong," Trevor assured them as the crowd chuckled.

"This is a special day for all of us. With yours and your GranPop's permission, I married your mom." He kissed Randi's cheek. "And we finally completed the firehouse project with no more problems. Can finally open the doors for business."

Everyone cheered.

"But there's one more thing. I asked Mr. Beckman to put together a document for me." He pulled a single sheet of paper out of this coat pocket. "It's a resolution and I hope you two will be willing to sign it."

"What's a resolution?" Sandy asked.

"Just listen," their mother said while everyone laughed.

"It says, we – Scott and Sandy Cavanaugh – are very happy that our mommy met and fell in love with Trevor Graystone." He looked at the boys. "Right?"

They giggled.

"We are happier that our mommy married Trevor Graystone." Once again, he looked at the boys. "Right?"

"Yeah," they both shouted, getting into the spirit of the moment, started to jump off the stand.

"Wait a minute, there's more." Trevor stopped them. "Since our mommy's last name will now be Graystone, we would like ours to be Graystone too."

Whispers and sobs filtered throughout the crowd.

Scott and Sandy frowned at Trevor. "You mean our last name won't change? Like Mommy's."

"Only if you sign this paper. Mr. Beckman has taken care of the legalities and if you two sign this sheet of paper, your last names will officially be Graystone, I will become your father."

Trevor dropped the paper to catch both boys when they leaped into his arms.

Randi's heart swelled as she smiled tearfully at them when Trevor turned to face her.

"I never thought I'd be this in love. Ever again."

She stepped forward to share a group hug while everyone cheered for the second time that day.

Thank You

Dear Reader,

Thank you so much for reading Newfound Love. If you enjoyed the book, I would be incredibly grateful if you could take a few minutes to leave an honest review.

Reviews from readers like you help other book lovers discover new stories and are deeply meaningful to me as an author.

If you're able to post a review, please consider sharing:

- Your overall thoughts and feelings about the book
- What you enjoyed most or what resonated with you
- Who else you think would appreciate this book

You may email the review to: kay@kaydbrooksauthor.com

Your support means the world to us.

With gratitude,□□□□

Kay

ABOUT Kay

K ay's love for books and organization started early, as she fearlessly tackled her uncle's extensive collection in his mansion's attic, despite childhood tales of a lurking boogeyman. Discovering the works of Georgette Heyer, Daphne du Maurier, Mary Stewart, and Victoria Holt only fueled her passion further.

With a double major in Library Science and history, Kay's career began by organizing a private school library in Virginia. Her success led her to establish a public library system in rural Caroline County, complete with a headquarters and three branches.

Amidst raising three children and juggling a full-time job, Kay discovered romance novels and began writing her own stories. Though her friend Nora Roberts seemed to snag all the publishing contracts,

Kay remained undeterred, honing her craft through writer's groups and workshops.

In 2007, Kay embarked on a new adventure, opening Grapes of Taste, a wine shop that showcased her love for wine and her knack for engaging newsletters. After retiring from the library in 2013, she revisited her old manuscripts, polishing them for publication.

Since then, Kay has published numerous titles, including the Row Series, the Victory Hill Trilogy, biographies, and stand-alone novels. With an endless supply of "what if" stories waiting to be told, Kay continues to pursue her passion for writing, inviting readers to join her journey through her website and social media.

Website: www.kaydbrooksauthor.com

Contact: kay@kaydbrooksauthor.com

Facebook: Kay Brooks – Author